WANTED —
DEAD OR ALIVE

Center Point
Large Print

Also by Gordon Young and available from Center Point Large Print:

Red Clark, Range Boss
Red Clark, Two-Gun Man
Red Clark on the Border

This Large Print Book carries the Seal of Approval of N.A.V.H.

WANTED — DEAD OR ALIVE

GORDON YOUNG

CENTER POINT LARGE PRINT
THORNDIKE, MAINE

This Center Point Large Print edition
is published in the year 2024 by arrangement with
Golden West Inc.

First appeared serially in Short Stories Magazine, July 25 – Sept. 25, 1948 under the title Hard Hunted.

First published in the US by Doubleday.

The text of this Large Print edition is unabridged.
In other aspects, this book may vary
from the original edition.
Printed in the United States of America
on permanent paper sourced using
environmentally responsible foresting methods.
Set in 16-point Times New Roman type.

ISBN 979-8-89164-107-5 (hardcover)
ISBN 979-8-89164-111-2 (paperback)

The Library of Congress has cataloged this record
under Library of Congress Control Number: 2023952094

WANTED —
DEAD OR ALIVE

CHAPTER 1

Jack Rodiker rode up to the old adobe, and hadn't left the saddle before a small tousle-headed, bare-legged girl ran out of the house and leaped at him as if thrown. He reached from the saddle to catch the kid, then heaved her high overhead. She squealed happily, and came down with her arms about his neck, clinging like a kitten and fighting against the pull that loosened her arms.

Rodiker, long-legged and high-shouldered, leaned low to set her on the ground, then stepped from the saddle and gently poked a finger against the end of her nose. "Sue, you're getting purt' near pretty," he said, though she wasn't, being freckled, tanned, skinny, with a copperish red in the curly hair that Arizona's hot winds combed, curled, and frizzled.

When Tex Clayton stomped out on his wooden leg, Sue said, "Now he won't have so many kisses for Bess!" She set her head at a birdlike tilt and told Rodiker, " 'F you'll just have sense enough to wait for me to be old as Bess, you'll like me best!"

Tex Clayton shook his head and puffed. "I maybe orta paddle her sometimes." The day was warm and he was fat, with the smell of whisky on him. It was always on him. "But I never yet laid a hand in anger on a young'un of mine." He rubbed the short gray fuzz on his fat cheeks. "Not even 'fore their maw went away." Tex solemnly looked far off, as if the Promised Land were where the sky met the colored mountains that some called the Cathedrals.

"Well, come in, boy. I've got to get wood chopped, an', whew, it's hot! How's all your folks?"

The 'dobe floor was earth, bare, but hard as slate, and slick-smooth from dancing feet. Any Clayton could make music out of anything that tinkled or squeaked, and there were three girls and one boy. The long-legged Rodiker was awkward about moving to rhythm, which made him feel a dullard when Bess tried to teach him, for she not only danced like a dust devil but fiddled better than her brother, who was a gangling, lazy, slow, loose-jointed fellow, until music moved him.

Bess met Rodiker at the kitchen door, with sweat on her face and the smell of dishwater on her hands. Sue's head was poked through the back door to comment on the love-making, but Bess didn't care, and Rodiker, blushing like a boiled beet, pretended not to care; so Sue, finding it no fun to jeer at persons who were deaf or acted like it, went off whistling, and climbed a bareback mule that she kicked into an aimless cross-country lope.

Bess was a pretty girl, and careful of her prettiness; she brushed her light-brown hair, scrubbed her face with moist corn meal, wore a bonnet outdoors, and of late the fellows who came to see her oldest sister were taking notice of Bess.

When she finished in the kitchen, she sat on the stoop and watched Rodiker cut and split wood. Old Tex, hearing the sound of the ax, smiled to himself, nipped at the bottle of white whisky, and took up the fiddle, playing dreamily.

Ann Clayton came along the back veranda and sang "Hello there!" at Rodiker, then laughed. "Tex sure knows how to get his wood chopped!" Ann was a tall girl with a merry loveliness, and the light in her blue eyes danced as starlight does when the night winds blow hard.

The fiddle stopped. Bess listened for a moment, then jumped up. "Somebody's coming!" Both girls caught at their long skirts, and scampered through the house. Rodiker chopped wood until Bess came to a back window and excitedly told him, "It's old Yank Arnold and a woman in a buggy. That sister-'n-law of his, I think!"

Rodiker sank the ax into the chopping block and went indoors, moving with the same sort of quiet as if up to thievery. He didn't know Yank Arnold except by sight, and had never been closer to the sister-in-law than across the street in town a time or two. Folks said she was the most beautiful woman ever to come into the Santsander. Now he edged up to the doorway where Bess and Ann were staring.

Old Tex Clayton would have asked the devil in, had the devil stopped before the adobe. He stomped out, hat in hand, to greet Colonel Arnold and the woman and to invite them in, though he knew that Colonel Arnold was about as unfriendly toward him as a man could be and not pull a gun on sight.

The buggy top was down, and Cora Arnold held a small, blue, lace-trimmed parasol in gloved fingers. She was wearing a heavy veil, but pushed it up as if quite willing to be looked at. Her hat was small and blue; it sat forward on her head and had bonnet strings. She was also enveloped in a straw-colored linen duster, and the Clayton girls couldn't tell what kind of dress she was wearing; but her complexion was white, startlingly white in this hot, windy country. Her face was pretty, but had the taint of snootiness, very like sullen discontent.

Bess whispered, "What's she so stuck-up about? Can't even ride horseback, they say!"

Ann murmured, "Wish I had skin like that!"

"Wish I had the money the old Arnolds have!"

Ann's tone was kindly. "Her husband's a half cripple, and sick much of the time, they say. Maybe that's why she don't look so happy."

"Yank's a widower. She ought've married him instead!"

"I'd marry a baboon sooner!" said the gentle Ann, who remembered the War.

Colonel Arnold was tall, thin, ramrod-straight, and hatchet-faced; a long mustache put his mouth in brackets, and there was a tuft of whiskers on his chin. His eyes were deep-set, with a hard directness. Now he didn't leave the buggy. One of his splendid black saddle horses was tied behind, and he held the high-headed team's lines with a steady, one-handed pull as he faced Tex Clayton.

Rodiker could hear his voice, but not what he said, and he didn't need to hear to know that he was laying down the law. Tex got huffy, and slapped on his floppy hat, then reared back, propping himself on the wooden stump as he folded his arms like a defiant man before a firing squad. Cora Arnold looked aside at him, listened, and seemed bored.

A barebacked mule with a rope halter loped down the road, and Sue's spraddled legs flung kicks at the mule, hurrying him so she could have a look at the company in front of the house. She pulled up on the off side where Cora Arnold sat, and leaned for a close look at the milk-white face on the blue-eyed woman.

Sue's "Jumped-up Judas, you're purty!" was a heart-felt compliment, but earnestly loud.

Cora Arnold looked about and, with the startled gesture of brushing away a wasp, swept the parasol toward Sue's face. That frightened the mule. He gave a sidling jump, and Sue slid from the slick back, landing in the dust. She came up as a ball bounces, and her small hands had closed on whatever they could grasp, which was sandy dust.

Sue now called her the unloveliest names known to such muleskinners as visited the Clayton ranch, and shrieking, "You done it a-purpose!" let fly with dirt she had grabbed from the road.

Cora Arnold screamed, dropped the parasol out of the buggy, and, throwing both hands to her dust-smeared face, cried.

Colonel Arnold half arose from his seat to look across to the other side of the buggy, and demanded, "What on earth?"

Sue began to tell him at the top of her voice, but he shook the reins and drove on, leaving a swirl of rising dust as if to escape in a cloud.

Sue picked up the abandoned parasol, daintily brushed a grimy hand at the dust-spotted silk; then, with it overhead to shelter her freckles, she began unhurriedly, and with what she assumed was a high-born lady's mincing gait, to trail her mule.

Tex Clayton stomped into the house, lifted the fiddle from the rocking chair, gave it to Bess to put away. He flung his hat on the floor, mopped his face with a bandanna, then sat in the rocking chair and drank from the bottle. He offered Rodiker a nip of white whisky, and wasn't offended by the headshake.

"D'yuh hear what all he said?"

"No, Tex."

"W'y," Tex shouted, "that ornery ol' scalawag said us Suth'ners better damn' well remember the Wah's over an' leave his cows alone or we'll git whupped again!"

"He talk like that?" Rodiker asked hotly.

"He sho' did!" Tex slapped his wooden stump. "Worser'n that! W'y, he called me ugly names I never heared before. 'Cat's-paw!' That's what he said I was! 'Tain't enough to have a blue-bellied Yankee drinkin' out of the river above yuh, but he come right up to my own front door an' called me a 'cat's-paw!' Called your own folks that, too, Jack! He said Ol' Jerym Bevarts is a-makin' cats'-paws out of all us Suth'ners. He said, he did, that Ol' Jerym hisself wasn't no mo' Suthern than a skinned polecat is a possum!"

CHAPTER 2

On a Sunday near noon, Rodiker dismounted at the Moheela livery stable, not far from the center of town. The town seemed deserted.

The stable hand asked, "Ain't you goin' to the picnic? They roasted a steer. They took ten, fifteen kegs of beer. The Claytons went by this mornin'. All but Slim was on mules, and old Tex fiddled as he rode. There's bronco bustin'. You could win yourself some money, like last Fourth."

Young Rodiker hooked his thumbs in his belt and, with a wry-lipped noiseless laugh, said, "I wouldn't top one like that man-killer again—not if he was dead and stuffed, I wouldn't! All I got was ten dollars, and spent that for liniment!"

The stableman swung a hand vaguely toward the length of dark stalls. "If you want to see a purty horse, go look at Yank Arnold's girl's. Near ever'body that can walk or creep has gone to the picnic—but not them Arnolds. I reckon she wouldn't mix with common folks."

"She's nothing but a little kid."

"Not too little to be snooty as hell, you ask me!"

"I never was close enough to know. But Yank sure looks mean and high-headed."

"He is," said the stable hand. "Just rode off a while ago. Him and the girl stayed the night at the hotel. It's theirn, so they don't have to pay board."

As Rodiker tramped along the board sidewalk his sharp heels and heavy spurs clanked and jangled in the sunny stillness. The sheriff's office was open, though no one was inside. He paused, wondering if there were new "Wanted" posters. "Dead or Alive," some had said, offering a pile of money.

On down the street was Bevarts' Cattlemen's Bank, and on a corner across the street the Bevarts' Hardware Store, with a new Winchester in the window. He stopped, pushed up his hat, put his forehead against the glass to see better. He was good with firearms. His father, a Confederate cavalryman, had seen to that.

A block farther down was the two-story Moheela hotel. A wide porch was in front, and over the porch an old sycamore of huge girth.

He stopped at the trough, pumped some water into a rusty cup on a chain, and drank, then climbed a few steps that led to the porch and went into the hotel. The bar was closed, not because it was Sunday but on account of the picnic, and he didn't see anybody about.

A girl's voice said, "Hello!" She was on the stairs coming down, and had paused. He bobbed his head and touched his hat, wondering that she had spoken to him, and then smiled. Though she limped in coming on down, she steadied herself at the banisters, and looked at him with dark-eyed interest. Just a mite of a girl she seemed, even in the long riding skirt, and the stable hand was wrong, for she wasn't snooty, not at all, but said quite cheerily:

"I sprained my ankle and can hardly walk. Would it be too much trouble for you to help me to the stable? There's nobody around here to send for the horse. Of course once in the saddle I'll be all right."

The ankle may have been weak, but didn't seem painful, for she looked as cutely mischievous as a kitten that wants to play; yet when she was at the bottom of the stairs and had left the newel post to take a step toward him, the ankle gave way, and she thumped down on the uncarpeted floor and lay still.

Rodiker looked at her and felt helpless, then he got down on his knees; her eyes were closed and the small tanned face had the placidness of death, but he touched her cheek and it was warm. He took her into his arms, and stood up. Not knowing what to do, he turned this way and that, holding her close. Her hat, loosely fastened by chin thongs, had slipped off, and her dark hair was a soft tangle of braided coils. The fragrance of cologne, faint as a mountain flower's perfume, came into his face.

When he started toward the wall bell behind the desk, she opened her eyes and smiled. "I never fainted before. It's not so bad, really not!" Her black eyes crinkled at him.

He held her close and said, "You oughtn't try to ride. You might faint again. On horseback that would be bad."

"Wouldn't it?" she agreed. "But I'm all right now. Honest." Her feet stirred the long riding skirt. "I can walk to the stable, if you will take my arm. Let me down, and I'll show you."

He set her feet on the floor, and she clung to him in going toward a chair. He said firmly, "You stay here. I'll bring your horse."

When he led the sidesaddled horse down the street, she was waiting outside on a railing of the veranda with her back resting against a low sycamore limb. He offered his hand to help her down the steps.

She said, "You'd better carry me," and helpfully put an arm about his neck.

He said, "You're pretty little to ride clear out to your ranch alone."

She crinkled her eyes laughingly. "Oh, I'm lots bigger than I look!"

He, tall and long-armed, lifted her onto the sidesaddle, and she said, "Thank you, Mr. Rodiker," which surprised him.

"How do you know me?"

Her dark eyes laughed, but her voice was

serious. "I've known you for a long time. I saw you ride that mean horse last July Fourth. It jolted even my teeth, the way he bucked. I bet on you too!"

She waved back at him as she rode off, and he thought what grit Colonel Arnold's little girl must have to ride with an ankle that hurt so badly it made her faint. He was pleased that she had known him by sight, and he liked it that she had bet on him when he topped the man-killer, though likely it was no more than a bottle of pop.

He made bets with Sue Clayton that were paid with soda pop and candy, and was careful never to win. Sue and Kate Arnold, he thought, were about of an age.

When Rodiker rode up to the Lazy S chuck wagon the following day in the predawn starlight, Bill Brody, the wagon boss, was pouring himself a cup of lye-strong coffee, and said:

"Get off that horse and eat. Then take a fresh one an' light out for John Henry's and ask where in hell is that wagon an' them riders he promised?"

Off south, the beef cut lay dark and lump-shaped on the ground, while riders moved at an encircling walk and sang wearily. Within a step and a jump of the wagon boss's feet were long, blanket-wrapped cocoon shapes, and some snored. The cook, a tall old fellow with joints that creaked, crouched under the lantern by the wagon and poked his fingers into a dishpan filled with dough.

Bill Brody had a weakness for "likker," and didn't sprain his back bending backward to keep a straight tally book, but he had been top man with the Bevartses for a long time. He now turned impatiently to the turnip-sized watch that was hanging on the side of the chuck box. The hands said twenty minutes of four, and the watch ticked; but he pried open the face and moved up the minute hand, rehung the watch, then let out an unjoyful roar.

"Haller-lu-yer! A new day has dawned! Up an' at 'em, you tassle-eared bobcats! Come a whoopin'!"

He strode among the cocoon shapes, giving a push with a boot's toe or stingless cut with the quirt. Men stirred, wriggling from blankets and unfolding the boots from under the "pillow." Sleep-husky voices grumbled—not complaining, just grumbling. The air was nippy. Men stamped into boots, rolled bedding into tarps, flung the lashed bedroll into the cook's wagon, and went stumbling toward the horses that the wrangler was heading in.

Men dipped into the bean pot, filled tin cups with coffee, soused hot biscuits into bacon fat: they hunkered down, chewing and swallowing, as if each tried to finish first.

A big man who wore a shabby overcoat against the morning's chill rode up slowly on a big horse. He owned the Lazy S, but wasn't much of a horseman. He owned a bank, too, and was more used to sitting on a chair than in a saddle.

Old Jerym Bevarts had a body thick as a barrel, a short neck, a heavy head that he carried in a lopsided twist, as if suspicious of what was going on behind him. He was gray, hook-nosed and hadn't many teeth. Tight-fisted, it was said; but it was said, too, that his sons appeared to have money and didn't do much work. The Bevartses might own cattle, but they weren't cowmen.

Rodiker, beginning as a kid wrangler, had worked off and on for the Lazy S for years without seeing a Bevarts once a year. They seldom showed up during spring or fall roundups. Bill Brody ran the outfit.

Old Jerym got down from the horse as if coming down a ladder. He took a plate from the cook, helped himself to beans, bacon, biscuits, molasses, then sat on the ground near Rodiker. He couldn't sit on his heels like a proper cowman.

"You're young Rodiker, ain't you?"

"Yes."

"Fine folks, the Rodikers. Um-hm, yes."

The old man lifted his face and stared about owlishly as he chewed. He watched men rise, scrape their plates into, or at least toward, the fire, then drop the tin plates into the bucket.

Old Jerym poked out a spoon toward the scraps that came from the plates, and told Rodiker, "I pay for ever' speck of that waste!" He sipped coffee and chewed. "You're purt' near the best rider in this country, ain't you?"

"I been throwed."

"You rode that bad-buckin' horse last July Fourth, didn't you? Dougal—you know my son Dougal?—he bet agin you. I told him he was a fool to bet agin a Rodiker ever!"

Rodiker flushed proudly, and Old Jerym chuckled; he had never before said anything of the kind, but it was a pleasant thing to say now, and didn't cost a dime.

Rodiker rode west, crossing and recrossing the snake-crooked Santsander. Yank Arnold ran cattle on both sides of the river. The Bevartses had come up from the south. There was lots of range, but not enough for both outfits and the little ranchers and nesters who squatted close to the water.

At fall roundup time Arnold sent a wagon to work under Bill Brody, but never showed up himself. His other wagons, with smaller outfits joining in, combed the valleys from the northern Cathedrals to the red and rugged Sierra Gordos on the west. He had three or four ranches, owned a half-dozen brands, and some said that he and his brother acted as if they owned the earth.

Rodiker had headed into the outskirts of the

colonel's range to reach John Henry's ramshackle place. Nobody was in sight. He hallooed, then pushed open the door and looked all about. Bedding was off the bunks. He looked around outside. The chuck wagon was gone. Fresh grease was at the edge of the can on a wagon shelf, so he knew they had greased up the axles and rolled off.

John Henry had most likely got word from Colonel Arnold to join up with one of his crews. Rodiker explained to his horse, "If I lived as close to Yank Arnold as John Henry does, I'd most likely want to do like he wants me to too."

About five miles on the way back Rodiker turned aside and rode toward an upland grove of piñons, where he thought he saw smoke. It vanished, but he rode on toward where it had been, until he heard the faint boom-boom of a double-barreled shotgun, and black puffs rolled up and floated off. He was near enough now to see the startled quail sliding down from shoulder-high flight into brush and behind rocks.

Since it was powder smoke and not fire, he hadn't any more interest, and was reining about when a voice hailed him. He saw a man on a boulder, and the man waved an arm, beckoning.

Rodiker rode up and, from having seen him in town, recognized Yank Arnold's brother, whose name was Craig. He was heavier than the colonel and older, with some kind of a war injury that kept him out of a saddle. He used a buggy for going about, and that was no good in roundup work. He liked to hunt, and two bird dogs lay at his feet when Rodiker stopped before where Craig was sitting on the lichen-colored boulder.

He had an embittered, pain-plowed face and, after eying the Lazy S shoulder brand, said meaningly, "You are a hell of a way from your own stamping ground!"

Rodiker looked back at him and said, "Yes," stubbornly, not explaining, because he acted mean.

"I thought you might be one of my men looking for me. That's why I waved." Craig's eyes and voice seemed demanding to know what Rodiker was doing up here. There wasn't any reply at all, so Craig asked, "What is your name?"

"Jack Rodiker."

"Oh, Rodiker, eh? I'll tell you right now, once and for all, it is best if you Rodikers, Claytons, and all the rest of the Bevarts' bootlickers keep the hell away from this range!" The shotgun lay across his legs, not pointing at Rodiker, but it could point at him very quickly, and Craig's look expressed a warning as he slapped the gun's stock.

Rodiker took his time, and his voice drawled with soft slowness, as nearly always when he was mad.

"I've heard tell that you are ornery mean. Some

say it's on account of your back hurtin' all the time. Some say it's just Yank cussedness oozin' out like resin from a pine knot!"

Craig Arnold's hard eyes slowly widened and sparkled, then he threw back his head and laughed. When he stopped laughing, he had a hand to his back and pressed there to ease pain, but he looked amused. "So your name's Rodiker? Well, from now on I don't care what the colonel says, no man who'll talk back like that to a double-barreled shotgun would steal a cow! Ride on, Rodiker. But come back if you ever want to work for a damn Yankee that oozes pine-knot cussedness!"

It was far past the middle of the afternoon when Rodiker found the Lazy S chuck wagon some ten miles from last night's camp. He'd been without dinner, but lukewarm beans were in the pot, and he piled up a plateful and drank stale coffee, then changed horses and rode out to find Bill Brody.

Some steers in the beef cut acted as if they had made up their minds that they wouldn't go to a Kansas City slaughterhouse, and were breaking in all directions from the herd. The men who were trying to head them off rode through as much dust as there is smoke in hell. It was a near thing to a stampede, and the wagon boss that lets his herd get away isn't likely to be boss the next morning.

Rodiker took out after a galloping longhorn

that had a tent-sized A on its side. He forefooted the steer with a thirty-foot throw and sent it into a somersault.

Bill Brody came alongside Rodiker and said, "We'll have fresh beef tonight! Sometimes I think Yank Arnold runs his meanest cows down where we'll have to handle them! And John Henry sent me word today that the Arnolds had told him to bring his wagon to them. Yank Arnold may learn someday he don't own ever'thing and ever'body in the Santsander. You had your ride for nothin'!"

CHAPTER 3

Rodiker was spreading his tarp, when a horse came pounding through the dusk and pulled down at the chuck wagon; and Slim Clayton asked the cook where Rodiker was.

Rodiker heard and called out, so Slim rode over to him and dismounted from the lather-wet horse, then pulled at Rodiker's arm. Slim's was a bean-pole build, and he had a sleep-eyed laziness, but now there was urgency in his quietness as he walked Rodiker well away from the camp before he said:

"Craig Arnold's been killed out in the piñons, and his wife says you done it! She seen you! It was today about noon!"

Rodiker asked, "You funnin' to scare me?"

"I near rode my horse to death gettin' out here to tell you what Colonel Arnold in town says she says."

"I stopped in the piñons coming back from John Henry's and I talked to him, but I didn't know she was around, and I never—"

Slim said, "Looky! What a woman says is so, allus, when she is pretty, and Cora Arnold's that!"

"I never before today spoke to Craig Arnold and hell, man, he offered me a job any time I want it!"

"Don't talk that way. It ain't so, and nobody'd believe it."

"I'm telling the truth."

"And I'm tellin' what the colonel says she says. And he's offerin' a thousand dollars for you! Dead or alive! I knew you'd just joined up to work for the Bevartses' wagon out here. If they's anybody else in town knows where you are, Arnold's riders'll have your neck in a rope before mornin'! So you light out!"

Jack Rodiker sat on his heels in the darkness and studied. "Why would I shoot Craig? I had a sort of liking for him after our talk."

Slim said, "Yeah?" unbelievingly, then squatted beside Rodiker and fingered the dust. Fifty yards away tired men were spreading their bedrolls. Here and there a final cigarette burned like a floating coal. Slim rolled himself a cigarette, and told more of what he had heard in town.

"It's bein' said somebody hired you to shoot him. Most folks would guess that 'somebody' is a Bevarts! As it's told, Craig was quail huntin' over in the piñons, and she was along an' dozin' in the shade. A shot close by made her jump up. Craig was plugged in the back, an' the man she says was you was ridin' off lickety-split. The horse you rode was a roan and branded Lazy S, the which means Bevartses."

"In the back—me?"

"It's what Yank says."

"She must've mistook me for—But in the back—*me?*"

Slim became impatient. "You rode in the piñons. Your horse was a Lazy S. She says she seen you. The sheriff is Arnold's old trail boss, and he'll pick damn Yankees for the jury. The judge of the circuit is a damn old carpetbagger!" Then Slim added recklessly, "Personal, I don't care where any Arnold gets shot, or who by, but I bet the Arnold riders'll be out here in a hurry. You've got to cut an' run."

Rodiker pondered some. "Slim, you tell my folks—and yours—I never done it. You tell them the Arnold woman's somehow made a mistake, and if I can get to talk with her, she'll know by seeing I'm not who she thinks."

He saddled with a stealthlike guilt and headed out into the darkness, seeming to confess by turning fugitive. Before midnight Arnold riders came in. They said Yank Arnold swore he'd keep offering more and more money until Jack Rodiker was killed, or caught and hung. And Colonel Arnold wasn't a blowhard.

Rodiker rode from the Santsander into the Requa country, and went to work for a man who raised horses. One afternoon the man came from town with some liquor in him and, after eying Rodiker, said, "You're him!" and started to pull a gun.

Rodiker reached out as a rattlesnake strikes

and twisted the gun aside. "How'd you know?"

"Reward poster there in town offers two thousand dollars. Tall, wide-shouldered, gray-blue eyes, and no man is a better rider. The name is Rodiker."

He shook off the posse, and after a long time made his way into Kansas, where he went to work for the Hayes brothers.

Here he felt safe enough to write Slim a letter, and gave it to a freighter. In town, before he got to the post office, the freighter saw a fresh reward poster that said, "Wanted for Murder!" The reward was three thousand dollars, and was signed by the sheriff of Moheela. The "Wanted" description not only fitted that tall fellow at the ranch, but his letter was addressed to a man at Moheela.

The freighter opened the letter and showed it to the sheriff. The sheriff rode out to where Rodiker was working, and caught him asleep. It was about midnight, so the sheriff tied him up and set one of the cowboys as a guard. In the morning Rodiker and the cowboy were gone. The cowboy himself was on the dodge, and had been hiding out at the Hayes Ranch.

Soon a bank was held up in western Kansas by two very bold men. The posse shot the Hayes cowboy to death, but the other man escaped with—so the bank said—twenty thousand dollars in gold.

Colonel Arnold again increased the reward, and newspapers began to make a big to-do over the young outlaw who couldn't be caught. Rodiker was being reported from many places at the same time: A half-breed outlaw in Indian Territory "confessed" that Rodiker had been among his companions in a train robbery; a stage driver out of Phoenix "recognized" him as the lone highwayman who had lined up his passengers. It was Rodiker and his bunch, so the newspapers said, that flagged down the Union Pacific outside of Denver and dynamited the Wells-Fargo safe, but when the four men were caught he wasn't among them. One night a man rode his horse into a Calabasas gambling house, leveled out two guns, and said, "I'm Jack Rodiker! Fill up my saddlebags with coin!" Somebody sneaked a shot and killed him. He had thought Rodiker's name would be more impressive than his own.

It was a name that began to flare in print clear across the country. One New York paper sent a correspondent into Huerfano County, Colorado, to confirm the story that Jack Rodiker did ride many muddy miles into town one rainy night and drag a doctor back with him for the croup-choked child of a woman he'd found when he stopped and asked for something to eat. The woman hadn't known him, but worriedly explained that she was alone with her sick child because her husband was out with a posse, wanting a part of that reward, now up to five thousand dollars.

The doctor said the outlaw told him, "I'm Jack Rodiker. I've got no money to pay you. I never in my life held up a bank or train or stage. But this sick kid looks like a little girl I used to know."

That was how it went for more than three years. Then Bill Brody of the Lazy S received a letter that said, "I'm scared to write my folks or the Claytons, on account of how they are being watched to get some track of me. I want somebody to talk with Mrs. Cora Arnold and find out why she thinks I killed Craig, because I never did. Will you?"

Bill Brody showed the letter to Dougal Bevarts, and Dougal made a whistling sound of astonishment. He said, "What a chance!" He was a big fellow with solid, heavy features and a liking for fancy dress, but he was good-looking.

Bill Brody said, "I don't care whether he killed him or not. I want that reward!"

"Sure," said Dougal, "but Cora Arnold told me herself she seen him. Old Yank would have a cat fit if he knew we'd been writing regular ever since she went back to Ohio." Douglas was a married man himself, but he said, "Yank'll have more of a cat fit when it's fixed so we can get married. Half of ever'thing was Craig's!"

Bill Brody had a few more drinks, and then went to the hotel room where Colonel Arnold was staying the night. His was a hawklike face, a tired face, but he was straight up and down as he stood in his stocking feet, and his shirt was off. He was so cool toward the Bevartses and all their friends that he didn't ask Bill Brody to take a chair.

Bill Brody said, "Colonel, how much is the most you will pay for Jack Rodiker?"

Colonel Arnold, knowing this man had been Rodiker's friend, thought he understood, and took his time, and didn't move his eyes off Bill Brody's face. At last he said, "Bring him in alive so I can see him hung, and I'll pay you ten thousand dollars!"

Bill Brody soon showed up in the little Wyoming town where the letter had come from, and asked his way to the Lone Star Ranch. There he said he was looking for a friend, and gave the name Rodiker was using.

The ranch owner was a lank, hard-bitten Texan who had moved into the tall-grass country, and he suspiciously looked Bill Brody over as he said:

"Didn't they tell you about him in town?"

"I never asked."

"If you had, you'd have learned he's a good man not to be lookin' for!"

"So?" said Bill Brody.

"Yes, so!" said the Texan. "Some days ago a blackleg gambler he'd knocked down an' kicked across the floor for cheatin' a damnfool dude laid for him. The gambler, bein' a sure-thing sharper, got a couple of friends to help. They wasn't enough! He downed the three of 'em in the fastest time I ever seen—and I seen it! Before I had my gun out to chip in, he was all through an' not scratched!

"He could've had the town on a platter, but he told me he couldn't stick around to be looked at close. Right then I paid his wages and threw in a horse too. Where he went I don't know, but our sheriff sure ain't lookin' for a man of his size! So if you've got a badge hid under that vest, you won't get any help from around here."

"His name," said Bill Brody, "is Jack Rodiker, and he shot a man in the back."

The tall Texan looked Bill Brody in the eye and said:

"He ain't that kind, so you are a liar!"

"He was seen do it!"

"Then who seen him lied!"

That was how the newspapers got hold of Jack Rodiker's name again and made a hullabaloo.

Ten thousand dollars was so much money that Bill Brody knew rich men who had less. He returned to the Santsander and visited Paw and Maw Rodiker's little mountain ranch, and to show what a good friend he was of their boy's, he let them read the letter; but he didn't learn anything. They were war-hardened, tight-lipped folks.

Bill Brody, from time to time, took along white whisky and candy to make up closer to Tex Clayton and the girls, but he had his face scratched when he tried to kiss Sue, who was growing into a good-sized girl with some weight on her bones and a strange straightforwardness in her violet eyes. She didn't like Bill Brody, just didn't, and said that there weren't enough bull whips in Arizona to make her.

Years went by—some seven, or nearly that—and Jack Rodiker was still talked about. Some said he was heading the bad bunch up around Deadwood; and some said that, rich from robbery, he had a big ranch in California; but there was also talk that he had joined up with a Mexican general below the border. Anyhow, Yank Arnold, keeping his word, kept raising the reward, though the old sheriff had died. Colonel Arnold had the kind of stick-to-it Yankee stubbornness that had worn out the South during the War.

CHAPTER 4

It was near midnight when the dogs began to bark because horses, coming fast, were on the rocky trail that twisted down through the pines to the Rodiker cabin. Paw Rodiker rolled off the corn-husk tick, and, rifle in hand, looked out. Thin clouds slid away from the moon, and against the forest's spire-tipped darkness he could see the splash of movement as men left their saddles.

Maw Rodiker was sitting up, and pushed the nightcap from her ears, to listen better. Their mountain ranch was far from neighbors, and night riders, looking for her son, had come before. She heard a voice call out, silencing the dogs, and told herself, *That's him!,* feeling dread but eagerness too. Then a half-grown boy tumbled down the ladder from the loft with the joyous shout of, "It's Jack!"

Maw Rodiker answered sharply, "Pray God with no hurt in him!" Her work-worn fingers squirmed together as when one in pain will not cry out; it was endless suffering to know that her son was hunted by men who wanted to kill him for the money on his head.

She was putting a match to the candle when Paw Rodiker stepped back from the open door, and the two men standing there had the quietness of strangers waiting for welcome.

Paw Rodiker was black-bearded, big, and bowed, and now stood barefoot in red flannels. Some of the buttons were off the undershirt, and the black hair on his chest was thick, like the curly hair between an old bull's horns.

He said, "Step in," and soberly shook hand with his tall son, who had changed enough to be indeed a stranger. Jack's face was darkened by a thick stubbly beard, his hair long and scraggly, his clothes weather-worn, and he was very tired.

Slim Clayton, just as travel-tired, was with him.

Maw Rodiker lit a second candle before pinching the first's burning wick with thumb and finger, taking off the crust, and then she relit it with the slowness of a ritual. After that she faced about, barefooted, in a nightgown, with the nightcap like a brimless bonnet tied under her chin.

Jack Rodiker thrust out his rifle for Slim to hold, then his spurred boots thumped hard on the doweled floor as he went to her, put his arms about her, kissed her wrinkled mouth, and held her back at arm's length, staring solemnly.

She reached out and took off his hat for a better look at his face. He was big, but had the lean, stripped look of a man who sleeps little and rides hard. His face was changed and strange, beardedly old. Always reckless, he had once been good-natured, too, with a smile ever close to his mouth. Now his mouth was hard, and the shimmer of unresting weariness was in his eyes.

The half-grown Ronnie blurted, "I wouldn't have known you to look at!"

Paw Rodiker, down on his knees, brushed the hearth with a wild turkey wing and blew life into the ash-smothered coals. Maw Rodiker fixed a meal. The men ate as starved men do, and nobody spoke. White ash thinly overlay the coals again. The candles burned smokily, making shadows jump and bounce, and the only sound was the shift of boots under the table and the hungry chewing.

Rodiker and Slim went out to the stable and wearily bedded down in the mountain hay, and the rest of the night Maw Rodiker turned from one elbow to the other, with head lifted and the nightcap pushed from her ears, straining her ears so that she could give warning if there were sounds other than the night wind. By her side Paw Rodiker lay wide-eyed and motionless.

The next morning Paw Rodiker saddled, and took Ronnie with him.

The two men sat in the sunshine, until it grew warm, then moved under a pine. Rodiker sat on his heels and somberly looked at nothing. His pockets were empty—so empty that he hadn't even tobacco and papers.

At noon Slim ate dinner fast and, never quite

at ease around Mrs. Rodiker, went outdoors.

Jack's mother sat on a stool across the table from her son, and they looked at each other, not speaking. When he opened his palms, as if showing something, she understood their emptiness and nodded; then she said:

"You sent me word last year from Mexico that if you ever come back it would be to kill Yank Arnold."

Their eyes met in a long-drawn-out staring before he asked tonelessly, "Hadn't I ought?"

"I guess you think then you'll go off with Bess Clayton—some'res afar off—an' change your name."

He told her steadily, "For over six years now I've been hard-hunted. I'm tired."

She put her fingers on the table's edge and asked point-blank, "Did old Jerym Bevarts send for you?"

He smothered, or tried to smother, his surprise behind a steady look, and his, "Why do you think a thing like that?" was cautious.

"Some time ago Tex Clayton rode up here on his mule to say Jerym Bevarts had asked Slim to get word to you. He had a jug of white whisky and his fiddle. He got drunk, and your paw lugged him out to the stable for the night and took off his pegleg so he would stay there. We've never let on to anybody that we've ever heard from you, but"—she jerked a thumb backward across her shoulder—"looks like Slim learned where you could be found. I reckon the fool Claytons eat out of old Jerym's hand like the jackasses they are." Then, breaking the words as sharply as glass breaks, "Jerym Bevarts is a copperhead!"

He raised his empty cup, looked into it, put it down. "I have to take my friends where I can find them."

"Friends? You can't have friends!"

"No?"

"No!" she said sternly, then went to the cupboard, where from far back she took out a large piece of paper that had been folded many times. All of it was water-stained, and parts were cardboard-stiff from having been once attached to wood. She unfolded the crackled reward poster before him, and her lean forefinger rested on the ten thousand dollars.

"That's why you can't have friends, ever!"

It was the first of its kind that he had seen, offering the largest reward. He reread the water-smeared large print that called him dangerous and gave warning that no chances should be taken in attempting his capture. Ronnie, she said, had sopped it off the board in front of the printshop in town one rain-whipped night last winter, and had brought it to her without Paw's knowing.

Rodiker looked up and smiled grimly. "From how this reads, looks like I'm a kind of fire-eater!"

She refolded the poster carefully, then said, "Plain speakin' may make you mad. No man likes the truth when its edge is against his own throat! While I can lift a hand, I'll do what can be done to shelter you safe, but while I've got a tongue I'll say what I think is needful.

" 'Twasn't no fault of yours that made you outlaw, but now I think you've got pride in it. You've been staring at this poster like it was a lookin' glass that made you feel handsomer than you are! Blood kin was before law, and is stronger, so whether you've done—or ain't done—all people say, you've got a home wherever me an' Paw have got a roof. But, because you are a hunted man, we have no peace. Right now him and Ronnie are out to watch the roads so you'll be safe."

Her plain speaking seemed one-sided, and thoughts lay within him like unhatched eggs he brooded over, but he had no ease with words and so remained silent until she, starkly direct, demanded:

"Why have you come back?"

He stooped to the blackened pot on the floor and poured more coffee, then turned about at the table, wishing for a cigarette. He sipped coffee, straining the grounds through his teeth, and became so lost in thought that he absently felt in his vest for the makin's that weren't there.

"I am a-waitin'," said Maw Rodiker.

He looked up, then stood up as if to walk away, but hooked his thumbs in his belt as he stared down at his mother.

"It took me a long time to figure that maybe Cora Arnold didn't make a mistake, like I used to think. That's because I was then too young to know how women lie."

"So?"

"She was so Eastern she didn't much more than know a burro from a cow, yet she said my horse was a roan and shoulder-branded Lazy S. And it was.

"But she says when she seen me I was ridin' off. I ought've wondered long before I did how she could tell what a horse, goin' hell-for-leather from her, was shoulder-branded with! God A'mighty hisself would have to squint pretty hard to read a brand He couldn't see!"

His thumbs were still in the belt, his shoulders were high and squared as he looked down at his mother and with stern slowness said, "She lied. Somebody who knew me and the horse had to put the lies in her mouth. Somebody that was there and seen me and told her what to say. Somebody that wanted the Bevartses blamed for maybe hiring me to do it. Somebody that killed Craig because him and her wanted Craig killed. And so, what man got the most from him being killed?"

Maw Rodiker studied awhile before she spread her hands flat on the table and said tiredly, "I've hated Yank Arnold for his spite an' malice, but it never entered my head that he'd maybe do a thing like that and put the blame on you!" She sighed wearily. "But I reckon what evilness can be thought of, man can do—and some woman'll help!"

He took his hat from the floor and put it on, again felt in his pocket for cigarette makin's that weren't there. "She left these parts, I hear, soon as Craig was buried. How much, I wonder, did she get from her husband dying? And Yank Arnold? Come a time soon when maybe he'll tell me all about it!"

Maw Rodiker stared until she understood fully, then she got up and rounded the table, and put a tight hand on his arm. "No, not that! If you shoot him, folks'll be just that much surer you killed his brother too!"

He walked to the door and looked out absently, but a wish surged in him to knock Yank Arnold down in front of people and to kick him into a confession they could hear.

When his mother said, "And what's more, you can't stay in the Santsander and not be known!" his hand went to his rough beard and felt about. He still looked from the doorway as he told her, "I've changed. I wasn't more than a kid cowhand when I left. The country's full of strangers. I'll play like one of them."

"It's dangerous!" she said. "You're outlawed!"

He turned about, and looked amused and hard and reckless too. "Down below the border they don't call you 'outlaw' unless you're on the side that loses. It's been a little of what you call 'dangerous,' too, but I didn't mind."

She said, "I know. I learned durin' the War." Her tired voice dropped to a weary monotone. "Danger for men like you is all the same as a no-good woman. She draws you on and on, takes all your strength and manhood, leaves you dead, or near it, then calls for some other fellow. And now by coming back into the Santsander you're bein' reckless out of pride in recklessness. That's the fool's way!"

"I'll lay low awhile."

"You can't lay low and not be meddled with. For one thing, the whole Clayton tribe'll know you're back."

"All Yank Arnold's money wouldn't buy a word 'gainst me from any one of them!"

Maw Rodiker looked half minded to say otherwise, and something of her opinion did come sharply with: "No matter what else, it takes only two dollars to buy a gallon of white whisky, and Tex Clayton can be heard a mile off when he's drunk. That's how I know he's Jerym's man—and so is Slim! There's no trustin' any Bevarts. No, nor anybody they hold a whip hand over!"

He said, "Jerym's too rich to need the money my scalp would bring."

She snapped, “But maybe not so rich these days as you think. I hate Yank Arnold purt’ near next to old Satan, but he’ll fight! The Bevartses don’t like out-an-out fightin’! They’d rather sneak an’ creep, like copperheads! So maybe Jerym would like to ease Yank Arnold’s grudge by giving him your scalp!”

“Could be,” he said indifferently, and looked about the room without taking notice of anything. Then he faced his mother. “All right, I’ll tell you the big reason I am back.” His narrowed eyes had a glint that gave her a startled shock, its cruelty was so unlike anything she had ever known of him. “Cora Arnold is coming to live out West again!”

Rodiker lifted his hand, and the fingers were stiffened like claws. “When I take her by the throat, she’ll tell what I want to know!”

CHAPTER 5

He rode off with Slim through the afternoon shadows, not taking the road, but leaving by a back trail out of the wooded pasture. As they went down toward the long and wide Santsander Valley, rashness gathered within Rodiker. He said, "I'm going home with you," which wasn't as planned.

Mountain twilight overlay Slim's face. In saying, "No place you'd be more welcome!" he felt like a liar, and in a way he was, because the kind of welcome that Rodiker wanted and expected would not be there. Bess had tired of the pride she once had felt in being known as the outlaw's sweetheart.

She was a honey-pot sort of girl, and did no more than a honey pot does to shoo away what she attracted. She was loyal in her way, but her way was not to nurse a lonely heart—not while the younger Bevarts boy was sweet on her.

Slim thoughtfully asked, "Why've you changed your mind to ride on in with me?"

Rodiker passed his hand inquiringly over the short thick beard as if feeling a mask.

"I'll not be known, not on sight—not by anybody. Think so?"

"You sure enough look like a bush-jumper."

The Claytons lived some three miles this side out of town and on the high bank of the Santsander. Tonight there were four or five saddled horses before the doorway. One was Zig Bevarts's.

Slim said uneasily to Rodiker, "You ride on around to the stable. I'll send Bess out."

Inside the house a fiddle swung its squawky tune, and there was the thump of booted feet, and swirling shapes passed by the open windows. Then laughing shouts reached Rodiker as he rode around the house and past the woodpile where, by way of showing what a good worker he was, he had often chopped wood as if hired to do it.

He reined up near the stable and listened to the splash of tinkling from the mare's cowbell, and wondered if it was the same mare that had been gray with age when he was a boy. He could hear, too, now dimly, the fiddle's chattering jiggle. Always he had found peace and pleasantness here, and the shiftlessness his mother complained of was unimportant.

Below him the bluff broke abruptly into deep shadows, dark enough to seem bottomless, and he knew that the river's crooked way was marked by trees and willow thickets that crept along the edges of the wide bed and were sometimes overwhelmed by the winter floods.

Slim came from around front, leading his horse, and he said, "Come on in the stable. A birthday party of some kind for Bess. Tex is drunk."

Inside the stable Slim put a match to the lantern, and offered tobacco and papers. "I borrowed the makin's. I told Bess you was out here. Near took her breath. She's comin' soon as she can slip away. You goin' to stay the night?"

Rodiker rolled a cigarette thin and tight, and drew on it, as if drawing his breath after being long without air. "Depends. Who all is the company?"

"Zig Bevarts and some fellows. It's his tobacco. You keep it. I'd better get back. You stayin' the night?"

Rodiker glanced overhead toward the hayloft. It would be a snug place to sleep, and close to friends. His horse stood outside with reins trailing. A strange horse, even if put in the stable, might draw questions; and a strange man, if glimpsed, might draw questions that would be even more embarrassing to the Claytons.

"No, I'll ride on."

Slim put out his hand. "If I don't see you again before you go—"

Rodiker pocketed the makin's. "We're strangers when we chance to meet."

"Sure. I won't let on. I don't know how long this shindig'll last. Don't be surprised if Bess don't hardly know you."

He went out, and the stable door swung shut.

Rodiker heard light steps outside, and watched the door. The lantern hung there, and Bess, with long skirts lifted to step across the log threshold, pulled at the stable door and held her breath. Her brown cheeks were on fire; she was curious, with a flutter of dread too. He had been her sweetheart, her first sweetheart years and years ago.

The lantern was between them, and she stared through its light and said, "You?" as if unable to believe that this big-shouldered, rough-bearded man could be Jack Rodiker, and her uneasy voice was without welcome.

Bess was pretty—prettier than ever, now, with flushed cheeks and loosened hair that was as soft and brown as dried corn silk. Her striped gingham gown had a billowy looseness. A double row of red beads that looked like coral added to the flush of her face, as her brown eyes widened in an unbelieving stare; he seemed so old, and had a haggard tiredness, his clothes were frayed and his hat shabby, his hair and beard as scraggly as a bummer's. Only his high, wide shoulders and steadiness of gaze gave him distinction, and she knew him readily enough, which made it seem the more incredible that he could have changed so much.

She came in slowly, letting the door close behind her, and whispered, "Why are you back?" Remonstrance was in her voice, and she was uncertain enough to seem a little fearful.

It was like reproach, and unexpected. His back stiffened as he hooked thumbs in his belt, covering over soured feelings. His was a cherishing memory that he hadn't let grow or change from the frolicsome girl who had teased and romped, but now he saw the change, for she was older and different too. The maturity gave her a sense of strangeness, and her startled anxiety seemed to express dislike of him, even fear.

Then her "I wouldn't have known you, Jack!" sounded as if it were a too-late effort at apology.

Quietly and with bitterness he told her, "So it seems!"

The silence between them sagged from the weight of unspoken thoughts, and their eyes met in much the same bafflement as if they had lost their voices and were untrusting. A hardness that she had never expected lay over him, and the smolder in his eyes made her afraid. But she was sorry for him—he looked so worn and tired and hurt.

Silence lay between them, but not for long, because the door was opened with a jerk, and a voice demanded in angered hoarseness:

"Bess, who is this man?"

"Why, Zig! How you scared me!" She tried a little laugh that wasn't easy because she was scared, and she smiled hard, drawing her lips frozenly, for the bare-headed Zig to see.

He was a chunky fellow with big hips and thick shoulders; he had the Bevarts darkness of skin, and the bull neck and knobby features that marked the family. He stepped over the split-log threshold, and the door that wouldn't stay open unless propped closed behind him. He was glaring at Rodiker as he again asked Bess, "Who is this fellow?"

Rodiker's was a tightening anger at what seemed the man's intimate right to question her, more anger when she put out her hand soothingly on Zig's arm and said, "Why, I don't know who he is, Zig! He came to see Tex, and Tex, you know, is—isn't—so I—he is a stranger that I never saw before!"

Her face was as earnest as truth-telling could have made it, and Zig wrathfully believed her. He hunched his thick shoulders and glowered at Rodiker. "All right, fellow! Who the hell are you and what do you want?"

Rodiker didn't move, not even an eyelid. Bess, uneasy from the quarrel sound in Zig's voice, begged, "Don't!" as she swiftly moved closer to him, and the billowy striped gingham stirred the litter about her feet.

Zig said, "Bess, go on out of here!" and put an arm about her with the naturalness of doing what he had often done. He indicated the door. "You go! I'll find out who he is and what he wants!"

Bess struggled from him and drew outside. "No, Zig, no! Don't have trouble!"

She indicated Rodiker's low-slung revolver. Zig, of course, had removed gun and belt when he had come into this friendly house, but he had put his cup to the liquor jug a few times, and now bellowed at Rodiker:

"You sonofabitch, I've got a right to know why the girl I'm goin' to marry is in this stable here alone with you this time of night!"

All of Rodiker's weight came up on tiptoes to get behind his fist. Zig jerked back, but the fist reached his chin, and dropped him as a club would have dropped him. In going down, the back of his head struck against the door. That, too, was much as if a club had hit him.

Rodiker slowly and absently rubbed his knuckles and stared at Bess, with his thoughts on the surface of his eyes. Her hands were high on her throat and she said, "No! No!" whisperingly.

What she meant he didn't know and wouldn't ask, but her cheeks weren't flushed now, and though her eyelids flickered under his mistrusting gaze, she did not turn aside.

"No!" she said again. "No, I wouldn't tell who you are—not to anybody, ever!" Her eyes begged before she asked, "You believe me, Jack? Don't you believe me?"

Zig lay as he had dropped, cheek down in the dust, with blood running from his nose, and the short neck had a twisted look as if broken.

Rodiker pointed, and told her coldly, "He'll not believe you!"

"What can you mean?"

"When he comes to, he'll think it over and know you wouldn't have met a strange man here—not here in the stable! Not when Slim is home and could have come! You've lied yourself into a bad fix, my girl!"

His was a sodden anger, remote and cold and studied. He gave no acknowledgment whatever of her loyalty in protecting him, and his "my girl" made her furious.

Bess clenched her fists and said, "Go away! Get clear away!" Her arms swung toward the door. She said, "You'd no right to come here and put me in such a fix!" Her brown eyes gleamed and the tinge of flame was back in her cheeks as she told him, "I'd die before I'd let a friend of Slim's be caught, but I don't want to see you ever again! Now go away and stay away from me!"

He looked at her and nearly said that was how he wanted it, too, but his lips stubbornly wouldn't move, so without speaking he stepped across Zig's body and pushed at the door, stooping to go out.

Outside, he gathered the dangling reins, swung into the saddle, and at a walk rounded the corral, then picked a zigzag way down the bluff and into the shallow river's bed.

Bess carried the lantern out into the moonlight, going with Zig into the corral, where she avoided the mud about the trough, then sat the lantern down and pumped.

Zig tramped into the mud. He sullenly washed his face with cupped hands that he filled under the pump spout, and after that he wiped at his face with a large bandanna from his hip pocket. He wouldn't say anything. But Bess took the bandanna from his hand, and with mothering care wiped behind his ears and neck, brushed at his hair, then rose on her tiptoes and kissed him.

"He hit you when you wasn't looking! Oh, cowardly!"

Zig said, "You know him!"

Her voice was swift and pleading. "I don't know a thing on earth about him, except he's one of old Yank Arnold's new men—or so he said!"

Zig growled, "You're lyin'!"

Bess said, "I'm not! I don't tell lies! Now you listen to me!" But indignation left her voice as, using the bandanna to wipe blood spots on the front of Zig's shirt, she explained.

"A while ago he rode right up to the back door and asked for Tex. You know how all sorts of men come. I said Tex couldn't see him, so he said all right, he'd talk to me. I told him my brother was home and to talk to Slim, but he said he didn't want more people knowing he was here. And he didn't want to be seen. There might be trouble.

That's why we went to the stable. He'd come, he said, from Yank Arnold to warn us Claytons we'd get pushed into the river—women and all!—if we didn't stop helping you Bevartses steal Yank's cattle! Oh, I was glad when you come into the stable! But he looked so horrid mean I was afraid to tell you who he was to his face—you not being armed! What a coward he was the way he hit you! Now you see just how it was, don't you?"

Colonel Arnold's name fitted so plausibly into facts that Zig said, "Yes," believingly, and with some uneasiness too. Also, Bess's sympathy and the affectionate touch of her fingers eased the shock of Rodiker's fist.

"Like you said, he hit me when I wasn't lookin'! If ever I meet him again I'll beat him half to death!" Zig showed a fist. "Just to teach 'im nobody ever gets the best of us Bevartses!"

CHAPTER 6

Rodiker, in the river bed, kept to the shadowed side of the bluff, letting the horse pick its way through and around the tall dark clumps of brush, mostly willows. Some of the old flood marks were saddle-high, showing how the Santsander could rise.

He rolled a cigarette from the Bevarts' makin's, and liked the tinge of soreness in his knuckles. It meant that his full weight had gone into Zig's face.

He'd never before had trouble with any Bevarts, and, wondering what old Jerym wanted of him, recalled his mother's "copperhead," which reminded him that there had always been talk of how the Bevartses were a tricky bunch and old Jerym a great finagler—as a Northern man would have to be to trade with the South during the War and not be hanged.

When Rodiker rode into Moheela the streets were empty, the town dark and quiet in the moonlight. He looked to the right and left, moving at a walk, the horse's feet nearly soundless in the dusty street. Much was changed, but many things were unchanged, and memories stirred within him. The wide-reaching sycamore still grew before the hotel, and the long water trough, as always, leaked and nourished the tree.

He got off and pumped himself a drink into the rusty cup on a chain, remembering the little Arnold girl he had helped into her saddle, and how she had crinkled her eyes at him. A black-eyed little thing, cute and pretty—but Yank Arnold's daughter.

A lamp with a low wick burned in the hotel office, but the bar was dark, and he judged the time to be well past midnight. What a clock said seldom had any importance for him. He got into the saddle again, and, still at a walk, turned on the next corner and rode along where there were some tall trees, and the houses had palings in front of them. He left his horse under a tree and opened a latch gate that grated on a broken hinge. His spurs jangled on boards that served as a sidewalk to the small porch.

He hit the door hard, knocking. Not hearing any stir within, he knocked again until echoes rattled within the old house.

When a woman's voice squawked at him from behind the closed door, demanding what he wanted, he asked for Mr. Bevarts.

"Who're you?"

"Somebody he sent for."

"What's your name?" Her sharp voice had the wire edge of habitual distrust, and Rodiker said:

"If Jerym Bevarts is so much coward he sends a woman to meet strangers in the dark, I want no dealing with him!"

The door's lock clicked, opening, but a chain was on the door to hold it against the sudden push of persons who might be dangerous, and a gruff voice said with no kindliness, "All right, Jenny, you get back upstairs."

Her voice, going away, quavered resentfully that no good was to be had from men who came in the dark and wouldn't give their names.

There wasn't any lamplight, and the moon's glow didn't reach onto the porch, but Rodiker sensed that a face was peering from behind the edge of the chained door. When the gruff voice dropped to confidential lowness, asking: "Who are you?" the answer came straight: "Jack Rodiker!"

That knocked a soft grunt out of old Jerym Bevarts. He said, "Eh? Eh?" stammeringly. "You are? Why—uh—what's you want?"

"To know why you've sent for me!"

"Uh. Hmm. Well—er—wait a minute."

Jerym put a match to an oil lamp and held it overhead as he peered through the opening. Rodiker moved up close enough to be seen. The chain fell from its hook. Jerym said, "Come in."

When he went in, Jerym pulled the door shut, then lifted the lamp overhead for a better look, the small, deep eyes peering from under gray bushy brows. He was a hulking stooped man, with a sidling twist to his neck, as if alert for what was going on behind his back. His thick nose had a beak-shaped curve, and he had lost so many teeth that the nose came down over the upper lip. His sparse hair was gray, and he had a bulging belly outlined by the nightgown of unbleached cloth that may have been clean but looked dirty. Jerym's mouth was tight as a steel trap, and with no more than a sprung trap's kindliness in its outline.

"I'd never known you. No, sir," he said, stretching his wry neck to peer into Rodiker's face. "You are a famous fellow now!" His eyes were intense, and his lips moved, shaping a grin that looked as if a worm crawled on his mouth. With confidential knowing he went on. "Yank Arnold thinks I hired you to shoot his brother!"

"So I've heard."

"That makes us need to stand together, eh?"

"It's took you some years to think so!"

Jerym, still holding the lamp, said, "Now, now, that's no way to feel about me." His pig-sized eyes were fixed on Rodiker questioningly. "It's a big risk for you to come right into town like this, ain't it?"

Rodiker's thumbs went to his belt, his shoulders stiffened. "No more risk for me than you."

Jerym's "Eh?" was as if another grunt had been knocked out of him. The small sunken eyes had the colorless luster of wet pebbles. Frost-white stubble covered his face. He still held the lamp with both hands, and raised it higher, the better to study Rodiker's look. "What's that you say, eh?"

"Why," Rodiker explained with matter-of-factness, "you sent for me. I have friends who know that if anything happens to me, you'll be to blame!"

"Ugh, so?" said Jerym, and, taking the lamp into one hand, he rubbed thoughtfully at his mouth. When his hand dropped, once more a smile wriggled there. "A good bluff. Yes, very!" He nodded approval and made a chuckling sound. "Let's set and talk things over."

He led the way into the room off the entrance, and put the lamp on an oilcloth-covered table that was used as a kind of business desk at home; account books were on it, ink and pens and letter paper of the Cattlemen's Bank.

Jerym said, "I'll draw the curtains." They were already drawn, but to make sure he went from window to window with whispering slip-slap of loose slippers.

Rodiker sat in a straight chair at the end of the table and rolled a cigarette with Zig's makin's. Jerym came back and sat at the table, placed his hands on his knees, and peered studyingly. "I thought I'd meet you out in the country some'res. I never thought you'd come right into town!"

Rodiker had evaded all kinds of traps by doing what people never thought he would, and now said, "Here I am."

"W'y—er—yes. So you are. And a famous fellow!" Jerym reached down and scratched a shin.

"How did you know Slim could reach me?"

Jerym held up a crooked finger and looked mysterious. "Ah, but we are all good friends, us Bevartses, the Claytons, you. All of us can work together fine, eh?"

Rodiker rubbed out the cigarette on the sole of his boot, and laid the stub carefully on the table. "What kind of things?"

Jerym wasn't easy to hook with questions, and again scratched his shin, then leveled out a forefinger. "We Bevartses are forethoughtful an' farseein'!" He screwed down an eyelid, as if he had made a confidential admission.

Rodiker tilted his hat back a little, crossed a foot over a knee. "All right, what's up?"

Jerym's chuckle was an ugly noise, having the rasp of malice as he evaded the question with, "Yank Arnold's going to purt' near wish 'twas him you shot instead of Craig!"

Rodiker drew himself tight, made no denial, said nothing.

Jerym lifted his eyes to the ceiling, spoke thoughtfully. "Craig's widow has been lettin' the colonel run her ranch like it was his own." His look dropped to Rodiker. "Dougal—you remember Dougal—since his wife died, he's visited back in Ohio, courtin' Cora Arnold.

And won't Yank have a fit? There'll be hell a-poppin'!"

Rodiker nodded. He liked the bitterness that Colonel Arnold must feel if his sister-in-law married a Bevarts. Farseein', these Bevartses. Maw Rodiker had warned him, "They'll use your grudge!" Also he remembered her guess that Jerym might try to make a kind of peace by bartering Rodiker's scalp.

He asked, "When are they marrying?"

"Soon, soon!" Jerym chuckled. "After the marriage, Dougal can take over what's hers. Wouldn't you like to see Yank Arnold's face when he hears about the weddin'?"

Rodiker studied that. Whatever hurt Arnold was all right and retributive. He said, "For all I care you can take Arnold's ranches away from him, lock, stock, and barrel! But let's get down to cases. Why'd you send for me?"

Jerym moved the lamp to one side of the table and rubbed his hands together. They were big pale hands, with ink stains on the right hand's middle finger. Jerym hunched nearer, and spoke with a kind of hissing softness.

"I'll protect you ever' way I can. You know that, don't you?"

"Would I be here if I didn't think it?"

"And them friends of yourn," said Jerym mockingly, "who'll hold me to blame if anything happens to you—*tck, tck!* Good bluff, eh?"

Rodiker thought, *Not so good!* but said coldly, “What do you want?”

“Eh? Why, I’ve been thinkin’ things over and—” He stopped, fingered the adjustment screw of the lamp’s wick, remained silent, but his eyes searched Rodiker’s face.

“Don’t take all night. Let’s have it, or I’ll be on my way.”

Jerym peered for a time before he nodded.

“My bank—I want you to rob it!”

Rodiker’s face showed no more expression than a calloused palm. He took up the cigarette butt and relit it. A foot was across his knee, and he spun the rowel, watching intently, as if doing something difficult. Then he lifted his eyes.

“Aren’t there any thieves left in the Santsander?”

Jerym spread his palms. “Not just anybody can be trusted.”

“How much?” Rodiker’s voice was toneless.

Jerym put a hand to his chin, scratched delicately. “Umm—for a morning’s work, eh? Say—um—well, say one—no, say two thousand dollars?”

Rodiker’s eyes were hard-set. He thought, *You’re lyin’!* and said, “A morning’s work? To cut and run and double back and dodge with a posse swarming on my heels and not a friend to hide me! A hardware store across the street where anybody can grab a gun and open up! You say two thousand. But how much will you say I took?"

"Sh-hh-h! Not so loud!" Jerym's pale hand moved silencingly as his head rocked this way and that with an anxious stare, as if eavesdroppers might be in the shadowed corners of the room. Then urgently:

"I'll protect you ever' way I can! And have the sheriff look where you ain't. It's a business deal. Just business! Just between us!" A savage glint slanted off the wet-pebble eyes, and the nearly toothless jaws came together like a snap turtle's. He studied Rodiker's silence and repeated, "I'll help you ever' way I can!" implying, or trying to, that his help was infallible.

Rodiker said nothing. There was no flicker in his eyes as he stared across the table. Farseein', the Bevartses? Hell, no! Old Jerym had just shown the pips of cards he thought he was playing close to his belly. Rodiker asked with slow fall of words:

"Business, you say, and just between us? And you'll protect me every way you can?"

Jerym studied as if he sensed something ominous in the way the question was shaped; but, after all, it only restated his own promise, so he said:

"Yes, yes, that's it. My word on it! My solemn word!" He put his hand across the table to shake on it.

"Good!" said Rodiker, ignoring the hand. "This

time it will be as big a risk for you as for me!" He stood up, and his forefinger tapped the table as he said:

"Write it out! Write, 'I, Jerym Bevarts, having sent for Jack Rodiker, hereby promise him two thousand dollars to raid my bank because it is so near broke that it has to fail, and I want to make people think it was Rodiker, and not me, that got away with the money!' "

Old Jerym had a shocked, palsied stare, then he shook his head and grinned, as if tiredly making the best of a bad joke. "No, no! That's goin' too far!"

Rodiker told him, "You promised your solemn word to protect me ever' way you can. No other way can give me so much protection. Write it out!"

"You think I'm crazy?"

"No, you're forethoughtful and farseein'! And you can foresee how much protection you'll have to give me if I have something like that in my pocket!"

Temper came into Jerym's sunken eyes, and they were evil eyes. "I ain't a fool!"

"But thought I was!" Rodiker lifted his revolver, thumbing back the hammer, as from over the top of the holster the muzzle pointed at Jerym, whose mouth popped open with the look of trying to yell, but not a sound came.

Rodiker said, "I want it in ink. I want it on

bank paper. And when the showdown comes, you can say I made you write it at the point of a gun. Most people will believe you. But if your bank fails before it is held up, most people will know that I made you write what is true. And if I show it before your bank is held up, you'll be in a hell of a fix—the way people'll rush to get their money out!"

Jerym drew his neck down between his humped shoulders and peered. He didn't believe Rodiker would shoot, but wasn't sure, for he was an outlawed man with the name of having done desperate things. Never in his life had Jerym been so tricked and caught before. He had big holdings, but he had big debts, too, and many speculations hadn't been lucky. He wanted the bank to fail before the Bevartses got hold of Cora Arnold's property; otherwise he'd be expected to bolster it up and pay creditors. And he didn't want people to know that failure had been brought about by fraud and speculation. There would be curses and hatred of the Bevarts name, with trust and prestige gone.

Jerym's eyes left Rodiker's face and went to the revolver; it was steady, and the fanged hammer was cocked. He lifted his eyes that seemed lidless as a snake's again to Rodiker's face and was half-minded to refuse. But Rodiker's was the cold hardness of a man who had indeed done desperate things.

Jerym warned, “You never in your life done anything you’ll be so sorry for!”

“Write, or be sorry your own self!”

Jerym said, “Goddamn your soul!” then took up a pen and pulled a stopper from the ink bottle.

CHAPTER 7

Rodiker left his horse and rifle at the livery stable, then went back along the empty street to the hotel with the sycamore in front.

A cord dangled from a bell on the wall, and he gave a jerk. The shallow clang brought an old man, whose eyes were blurred with sleepiness, shuffling out of the shadows. From behind the counter that served as a desk he pushed the register at Rodiker and handed him a pen. Rodiker signed. The clerk turned the book, peered at the squiggly signature, and said, "Room seven, Mr. Jackson. Four bits, please."

Rodiker laid down the coin. The clerk leaned over the desk, pointed, and spoke mildly.

"Don't make much difference this time of night, but the marshal don't want guns wore in town."

Rodiker said, "Thanks," took the key that was tied to a short piece of broomstick, and climbed the unlighted stairs. He struck a match in the dark hall and went in to number seven. It was hot and close and musty. He raised the window and looked out, leaning over. He didn't expect to have to jump, but he liked to know about where he'd land if he did jump. He undressed without lighting the lamp, had another cigarette from

Zig's makin's, and smoked, sitting on the side of the bed, wondering what Bess had said to Zig. Rodiker felt bitter toward her, but not mistrustful. All Claytons had been like close kinfolks; a man might get mad at his kinfolks, but treachery wasn't thought of.

He had a long, restful sleep, and on awakening with a dry mouth, drank stale water from the pitcher in the washbowl, and judged that it was afternoon. Gazing at himself in the cracked looking glass, he fingered the dark, thick, half-grown beard and decided better not, though wishing for a shave.

On the way downstairs Rodiker took off his hat and drew himself to one side of the dim stairs as a woman, coming up, passed. She didn't seem to look at him, but murmured, "Thank you." There was a satiny rustle about her, the vague fragrance of cologne, and though her veil was bunched along the brim of a small hat that had a feather in it, he didn't have a clear look at her face.

Outside he found rather a crowd on the veranda, for the stage from Woodward had arrived, and townspeople clustered about to look at who had come and to hear news. Rodiker, loitering there with a shoulder against the wall, heard a passing man say to the fellow with him, "Funny nobody was here to meet that Arnold woman!"

He strained his ears for more, but that was all

he heard. So far as he had seen, there was only one woman who might have left the stage, and his heart thumped like a fist knocking when he thought that on the stairs Cora Arnold had been close enough for him to have taken her by the throat.

The stage rattled on toward the stable, and men drifted back to their stores or into the hotel bar, or over to the New York Store, where the post office was, to wait while the mail was sorted.

Rodiker went there, too, wanting a fresh shirt or two and underwear. Among the group of men waiting before the closed post-office window while the mailbag was being sorted was Zig Bevarts. His face had a dirty, discolored, swollen, and bruised look.

Rodiker stopped short, eyed him, silently asking, *Do you want more trouble?*

Zig stared back sullenly, as if ready for the trouble, but under Rodiker's gaze defiance faded from his eyes. They wavered down, paused on Rodiker's revolver, and turned aside until Rodiker went along the counter. Then Zig went outdoors.

Soon a man came in with a marshal's badge on his vest. He spoke genially to the men waiting for their mail, then stepped along toward the end of the counter where a clerk was wrapping Rodiker's two shirts.

He was a thin man, this marshal, with a long

neck, droopy mustache, pale eyes, and was so hipless that he wore galluses.

In a friendly way he said:

"You're a stranger, mister, so I reckon you don't know that here in town we like for folks not to wear guns."

Rodiker listened politely, and was ready to say that it was all right with him, which it wasn't, but the marshal added in mild earnestness:

"Funny the colonel didn't tell you."

"Colonel?"

"W'y, yes. It's him that raises so much billy-hell if one of the Bevartses' men don't unbuckle himself as soon as he hits town."

Rodiker cautiously intoned, "Colonel Arnold?"

"You're workin' for him, ain't you?"

Rodiker played the hand as dealt and, poker-faced, asked, "How'd you come to learn?"

"Zig Bevarts said you was a new Arnold man. Just kicked to me about your gun. I sure make him take off hisn! Sorry you two outfits are so stiff-legged with neck hairs bristlin'!"

Rodiker smiled a little, a very little, as he unbuckled his heavy gun belt, wrapped it about the holstered gun. "This be all right until I get back to the hotel?"

"Sure will." The marshal let his eyes run friendly-like up and down Rodiker's long body. "They call the colonel 'Yank,' but he hires some Southern boys. I guess he found out how good they was, tryin' to whup 'em during the War!"

"You think I'm Southern?"

The marshal told him, "How you talk is, anyhow."

At the hotel Rodiker took off his clothes for a wash, and kept trying to figure why Zig Bevarts had told the marshal he worked for Yank Arnold. *Just his ornery way of lying, maybe.*

After the marshal had spoken to him in the store, Rodiker bought a soft buckskin belt; and now, when dressing, he ran this belt through the holster loop, then put the belt over his right shoulder and set the holster under his left armpit. He tied the thongs which were attached to the end of the holster around his waist, then he slipped the revolver into the holster. When he put on his new blue shirt, he left the three top buttons unfastened. The gun was long and the butt made a lump under his shirt, but the lump wouldn't show much after he put on his vest. He had high, wide shoulders and his waist was lean, which helped to conceal the gun.

It wasn't easy to make a quick draw, because he would have to reach down inside the shirt and lift the gun straight up from the holster and alongside his jaw, but at least he wouldn't be unarmed. It was a trick he had used before.

Even as he stood in front of the cracked looking glass and told himself he oughtn't to stay in town, he knew he wouldn't be riding out, not while

Cora Arnold was maybe here within a hand's reach of him.

Downstairs he had a look at the dog-eared register, but there wasn't any "Arnold" on the page, not any woman's name at all.

A man behind the desk had his hat on, and was reading a newspaper. Rodiker asked who was the woman that had come on today's stage, and the man scarcely lifted his eyes from the paper to say, "Don't know. I'm not a clerk. I'm just helpin' out."

Rodiker went through the double doors to the veranda and turned toward a restaurant up the street, then right off changed his mind and swung about at the hotel bar's entrance, meaning to wait and eat in the hotel on the chance of seeing the Arnold woman again. The dining-room doors weren't open yet, so he'd have a drink.

He cut from the street door straight to the front end of the bar that made an L to the wall. The bartender, a dumpy man with a round red face, touched the pigtail-tight curls of his black mustache, then set out a bottle.

In no time at all Zig Bevarts, followed Indian file by two fellows, came through the swinging doors and brought up halfway down the bar, where they stopped side by side, not talking, but drank from the same bottle, with Zig paying.

Rodiker took note that Zig didn't look at him, which was all right, but the two fellows kept sneaking glances toward the bar's L. They were strong, rough-looking men, and though they were not armed, Rodiker, cat-cautious, smelled trouble, guessing that Zig, having brought help along, was set to beat him up.

It wasn't quite dusky enough for lamps to have been lit when the supper gong rang, and at once there was a scampering rush for the side door that opened into the hall before the dining room.

Rodiker waited for Zig and his friends to go first, but they stood as if they didn't care anything about eating. The saloon was about empty when Rodiker started down along the bar, and wasn't at all surprised when one of Zig's men spun about and made an encircling grab from behind to pin Rodiker's arms.

Zig, all set for just that, whirled and let drive at Rodiker's face, as the third fellow yelped, "Git 'im, Zig!"

Zig didn't, because the shaggy man who had grabbed from behind for Rodiker's arms found his own hands caught in a beartrap's grasp, as Rodiker ducked down with a bucking heave and threw the fellow forward, heels over head. He hit the floor as if he had been dropped on his back from a beam, and he hadn't any more breath in him than a busted bladder.

Even before the fellow hit the floor, Rodiker had swung about, straightened, and turned on

Zig, whose lump face wore about the same astonished look as if the roof were falling in on him. But Rodiker, a quick-seeing man, hit the other of Zig's companions first, because his hand had closed on the neck of the whisky bottle, and he was set to use it as a club. Rodiker's fist rocked the fellow's head back over the bar, then straightened him up with a belly punch, and let him fall. The bottle fell, too, and gurgled gurgled over the floor.

When Zig saw that his two friends were both going under, he scrambled, belly down, up on the bar, then on over, with the look of frantically trying to get down behind it and hide; but the pudgy bartender yelled, "Look out! He's after the gun!"

Zig's face was turned over his shoulder and had a spasm look of terror as he groped behind the cash box on the back shelf.

Rodiker had jerked a button off his new shirt when his hand started for the concealed revolver, but it came to him that if he killed this Zig, however much in self-defense, he couldn't then evade questioning, and would be looked at intently by a lot of people, some of whom would know him, beard and all. So he slapped his hands palm down on the bar, vaulting up, and as he went he swung his long, saddle-hardened legs around and up in such a way as to hook his spurred boots' toes about Zig's short neck, then jerked him so hard that the gun dropped out of Zig's hand.

The pudgy bartender said, "Holy Moses!"

When Rodiker got down behind the bar, Zig was hemmed in like a steer in a chute, and Rodiker batted him. Zig kept backing up until he came against the L at the front, and was trapped. Rodiker let drive from the shoulder, throwing his knuckles against the discolored spot on Zig's jaw, and as Zig slumped to the floor, old Jerym, from right across the bar, shouted:

"Punch him good, stranger! Punch him good! He deserves it! I seen 'im jump you!"

Men had forgotten supper, and swarmed back in to see the fight, and they heard Zig's father saying that.

Rodiker eyed old Jerym with suspicious steadiness as Jerym lifted his voice to tell the barroom, "I seen it all! Was just comin' through the street door. That fool Zig of mine, and Pete and Mark here, picked on this stranger who was mindin' his own business!"

It had grown darker in the barroom, and no lamps were lighted. Jerym was still talking loudly when Rodiker stooped to hands and knees, passed under the L, and went out to the street. He didn't want to be stared at, and now wouldn't go into the dining room.

His mouth carried a crooked smile as he stepped along the sidewalk. *Forethoughtful and farseein',the Bevartses!* Old spider-shaped Jerym certainly was! Print couldn't have made it plainer that Jerym had instructed Zig to gather a couple of helpers and knock Rodiker senseless—or worse. And Jerym had lurked near so that he would have the first chance to go through Rodiker's pockets. When the plan didn't work out, the farseeing Jerym at once announced that Zig had been in the wrong. That, of course, was to pull the wool over Rodiker's eyes. *He don't dare have me bad hurt unless he's close enough to get into my pockets first!*

Rodiker sat at a back table in the Busy Bee, and was finishing a big supper when the marshal stood in the door and looked all about, then came toward Rodiker, who thought there might be some trouble. But the marshal smiled, drew out a chair, sat down, pushed back his hat, and pulled at his drooping mustache.

"Jackson, from how I hear, you sure cleaned up! That ought to make you ace-high with the colonel!"

Rodiker took a piece of dried apple pie in his fingers, bit off a mouthful, swallowed it with some coffee, nodded, and said nothing.

"But old Jerym Bevarts is a mighty fine man," the marshal explained. "He heard me askin' around for you, an' he said not to bother you. Said it was all Zig's fault on account of a lickin' you give him a night or two ago. Not many men would be that fair against their own son, now would they?"

Rodiker ate more pie.

"What I come for, Jackson, is that the colonel's daughter wants you. She sent for me a while ago, because nobody showed up here in town to meet her. I told her about you—you bein' one of the colonel's men—and she wants that you come to the hotel right away. That's why I was askin' around to find you, but Jerym thought maybe I was takin' sides agin you on account of the fight."

CHAPTER 8

The marshal went ahead on the hotel's dim stairs and walked down the hall to number four, a corner room facing Main Street, and Rodiker thought, *Maybe this is a trap!* and that stirred his wariness.

Trap or not, he wasn't being smart to come up here as one of Colonel Arnold's men and be found out a liar, but he had seen the colonel's daughter on the stairs and, while he'd much rather she had turned out to be Cora Arnold, he couldn't help wanting to see her again. He had once held her in his arms; she had been cute and pretty years back when the sprained ankle made her faint, and he had brought the sidesaddled horse from the stable. The dim glimpse he'd had of her on the stairs helped him to think she would be prettier now. He knew, or thought he did, that he was so changed in size, years, and with a beard, that she wouldn't remember him, not from the brief meeting so many years ago when she was just a kid, and he told himself that maybe he could learn something from her about Cora Arnold.

The marshal knocked lightly and the door opened.

They were invited in, and the marshal pulled off his hat and put on manners to say, "Jackson, this is Miss Arnold. She knows I'd do anything for the colonel, so she sent for me to ask about gettin' to the ranch, and I told her you was in town an'—"

The dark-eyed girl closed the door, not listening to the marshal, and she looked so steadily at Rodiker that he began to wish he weren't there. She was small, white-faced, pretty, and her black eyes seemed judging him, but without recognition. He did look rather a hard case, being big, and in old worn clothes, except for the store-new blue shirt that had some buttons off. Scraggly hair lay around the back of his neck, and the thick untrimmed beard overlaid his face. His gray-blue eyes held the unwavering pin-point stare of one who must watch closely, think quickly, and be right.

She gazed at him, meeting his look, and seemed doubtful, until suddenly she put out her hand, crinkled her eyes in a curious laughing way, and said cheerily:

"I am Kate Arnold, and will you take me home?"

Without waiting for a reply, she then turned and thanked the marshal, opening the door for him as she said good-by, all with a kind of gracious impatience. Rodiker sensed that she might readily lose the graciousness if she didn't have things the way she wanted.

As soon as she closed the door, she turned back

and told him to sit down, adding rapidly, "I've been in prison for years, and just escaped!"

Rodiker had a literal mind. He didn't believe what she said, but he didn't know what she meant, and regarded her with a soberness that made Kate exclaim:

"Don't look so shocked! A 'ladies school' *is* a prison of a kind. Worse than any other kind! In a good, lively penitentiary you have riots and fights and interesting companions! At least you're with persons who have done what they wanted, instead of with Miss Mealymouths, who are supposed to do only what other people want! So will you take me home?"

Rodiker sat down and drew his feet back alongside the chair, and hooked his hat over a knee. He had never seen another woman who could laugh so with her eyes as she did.

"Miss, I'm not working for the colonel, and never said I was. Seems like Zig Bevarts has told around that I was, maybe getting me mixed up with somebody else. And you didn't register today when you came."

"Didn't I, hm?"

"I looked to see who you was after passin' you on the stairs."

"Did you now?" Her eyes laughed at him but not in a way to make him feel uncomfortable. "But why should I register in a hotel my father owns? I used to be proud he did, but now it's run down. So Zig thinks he said something bad about you when he said you were working for the colonel?"

"Maybe so."

"I am surprised Zig tried to fight you with only two men helping! That's really very brave of Zig! Who *are* you working for, Mr. Jackson?"

"I'm sort of a stranger. Just drifted in a day or two ago."

He liked to look at her; she still wasn't much bigger than a minute, and may have been older than he thought that time, years back, when she had crinkled her eyes at him and said that she was bigger than she looked. She was slim and straight and quick, with lots of dark hair coiled about her head, and there was something of a race horse's glowing aliveness about her, but it was the sparkle in her eyes that interested and pleased him.

She said, "All right, Mr. Jackson, will you get a livery rig and drive me to the ranch? I could drive myself, but I'm not going to. Maybe I'm afraid! Years back East, having to be polite to everybody, takes the starch out of you. Or out of me! If I'd been Eve, and there was one of those Eastern fellows in the garden with me, I'd have fed him a prickly pear!"

She turned aside to peer into the mirror and put a hand to her cheek, then whirled toward him. "Just look at me! I'm as bleached as something that crawls out from under a wet log! And they told me back East that I ought to be happy because I'm now not brown as a Mexican! But I like Mexicans. I played with Mexican kids, till the colonel had the idea that I ought to be a lady! If being a lady is doing needlework and learning French when you don't know any Frenchmen and singing silly songs in a weak voice and looking at your toes when a strange man looks at you, then I'd rather be an Apache squaw!"

The earnestness of what she meant shimmered in her homesick jesting, and he laughed without a sound and liked her. She came nearer to him and said:

"It's not ladylike for a girl to ask a strange man to drive her fifteen miles, or nearly that, this time of night, but I want to go—I'll pay what you ask—and will you?"

The table with the lamp on it was between them and the window; the window was raised and its curtains were back to let in more air. When, hat in hand, he stood up, she wasn't an arm's length from him, and he shook his head, but wanted to do as she asked. It would be pleasant driving fifteen miles with her, but he'd be a fool to drive right into the colonel's home ranch; so he told her:

"I don't hardly see how I can."

"You aren't working? You want a job, don't you? All right, go get the buggy."

Those words weren't more than across her lips when a bullet smacked into the room, its thud jarring the doorjamb. The bang of a gun seemed thin and far away.

A gasp was the only sound she made as she whirled toward the window and back again. A revolver was in Rodiker's hand, and she hadn't any idea where it came from. Then his hat fanned down over the lamp chimney and stayed there, bringing darkness into the room as he lurched forward, giving a shove to put her out of the line of fire if another bullet came. He crouched at a corner of the window and peered out.

Kate scrouged close beside him, and the faint fragrance of cologne floated into his face. "You or me?" she asked.

"Who'd shoot at *you?*"

"Nobody, I hope!"

"Me, of course. Zig's evening up!"

"I'm surprised! Your back wasn't toward him!" Her voice had a lively scorn, but she was trembling.

"A rifle from the roof of that bakery across the street. Nobody's there now, but it's my bet that if you open the door and scream, Poppa Jerym will be the first man in this room!"

"Why? Why do you say that? Want me to try?"

He believed that she would have gone to the door and screamed if he had said yes, but he told her no, adding, "It would make old Jerym feel bad to be caught snooping out there in the hall."

"Why should he be?"

"Because they're copperheads, the Bevartses!"

"Why, that's what the colonel calls them!" Her fingers closed hard on his arm. "If that's how you feel, you ought to be working for the colonel!"

"Be fine, that would!" he said ironically.

She stared tensely at him, and couldn't see in the dimness, and anyhow his face was covered with the heavy smudge of half-grown beard that was like a mask. She wasn't sure of the irony, but she did wonder that he, with his Southern voice, would call somebody a "copperhead."

The gun's report hadn't caused any disturbance on the street; no outcry followed, no other shots were fired, and men who had paused to listen tramped along the sidewalk again and resumed their talk.

He said, "I reckon for sure now that I'd better not drive you anywhere. They seem to want me. May want me bad enough to follow. Or cut cross-country when they know we're going. You might get hurt. Like just now, you come as near gettin' hit as I did!"

"From where on earth did you get that gun? One minute you weren't armed, the next—presto! You in cahoots with old Satan?"

He didn't say anything, and she told him, "But you can't be, because the devil loves his Bevartses too well not to let them have their own way, if he can. I talk too much! But I'll be nice, and won't. Only please, you are Southern, so why did you call them 'copperheads'?"

His answer was surly. "Because they are!"

He stood up, thrust the revolver into his waistband, took his hat, then, lifting the chimney, struck a sulphur match and put it to the wick. She moved away from the lamp and watched uneasily, dreading a second shot, but he told her:

"That fellow's scrambled off the roof by now. Afraid he'd be caught."

"How can you know?"

"I know how cowards act. And I can't take you. I'm a stranger. And Southern, like you say. Even if we don't get shot at on the way out, Yank Arnold maybe won't like it for a stranger and a Southerner to be bringing his girl home."

Kate said, "So?" and lifted her head stiffly.

His eyes had a gray-blue brightness, metallic, hard, stubborn. She studied his look for some way to push by his stubbornness and get what she wanted, because she always got what she wanted, any way she could.

"You want to know something?" Her face was slyly mischievous. "The colonel hasn't a dislike of all Southerners! I'm partly one myself! He met my mother in New Orleans, and married her before the war was over! So there!"

"I never heard of that."

"How could you, just drifting in a day or two

ago? Not many know. He doesn't tell much about his family. But he's a fine man. I love him. You don't think I could love a man that wasn't fine, do you?"

Again her earnestness was overlaid with the sparkle of pleasantry and the curious crinkling at the corners of her dark eyes, and he liked her, though he said:

"No matter, I just can't take you. Why, if we are stopped on the road—"

He didn't finish. She waited, and when it seemed that he wouldn't say anything more, she exclaimed in the manner of seminary theatricals, "Oh, Mr. Jackson! How dreadful that would be! You are so small and weak and timid! You would just sit there with hands in the air and say, 'Please don't hurt me!' "

Laughter then tinkled at him derisively, but almost at once her face sobered, and Kate snapped, "I never yet put my fingers in my ears so I wouldn't hear a gun go bang!"

Rodiker gazed solemnly at her, then laughed soundlessly. "You sure *are* lots bigger than you look! I'll go for that livery rig."

He went out, and she watched the closed door with a bewildered stare; then she rubbed at her forehead and frowned in an effort to make her muddled thoughts take shape.

Kate turned to the alcove and dropped on a sofa. "I am bigger than I look" had been her little-girl's way of maintaining that she was grown up enough for whatever she wanted to do. The inflection he used implied that he knew it was what she used to say. A stranger in the Santsander, yet he called her father "Yank," the Bevartses "copperheads," and pointedly repeated her childish assertion that she was bigger than she looked.

CHAPTER 9

Loafers in the half-darkness of the hotel porch watched Rodiker come down the dim, dust-soft street with a pole buggy and his own saddle horse jogging behind on a lead rope.

Presently Slim Clayton, deep in the shadows, gawked to see Rodiker follow Kate out of the hotel with valises that he stowed in the back of the buggy, before he cramped the wheels and helped her on the step.

Rodiker then put down the buggy top. Kate asked him to. She wanted a full view of the stars and night-blackened hills and the great sweeps of dark flat land where the yuccas held up their clusters of white flame; and she wanted to feel the warm breath of the sweet wind as they drove toward her home.

When the team trotted off with whimpering creak of harness, Slim came out of the shadows to head for the bar, feeling the need of liquor to help him guess at what Rodiker was up to in going off with Yank Arnold's girl.

Jerym Bevarts's big pale hand reached out and closed on Slim's arm. "I want you!" said Old Jerym with the look and sound of the devil laying hold on somebody he had the right to claim, body and soul.

The team went at their own speed, walking or trotting as pleased them, while Rodiker, looking straight ahead, sat with a stiff back, a rein in each hand, a hand on each knee, rather as if he didn't know much about driving, but wanted to make sure the horses wouldn't bolt.

A thin lap robe lay over Kate's knees. She was merry, as if at a picnic, and had taken off her hat, tilting her face to the sky, and chattered like a magpie. He liked the lilting sound.

She couldn't imagine, she said, why the colonel, or some of the ranch folks, hadn't met her, but there wasn't any worry in her wonder. "I'm going home!" she chanted rejoicingly.

She moved a foot, and it struck the barrel of the rifle lying on the floorboard, and that reminded her of why it was there. She raised up and looked back over the folded-down buggy top.

"I'm not afraid, but do you think they'll follow?"

"To follow they'd be seen. If they can't dry-gulch a man, they'll let him be."

Uneasiness tingled through her, but she assured herself that it wasn't fear. *I'm just excited,* she thought, and said, "How the country's changed! When I was little, the colonel let me ride where I pleased. He said nobody would hurt a girl, however much they had it in for the girl's father. When I was little, even Jack Rodiker was good to me!"

His eyes stayed straight ahead. “You mean that outlaw?”

“They say he killed my uncle, but I don’t believe it!”

He droned, “From how I hear, most people do.”

“The colonel thinks the Bevartses hired him to. And you can’t argue with the colonel!”

Rodiker’s face turned toward her. “As I hear tell, some woman saw him do it, didn’t she?”

Kate said, “She saw a man she thought was Jack Rodiker. But she didn’t know him very well. Didn’t know him at all, really. The Fourth of July before, there in Moheela, we had seen him ride a horse that men bet he couldn’t!” Her voice trilled laughingly. “I made the colonel so mad he licked me good when we got home!”

“Whipped you?”

“Larruped me! Indeed, he did!”

“Why’d a man do that?”

“I needed it, that’s why!”

“W’y, you was only a little tyke.”

“Big enough to coax twenty dollars out of him to buy a dress and things, then I gave it to our cook to bet that Jack Rodiker could ride that horse! He did! He did it easy too!”

“Ah, ‘easy,’ hm?”

“Aunt Cora and I stood in a wagon to look over the crowd. The horse was a big devil, and trained to throw or kill a rider by falling back. But Jack rode him into a lope! I had the colonel’s glasses and could watch close. When he tried to r'ar back, Jack whipped him down—like this!"

She leaned forward, and her hand flew out in a rapid criss-cross, pantomiming the slash of a quirt over the killer's head.

"You knew this Rodiker?"

She laughed. "Oh, well enough to be desperately jealous of a white-trash girl who folks said was his sweetheart!" Kate added merrily, "I bet I was prouder of him that day than Bess Clayton was!"

Rodiker sat remembering. He had known some women looked on, but he hadn't known who they were, or cared, excepting that Bess was in the crowd. He'd taken the chance, wanting to make her proud; that more than any other reason had put him in the saddle.

And Kate was wrong; it hadn't been easy. He had topped all sort of unbroken horses, but this was a trained "outlaw," and nearly tireless. Pain had knifed Rodiker's side and his neck seemed broken by the whipcracker back-bumping of the big brute. Afterward Rodiker coughed blood. He had been paid ten dollars to make the try and hadn't bet on himself, not having any money. The horse was a killer, just horsehide stretched over the bones of a devil that tried to trample a man when he threw him.

Kate said, "The colonel doesn't believe in his daughter gambling. Though it was lying to him that brought the lickin'! I wasn't yet half grown, but I thought Jack Rodiker the handsomest boy in the country, having seen him about three times! Spoke to him just once. Pretended my ankle was sprained so I could ask him to bring my horse from the stable. Then I played like I fainted! What a girl won't do!"

"And he?"

"He picked me up off the floor and held me close! And my little heart bobbed like a cork when a fish nibbled! I had fainted so convincingly that he wouldn't let me walk to the stable with him! See how a girl can overplay her hand?"

"I see. And your betting on him made the colonel mad?"

"My betting not so much, but the lying, yes! He won't stand for lies of any kind from anybody! And of course he fired poor Bob. The best range cook we ever had! But you'll like the colonel. He looks so stern, with shoulders always just like this." Kate threw her shoulders back as stiffly as she could, made a sour face, pulled an imaginary mustache, but said, "He's really soft-hearted. Honest, he is. Only it makes him mad if he thinks anybody thinks so! He'd rather die than ever admit that he's wrong."

The horses plodded at a head-bobbing walk. Coyotes were yipping. How many, no knowing: two or three could sound like a wide-ranging pack, throwing their voices to confuse the game they chased. An owl flew across the road, coming to the ground with as heavy a flutter as if thrown.

Rodiker asked, "About your uncle, why didn't you think Rodiker had done it?"

"I did at first. Cora had seen him, she said. I was only thirteen, about. And not very bright. Not like now—after I've been away for years to school! And when the other girls there found that the little savage from Arizona knew Jack Rodiker—I bragged about how he had picked me up when I fainted!—they begged for stories and to read my clippings. I said he never shot my uncle. I'll still say it to anybody but the colonel!"

"You've not said why you think he didn't."

"For one thing, I liked him!" Kate seemed earnest. "I don't believe I could like anybody that was mean!" Then she laughed. "All women feel that way—which is maybe why we are so easy fooled! But you'll never make me believe that a man who'd go through mud and rain to fetch a doctor for a child he didn't know—when the child's father was out with the sheriff hunting him—would shoot anybody in the back!" Then she asked sharply, "Would you? Believe it, I mean?"

He didn't say anything, but shook the team into a trot, and the road was rough and joggled her about.

The lights of Whitman's lay ahead, just this side of Apache Flat.

A lighted door was wide open, letting moths and winged bugs come in with the fresh air. As soon as the buggy stopped, Kate threw the lap robe aside and jumped out. Her small feet scrunched the gravel as she ran toward the doorway and with a merry squeal announced her escape from the East.

Voices answered welcomingly, and Rodiker heard a deep-throated, "It's my little Kate!" Her small silhouette merged into a big man's encircling arms.

Rodiker meant to keep away from the light here for, though now his appearance was greatly changed, he didn't care to come under the keen eyes and remembrance of an old-timer such as Whitman. He drove on to the water trough and pumped. When the horses had drunk, he uncinched the saddle on his horse, then sat on his heels and smoked. Now he had tobacco and papers stowed in a saddlebag, and in his pocket still some of Zig's makin's.

His thoughts went round and round Kate, and a lingering smile warmed his dark face that she should have pretended a sprained ankle when such a mite of a kid, and he thought how little a man can know of what a woman's up to, big or little.

When Kate stood in the lighted doorway and called, "Mr. Jackson!" he rose up and pulled the uncinched saddle from the horse: "Come here," she said, "and meet old friends of mine!"

"Just a minute, miss. I've got some fixin' to do on this saddle," he explained, using his prepared excuse to keep out of Whitman's lamplight.

Kate then came into the moonlit yard with two men and a woman. The woman was a stout Mexican with long, swaying colored skirts, and Kate's arm was about her waist. One man was a small wrinkled Mexican, the other a burly fellow.

Kate said, " 'Nita was nearly like my mama, except she never spanked!"

Rodiker pulled off his hat, bowing to Anita. The burly man rumbled, "The times you've needed it, darlin'!"

"And Mr. Jackson," Kate said gleefully, "this is Bob, the cook I told you of!"

Bob had the girth of a good cook and was more jovial than most. He called Kate a "gamblin' wench!" and told Rodiker, "The men she's tied to a snubbin' post before she was knee-high to a pack rat!"

Rodiker shook hands with the small, wrinkled Mexican. Kate explained, "He and 'Nita came to help look after Mr. Whitman before he passed away last spring. And they are staying on here."

The cook said, "And if you don't mind, Jackson, I'd like to drive the little lady from here on in to the ranch. We're old sweethearts!"

"The colonel hired him back after I went away!"

"Yes, mister," Bob the cook rumbled, "and I hear you been hired too. Y'see, Zig onct tried to make love to her, and your punchin' his nose has dealt you aces!"

"He punched three noses, I told you!" Kate corrected. "And it wasn't Zig's trying to make love to me that I minded—it was his not knowing how!"

"He ought to do better at it now, since I hear Bess Clayton is learnin' him. And, darlin', why didn't you let us know you was comin'?"

"I couldn't do more than write, could I? I expected somebody to be at Woodward, and nobody was even at Moheela. So I coaxed Mr. Jackson here to drive me out. And," she added to Rodiker, "you are to follow us."

The buggy drove off. Rodiker slowly resaddled. He had lifted the rifle from the buggy's floorboards and replaced it in the boot, and now he dawdled in an argument with himself over his lack of good sense if he went on to the Arnold ranch. There was wariness enough to feel that he would soon be suspected, somehow found out, but the dark-eyed girl made him want to go. The lure of her high-tempered liveliness drew him on, though he wondered doubtfully about how she would feel now if she learned that he was Jack Rodiker, who had once held her in his arms.

He pumped himself a drink and leisurely had another cigarette, thinking of Zig as he flung the empty sack aside. *The girl I'm going to marry!* Zig had said that, and Bess made no denial.

A smile touched his mouth when he thought of Old Jerym, and he shook his head in recalling the offer of two thousand dollars. That promise, of course, had been a pure lie. *He'd probably have tried to fool me with washers in canvas bags, and claimed I got away with big thousands.*

CHAPTER 10

He swung into the saddle and looked ahead. There wasn't any dark spot wavering on the road that within a mile or two slipped from view at the Flat's downgrade, and he was half-minded not to follow the buggy, but he did, riding slowly at first, then at an easy lope. His incurious glance drifted over the shadow-studded land where sprawling clumps of cactus were fanged as a nest of snakes, where the shaggy yuccas lifted their glowing candelabra and, in some directions, the haze of smoke trees blurred the moon-etched sharpness of the night.

The gun's report was thin and not near.

He at once reined up, rising in the stirrups with a listening tenseness, as a hand dropped to the rifle stock. Right off another shot was fired, then others, and his keenness placed the sound as from dead ahead, for the wind was in his face and he heard, or thought he did, a scream that was as faint as a dying echo.

Rodiker pulled the rifle free, put the blunt rowels into the horse's flanks, and held them there, asking for speed, while he leaned low and peered along the road that curved and disappeared as abruptly as if at the end of the world. The horse's shod feet beat the dust with about the sound of rapid fists on a wet drum, as he rode headlong, not knowing, and for once not caring, what he was getting into.

He swung on the curve of the Flat's sharp downgrade and, as he passed her, Kate's wild cry told him. "They killed Bob—"

What else she tried to say was unheard. He didn't slacken except to swerve aside from the stalled buggy, where one horse still struggled in the tangle of harness and both were down. He straightened with a quick look to right and left and saw three horsemen; they had dodged off the road, one turning to the left and two to the right. These two would be circling for the river, and he followed them.

As they streaked in and out of the brush shadows, they lashed their horses, and he guessed that the horses were already tired by the long, fast, roundabout ride from town. His own horse was fresh, and he gained.

One of the fellows rocked back in his saddle and fired.

Rodiker's was a grim contempt. Firing a revolver from a running horse at a horseman nearly two hundred yards away was about like throwing rocks at a bat. But the man fired three times, and not a bullet came near enough to whistle.

Rodiker leaned forward, giving his horse a loose rein, and pressed in the spurs, again asking for speed. He got it, bound on bound, closing in; and when the man once more leveled his revolver behind him, as if desperately sighting, Rodiker swung up the rifle, fired, and the fellow lurched sidewise and backward, falling head down, and lay on his back.

In galloping by, Rodiker leaned low, but he couldn't see well enough to recognize the fellow, even if he had known him. He didn't pause, meaning to kill the other man who had veered sharply and was now flogging his horse. The horse was very tired.

Rodiker rode hard, gaining fast, and soon pitched up his rifle, lowered it, then peered frowningly. He muttered, "It can't be!" and drove in the spurs.

The man was circling a wide patch of brush. Rodiker didn't follow him, but tried for a short cut by dropping his head to one side of the saddle horn as he crashed into the chaparral, going through with crackle of dried limbs, with lash and tear of thorny branches that beat at him. When he got through he was so near the fleeing horseman that he yelled, "You, Slim!"

Slim pulled up, faced about, raised his arms. He'd lost his hat, but his face was still masked with a handkerchief.

Rodiker rammed the rifle into its scabbard and rode up, almost leg to leg, facing Slim, and hell was in his eyes as he reached out and jerked down the handkerchief's triangular fold from his best friend's face. Slim didn't say a word, but his eyes begged like a hurt dog's.

Rodiker said, "Even you!"

Then he reached over and pulled Slim's revolver.

Slim choked up and swallowed, and gasped, "I ain't fired!"

Rodiker lifted the barrel to his nose, sniffed, and replaced the gun in Slim's holster. After that he slowly drew back his hand, and slapped Slim across the face as hard as he could.

"I'd have believed it of my own brother as quick!"

Slim's words came with a hurt whimper. "He said you'd throwed in with Yank Arnold! Looked like it—you goin' off with that girl! And I purt' near have to do what Jerym says. He's got a holt on me!"

"I thought friendship had a hold on you!"

"Hones', I—"

"I felt I owed you more than I could ever pay, but now you're paid, you Judas-hearted bastard! Go on, get back to town and tell that I'm Jack Rodiker, then join up to hunt me down!"

Slim pleaded, "I won't tell. 'Fore God, I won't, ever! An' Jerym hisself don't want it made known that you're back. He made me come with him and Pete. 'Twas Pete you shot back there. Jerym hisself killed that man in the buggy before he knew it wasn't you! Then him and Pete shot the horses 'cause that girl grabbed the lines to drive on fast and—and—"

"Keep on! Talk fast!"

"Then he made out like one of us was *you* and layin' for Yank Arnold, pretendin' to think 'twas him bringin' his girl home!"

Jerym had worn a mask and a duster, fully concealing himself. The horses' brands were daubed over with wet clay that dried. Slim said that Mark hadn't come because his back was hurt too bad for riding after Rodiker threw him heels over head to the barroom floor. And Zig—Zig had got out of town.

But Jerym had brought Slim, and now Slim nervously tried to sound proud in saying, "I made him promise nobody would be hurt, b-b-but he lied, an'—"

"And did he promise, too, that *you* could have the reward for catching me?"

Slim mumbled and moved a hand, pleadingly. Rodiker reined back.

"Get the hell away from me and stay away! Next time we meet, I'll kill you! And tell old Jerym I've more than half a mind to join up with Yank Arnold and ruin all the Bevartses in the Santsander! He'll know what I mean! At least Yank Arnold never pretended to be a friend!"

Rodiker turned his horse and rode away with the feeling of having seen worse than death come to the one he had always thought was a friend who could never be distrusted.

When he rode back through the snow-white moonlight to the buggy, he led a horse with a dead man roped across the saddle.

Kate came from beside the buggy, not crying now, but with the smear of tears on her face. He stepped from the saddle and stood beside her. Her dark eyes looked up steadily when he asked if she had any idea who the men were. She didn't speak at first, but her voice wasn't steady when she said:

"They all wore masks and one was—was Jack Rodiker!"

"Masked you know him?"

"No, not that. But the big man who shot Bob rode close to the buggy and he called out 'Rodiker, this is not Yank Arnold!' "

"And what did Rodiker say?"

"Why, nothing. And how could he have thought my father would be with me?"

Rodiker's slow voice droned: "Rodiker was masked to keep from being known, yet didn't say anything when his name was given away?" Her eyes stared blankly when he asked, "How do you figure that?"

"I don't know," she said wearily. "I just can't think. Poor Bob! No warning at all—they just shot him!"

"Then Rodiker and his bunch cut and run when

they heard a lone horseman coming! That outlaw you've been braggin' about once holding you in his arms don't appear to be so much man after all!"

Kate leaned against him as one in weariness leans against a post, and said in a small, discouraged voice, "Oh, he's as measly mean as the colonel says he is!"

Rodiker angrily told her, "Come here with me."

He pulled the rope's slipknot from the dead man on the saddle, letting the body flop heavily to the ground, and said, "Bend down and look. Do you know this one?"

She didn't want to look, but came nearer, peeringly stooped, then shook her head. "I have been away so long."

"This is one of the Bevarts men I had trouble with in town."

Kate lifted her face. "The Bevartses and Rodiker are friends. The colonel always said they hired him to kill Uncle Craig."

He felt like shaking her, and said, "Haven't you a lick of sense? They never thought it was the colonel with you. They saw us leave together and rode from town to cut off the buggy. They killed the cook, thinking he was me."

She gazed staringly, with mouth O-shaped and noiseless until she got her breath and said, "Why would Jack Rodiker want to kill you?"

And he, exasperated and reckless, said,

"Because I know him! Windbag and coward! Shoots from the dark and runs—like tonight! He knows I know him!"

She gasped. "You—you know him?"

Rodiker walked away with her, not replying.

The horses lay in a tangle of harness on the road. The cook's frightened horse had broken from the lead rope and run. The cook was slumped forward, knees down, on the buggy floor. His hat had fallen off, and his head hung over the dashboard. A nearly full moon made the land bright as early morning.

Rodiker picked up the lap robe from the dust, shook it well, then spread it over Bob the cook with an unhurrying gentleness; and after that he said:

"Whitman's closer, but we're goin' on. These saddle horses might kick the buggy to pieces if I tried to put harness on them. Anyway, the harness is broken. We'll leave things just as they are."

Somberly, and without another word, he simply took Kate into his arms and lifted her to the dead man's saddle. She was surprised at the way he lifted and held her, yet she didn't flinch and wasn't startled, but liked the strength and possessive gentleness with which he raised her high in the air.

The saddle seat was much too wide, the stirrup leather hadn't notches to bring the stirrups to her feet. She put her feet between the leather.

The long skirts were rumpled high above her knees, and she pushed at the skirts, but couldn't do anything about the way they hiked up, so she let them be and told him quietly, "I never rode astride in all my life. The colonel wouldn't let me. It wasn't ladylike."

A mile later she said, "So he is back in the Santsander. And he is a friend of the Bevartses. After you thrashed Zig, they got him to lay for you—just as they did for Uncle Craig."

He said, "You are a fool"; and wouldn't answer when she tried questions as to why he had said it.

CHAPTER 11

They rode on to the house, passing through the lacelike shadows of the wide paloverde before the long adobe. Some of the dogs leaped stirrup-high with friendliness toward Kate, but some kept up their yapping and wouldn't quiet down at the sound of her voice.

A big dark figure lumbered out on the balcony overhead, and with the manner and voice of swearing at them, demanded, "What's yuhal want?"

Kate's pale, uplifted face glowed in the moonlight.

"Oh, Sam!"

The big Negro's "Who's 'at?" was a startled shout, and the breath seemed knocked out of him as he leaned low on the balcony to peer. "Miss Kate—home?" sounded as if unsure of whether or not he was dreaming. Certainty came with "B'ess mah soul!" He whooped at the dogs, calling them weird names for not knowing their mistress, and he told her the colonel sure had been poorly, but would come downstairs right away, and then disappeared.

Kate's feet weren't steady. Rodiker held her arm and the dogs crowded about, pawingly. The heavy door was unfastened, and opened into an unlighted hall. As they went in, some of the dogs charged by them and scrambled through the hall and on up the stairs.

When there was a hard clack of heels and jangle of spurs on the stairs, Kate said in a hushed tone, “That’s Papa!” His long shadow fell grotesquely far ahead of him, for Sam followed with a candle in a shell-shaped silver reflector.

Sam was big and fat and glisteningly black, and he grinned like a candle-lit pumpkin as Kate flung her arms about the colonel, who said, “Kate!” and embraced her tensely.

Rodiker had seen the famous Colonel Arnold on the streets of Moheela, and now perceived that he had aged greatly: the bridge of his thin nose was thinner, his nose longer and sharper and his eyes more sunken, the long hair had much gray in it, his mustache and chin whiskers too. A tall man, thin and straight-shouldered, he didn’t appear well. Dressing hurriedly, he had drawn pants over his nightgown and stamped into boots.

After he looked searchingly into Kate’s face, he said, “You have been crying!” and gave Rodiker such a glance as seemed to accuse him.

Rodiker couldn’t afterward recall just what had been said first, what next, but after Kate had leaned against her father with both arms around his neck and told how Bob had been killed, he asked abruptly, “Why are you home?” and sounded reproachful.

Kate looked toward Sam, and the big Negro, from behind the colonel's back, waggled a desperate pantomime of protest; so she replied, "I wanted to come!"

Colonel Arnold surprised her with, "I wanted you home, but wouldn't ask you to come, thinking you wanted to stay."

She rose to tiptoes and held to him. "Papa, I hated it there, but pretended not to, wanting to please you! But I'll never be a lady—not a real one! And I so wanted to come home!"

"Why didn't you write?"

She had written, she said—of course she had written—and why he hadn't received the letter she couldn't imagine.

He said, "Your aunt Cora's letters come. She is coming herself next week."

Sam had placed the candle on a stand and put a match to a big-bellied lamp with a round wick. He shook the lamp, judging the amount of oil in it, then replaced the chimney. After that he rolled his eyes as he made low moan over Bob and mumbled maledictions at the Bevartses, all with a ritualistic persistence in a guttural rumble, soft as distant thunder.

The colonel paid no attention to the muttering, and turned on Rodiker, who looked more of a hard case than ever, after the headlong ride through chaparral branches that had lashed at him like whips and torn his new shirt to rags.

"So they think you are working for me?"

"That's what the marshal says Zig Bevarts told him."

The colonel stepped closer and stood with feet together, shoulders stiffly straight, head up, and Rodiker noticed that he was breathing hard.

"And you know Jack Rodiker?"

No denying it now, not here with Kate's dark eyes on his face, and the wish that he had kept his mouth shut was useless, so he said, "Yes, I've seen him."

The colonel's deep eyes held a piercing focus in the studying silence before he said, "Jackson, when I hire a man I don't ask questions. Soon as he hits the saddle, I know if he knows his work. As long as he does his work, he is my man. If you want to be, you are working for me!"

The queerness of it twitched Rodiker's lips into a vague smile, but he didn't say yes or no. When the colonel told him, "Think it over!" and moved aside, Rodiker's glance drifted, found Kate, and paused.

Her lips were parted, fingers lightly touched her chin, and she stared frozenly in asking:

"Where did you ever know Jack Rodiker?"

He hitched his thumbs into his belt, straightened his shoulders, and his thoughts spun, trying for a story that would fit, but the colonel wheeled about, and spoke sharply.

"Never you mind! I've offered him work. No questions asked!"

Her "Yes, Papa," was submissive, as she lingeringly pulled her eyes from Rodiker's beard-masked face.

A little old man with fuzzy whiskers limped in, and a good-looking dark and not old woman was with him.

Kate said, "Why, Johnny Grant!" and almost hugged him. The wizened old soldier introduced his embarrassed wife. Kate and Mrs. Grant, though strangers, exchanged glances like confidants, which, in a way, they were, and presently they started upstairs together to air and make ready Kate's room.

In the dimness of the stairs' landing Kate turned and looked down on Rodiker, now rolling a cigarette. There was a heedfulness in her stare, a kind of questioning amazement, but decision, too, as she held her breath, bit her lip, and nodded. Her fingers were clenched.

Johnny was one of the colonel's pensioners; he lazed about, being greatly afflicted by the ache of old wounds when he didn't want to work. Now he was sent to arouse the bunkhouse.

Sam fetched a lantern. The horse Kate had ridden in was led around to the kitchen pump, where Rodiker threw water on the dried clay and rubbed the smear with his hands. The dirt came away, and a Lazy S appeared on the horse's shoulder.

Rodiker said, "Enough of a brand blot to serve in the moonlight."

The whites of Sam's rolling eyes glistened as he mumbled. Colonel Arnold plucked at his goatee and said nothing, until he turned to meet the four men who came from their bunkhouse in a stiff-legged hurry.

Rodiker cleaned his hands under the pump spout, dried them on a handkerchief from his pocket, and, listening, soon understood that most of the hands were in line camps or working out of Old Place.

The colonel, as stiffly as if speaking with strangers, said to put a team to the buckboard: they would take the Lazy S horse, pick up Bob and the dead Bevarts man from the road, and carry them into Moheela. That was all. No anger, no bitterness, no threats. He merely gave instructions. Rodiker thought, *Don't he feel, or can he hide it?*

Old Johnny's dry, thin voice rose angrily. "Colonel, they'll lie outa it somehow!"

"They" meant Bevartses, of course, and Colonel Arnold's reply was matter-of-fact. "Most likely."

He had Rodiker accompany him into the house, and lifted the round-wicked lamp from the table in the hall, then led the way into a small room that had the look of an office.

"Sit down, Jackson."

Rodiker took a straight-backed chair, laid his hat on a knee. Colonel Arnold said, "Wait," and left the room. Rodiker rolled a cigarette and, except for the movement of smoking, did not stir. He had much to think about.

When the colonel returned, he was dressed for town, having changed from the nightgown to a shirt with a narrow black bow tie at the collar. His wide black hat had a crease through the crown.

He took a bottle and glasses from the shelf, poured without friendliness, and handed Rodiker a filled glass, then downed his own drink as if dutifully taking unpleasant medicine. After that he asked, "Are you working for me, Jackson?"

Rodiker looked at the untasted whisky in his glass, thought it over, looked up. "What kind of work?"

Colonel Arnold's eyes narrowed. They were deep-set, bright, and hard as nailheads in a plank. "Your kind!"

Rodiker turned that over and over in his mind, and wasn't sure. "Meaning?"

Arnold nodded curtly. "All right, if it will make you feel more comfortable about staying on here, I'll put it into words. You are not a cowhand. You are, I think, on the dodge. Why, I don't care and won't ask you, because you've got grit in your gizzard!"

Rodiker said, “Thanks.”

“Since you’ve admitted knowing Rodiker, my guess is that you’ve rode with him, but are now at outs.”

The way he said it was a kind of question, but Rodiker’s eyes didn’t move, nor his lips.

Colonel Arnold was breathing hard, but not excitedly, as he continued. “Since you are a stranger, you may not know some things. I’ll tell you.

“That Lazy S belongs to the Bevartses. They made use of a Lazy S horse some years ago when they hired Rodiker to kill my brother. They never thought that horse would be known—not any more than they did this one tonight.

“Over the years they have crept up from the south and, to crowd me off my range, have put squatters on the water, nesters where my cattle run, and in every way they have schemed to increase the feud that always exists between a cattleman and farmers.

“There’s a sheriff now in office who is their friend, but who is also afraid of me. So you may as well say there is no law at all. I want law and order, but there is none now; so from henceforth, sir, I am going to shoot rustlers and hang those I catch! I have no other way to protect myself. And I need such men as you’ve shown yourself tonight!”

Rodiker drawled tonelessly, “I’m Southern,”

which didn't say anything in words that his voice hadn't already revealed.

"I'm not bitter against the South. My foreman is a Texan. But I am bitter against such copperheads as the Bevarts family, and against such shiftless white trash as the Claytons and the Rodikers, who use the War as an excuse to rob me because I am a Northern soldier!"

Rodiker's fingers tightened about the glass of untasted whisky as, staringly, he shifted his feet to rise from the chair, meaning to fling the glass and all into Yank Arnold's face and here and now have his quarrel, but the colonel had turned to the door where Sam appeared.

"Dey am ahready, Colonel, suh!"

The colonel, walking by Sam, said, "Show Jackson where to bed down." The march of his jangling boots along the hall grew faint. Sam had followed.

Rodiker stood up, slapped on his hat, then splashed the untouched whisky to the floor, and tossed the glass on the table. It bounced, rolled, fell to the floor.

Outside there was the sound of horses as men, riding from the stable, passed the house and were followed by the buckboard's rattle. Rodiker meant to leave as soon as they were well away from the house, but Sam hurried back to him.

The satin-black face glistened like wet mahogany when he bulked in the door and looked worriedly at Rodiker. Anger was in Rodiker's brim-shadowed eyes, but Sam wasn't noticing that. He blurted:

"Miss Kate, she want ter see you. See you upstaihs in her room, an' dat ain't no right way foh to do!"

"What does she want of me?"

"Foh you ter come. She say awhile ergo foh me ter tell you jes' as soon as de colonel he rode foh town." The big Negro hurried to explain. "But Mist' Johnny he's drivin' de buckboard, so you an' me is the on'y men left on the ranch, an' it ain't fittin' foh you ter go ter her room, suh!"

Rodiker said, "You're right, and I won't."

Sam's face brightened. "I tol' her you is a gent'mum an' wouldn't! No trick ter know a gent'mun when you'se been wid de colonel long as I'se been!"

The dogs that followed Sam stirred, and Rodiker, quick to take heeds of signs, said, "Who's that?"

Kate came out of the shadows, looking very small. She had tidied herself a little, straightening her hair and using rice powder. "I thought you wouldn't come, so I did!"

She looked at Rodiker carefully, drew a long breath, then turned. "Sam, go build up a fire and heat some water, and get a good sharp razor. Mr. Jackson wants to shave!"

She didn't smile. Sam gaped with flustered

amazement. Kate said, "The colonel often shaves with unheated water, but Mr. Jackson might protest. Go on, git! Or you will be hung up by the heels over that slow fire!" She was pleasant in her threatening, but her black eyes seemed to give warning that she meant to be obeyed, however pleasantly she threatened.

When they were alone, Rodiker looked at her steadily, and she looked steadily at him, their glances struggling. He knew what she meant by sending the Negro away so they would be alone. For a long time neither moved an eyelid, then Kate leaned toward him a little and whisperingly asked:

"Have I guessed right?"

"Why do you think so?"

She said at once, with swift frankness, "I really didn't think. It came to me suddenly, as if thrown from the dark through a window! I should have known from the first that there is something about you that I ought to have remembered, but it's been years, you know!"

She paused, and he said nothing, gave no sign; then she spoke fast, her lips rippling.

"You've changed, but not completely. When you first smiled I should have known. Then you said you were a stranger, but called the Bevartses 'copperheads,' and knew about the colonel being a Yankee. *And me!* No stranger could have known how I used to say, 'I'm bigger than I look!' But

I'm not bright, not really—so I didn't think. And are you going to shave and let me see, or would you rather admit right out?"

Rodiker's thumbs drifted to his belt, his hands hung there; he studied her dark eyes and shook his head.

"You said that fellow and the Bevartses are friends. I sure as hell am no friend of theirs!"

She answered whisperingly, "I know—know now! But I told you I wasn't very bright, so—won't you trust me?"

A kind of weakness crept inside him, moved about, and made him feel like taking her into his arms; but wariness came, and a renewed flush of anger at remembering, "Shiftless lazy white trash like the Rodikers, who use the War as an excuse to rob me!"

He told her coldly, "Lady, my name is Jackson."

"No, no!" she said, and caught at him, but he pushed by her without so much as a sidelong look, and tramped down the hall and out of the house.

He rode away, not hurrying.

Sam came with hot water, soap, shaving brush, a razor and its strap.

Kate sat at the desk, her chin resting on the knuckles of a clenched fist.

"You slowpoke, you! Too late!" she said, and her dark eyes glittered. "I wanted that razor to cut his throat!"

“W’y, whar is he gone, Miss Kate?”

“It took you so long that I couldn’t wait, and choked him!” She showed a small clenched fist. “Choked and dragged him out and scooped up sand to hide his body! He’ll never be seen again, but don’t tell anybody! We’ll just say he rode off to overtake the colonel!”

Sam, a ponderously fat black worshiper of the ground she walked on, looked at Miss Kate with bewildered gentleness. “Honey, hucome he made you so mad?”

“Why,” she said as fiercely as if it were true, “the insolent brute told me I wasn’t nearly as pretty as Bess Clayton!”

CHAPTER 12

Rodiker headed cross-country, making for the Santsander, where dense willow thickets would be the best hiding place he could find within an easy ride. He saved his horse by not going fast. No man was left at the house to follow—but tomorrow? He dreaded the hunt and chase, but felt that it must come. Old Jerym knew, the Claytons, too; also Kate Arnold. And he couldn't go near the Rodiker mountain ranch, because pursuers would look there first and watch afterward.

Many angers stirred within him like teased snakes in a basket, and his flesh burned from the mingled wrath and shame that two women, hand running, had made him feel the fool, and such a fool! Slow riding gave him time for reflection, and it rankled to remember how he had returned to Bess and what he had found. Now he knew that Claytons had Judas blood in them, and all trust had gone from her promise that she wouldn't tell who he was; she had made that promise when afraid and wanting him to leave. His bitterness toward Slim was the distorting bitterness of a brother's painful hate.

As for Kate, he had known better, which made him an utter fool to accompany her; and she had lured him with pleasantness and teased for his admission that he was Jack Rodiker, which was a woman's tricky way of being treacherous.

He wasn't many miles above the Claytons, when he reached the river after daylight. He rode into the shallow water as if heading upstream, then turned down to throw off trailers, and at last came to a narrow, brush-covered islandlike sandbar. He meant to ride at night, so would spend the day here.

When the afternoon was nearly gone he saddled and headed downstream. The river was crooked as a sidewinder's trail, and he didn't like leaving tracks along the sandy edge, but it would be tedious to pick his way through thickets. He rode slowly and watched the twilight deepen. Coyotes began yip-yapping on the mesa above the river bed.

The stars were out, and the darkness was heavy among the clump shadows, but in the open space of the river's bend a half mile away he saw a rider. He turned aside and stopped where he could watch, then dismounted and put a hand to the muzzle of his horse to prevent a whinny. Soon he heard singing, and knew that the rider was a girl astride a bareback horse. This was a chance to learn if the country was searching for Jack Rodiker. He rode out of the shadows and on into the water, as if he had come down to let his horse drink.

The girl checked her singing, but with no uneasiness, and her spurless heels kicked the horse into a canter toward him. She pulled up, saying, "Hello," with a musical questioning tone, and he lifted his head politely, knowing who she was before she said:

"I'm Sue Clayton, but I don't know you. I thought I knew all the good-lookin' fellows hereabouts—leastwise, I want to!" She laughed with the ease of a meadow lark singing. "It's awful hard to catch and hold a beau—you want! We steal 'em from each other, my sister an' me. One sister's gone away, and Bess picks the gosh-awfulest uns. Not worth stealin'! You new hereabouts?"

Rodiker, hat in hand, stared at her. This kid Sue had been a lanky, awkward, freckled tomboy; now she was big, quail-plump, and, in the starlight, pretty, but still seemed recklessly tomboyish. It never entered the Clayton girls' heads that they should be shy.

Sue rattled on. "The only one of Bess's beaus I ever honestly wanted for myself was Jack Rodiker. You know who he is?"

Rodiker carefully roughened his voice to say, "I've heard."

"I can't get him, so I have to do the next best thing. Are you a stranger, or is it that I just ain't met you before?"

"Pretty much of a stranger." He was thinking

bitterly of Slim and Bess and the Claytons as a whole, when he said, "Too bad you can't get him. I hear there's a big reward!"

Sue's was an instant fury. She kicked the horse up closer, as if about to use her fists; her face writhed and the words came as a cat spits when its back is arched and the fur is on end.

"You are weak-minded as a baboon to think us Claytons would think of a reward! He was our friend, and is! Will allus be! I've known him since I was big enough to fall outa the cradle! Reward, fiddlesticks! We're Texans, us Claytons are! Texans take up for their friends, and there ain't money enough in all the Yankee banks to make us not do it!"

He put on his hat. "I didn't mean to rile you, but hasn't there been some talk of him being back in the Santsander?"

"I can't tell what talk there's been! Fool folks talk of ever'thing from why the Lord made the world outa mud to what's the best salve for corns! But he ain't back. I'd know near the first of anybody. He'd come to our house on account of his knowin' we're his friends! More'n that, Mr. Nosey, I play like his own brother is my beau, 'cause he is sweet and looks like Jack, but is too young for me to be serious!"

Sue neck-reined the horse and clucked, meaning to ride on, but he asked, "I suppose you heard about Yank Arnold's man killing a Bevarts at 'Pache Flat?"

Sue said, "No such thing!" with certainty and impatience. "The Bevartses had nothin' at all to do with the shootin' of that cook, though old Yank Arnold wants to make out like they did!"

"No?"

"No! The way of it is that one of Arnold's men had a fight in town with Pete Croy. Pete got licked. Then he stole a Bevarts horse and went out on the road to lay for this Arnold man who was takin' Miss Snooty Arnold home. She's stuck-up and strait-laced and a mealy-mouthed scarey-cat, with a little pinched nose, and ugly as sin with its face washed! Well, Pete made a mistake and shot the Arnold cook who was in the buggy. Then this Arnold man shot Pete in the back. That's the kind of men ol' Yank Arnold has workin' for him! What's your name, mister?"

He gave the first name that came to mind, and Sue told him, "You are sure big, and might be good-lookin' if you shaved. I don't like pigs in a poke or men behind a beard!"

She laughed and rode on, and was whistling gaily before she was a hundred feet away, and he had to think about Slim's treachery to keep from overtaking Sue and gladly telling who he was. She seemed changed in appearance only, being still impulsively frank and quick-speaking; and he liked her, but wouldn't trust her.

He returned to the shadows along the bank, left the saddle, sat on his heels, smoked, and let his thoughts roll about, unsure of what to think. The story of Pete Croy was unbelievably false, yet with partisan aggressiveness Sue accepted what was evidently the Bevartses' explanation. They called Yank Arnold the liar and trouble-maker. He smiled grimly, in the hope that the Bevartses and Yank Arnold would claw one another into shreds.

When he left the river, he rode in the opposite direction from Moheela, staying on the Arnold range. It was an often used trick of his to double back and lay low, the same as that of wolves and foxes. He didn't want to leave the Santsander, not before Cora Arnold arrived and he had talked with her. And his bitterness toward Yank Arnold was increased because Yank had not only called Rodiker's doggedly honest folks white trash and thieves, but, thinking Rodiker was a man named "Jackson" and on the dodge, had offered him a job with no questions asked. *To be an outlaw is all right as long as Yank Arnold can make use of him, which shows he's no damn good his own self!*

In the distance he saw a block-shaped shadow with a pin point of light through it. He headed that way and, finding a small field of fenced corn, he knew it was a nester's place, and no friend of Arnold's would be there.

A dog came at him before he hallooed. Then a man appeared in the lighted doorway and a tow-headed, knee-high girl clung to her daddy's leg and peered at the tall horseman, who asked could he get supper and stay the night. Rodiker let on that he was a stranger who got turned around when he wanted to reach town, and now his horse was too tired to go farther.

The rawboned farmer hemmed and hawed. His chunky wife came to the door. The moon was rising, and she looked him over distrustfully, but as if it was her duty to feed the hungry stranger, she said, "Supper's long since done, but you can have some leftovers. And you'll bed down in the stable."

Next morning the horse limped when brought to water, and Rodiker made out that he was just a stray cowhand with a horse that had gone lame; but, wanting to earn the Baddens' good will, he heaved up well water on a windlass and carried it to the garden for onions, turnips, squash, and such. And he chopped wood. The wood was mostly mesquite roots that had been dug up and snaked in. The dog and little girl tagged him, the tiny child chattering. But Rodiker could tell that the Baddens, and especially Mrs. Badden, were untrusting.

About suppertime on the third day he carried in an armful of wood and dumped it behind the stove. Mrs. Badden wiped biscuit dough off her fingers before she turned and asked:

"Did Colonel Arnold send you here?"

"Why do you think a thing like that?"

Pent-up anger blew words at him. "Your horse ain't no more lame than I am! You got a piece of chip fitted in the left front shoe. I was raised with horses and I looked!"

He grinned. "That was so I could stay on here and get good food for a little or nothing."

She showed her spunk with, "I don't believe a word of it! You ain't never left off that gun a minute—which ain't a good sign in a stranger. And you're the first cowhand I ever saw that helped around a farmin' place instead of squattin' on his heels an' smokin' while other folks worked. So you must be up to somethin'! Did Colonel Arnold send you?"

"No. Why do you think he might've?"

"You would lie, wouldn't you?"

"Most likely I would, yes, ma'am."

"Well, that's more honest than I thought you'd be! So I'll just show you!" She washed her hands and dried them, then took a piece of paper from under a plate on a shelf. "Last week this was stuck on a gatepost out front!"

Rodiker read: "This is a warning. Nesters, pull your freight. Get the hell out because I'm moving in. Colonel Arnold."

Rodiker fingered the paper and asked, "Do you think Yank Arnold would send somebody like me in as a kind of spy to learn what you folks were going to do about it?"

Mrs. Badden came up close and, being short and chunky, she tilted her head to look straight into his face.

"I don't know. But you are up to something! Your horse ain't lame. Cowboys afoot are the laziest fellows on earth, yet you've worked like a horse—so it must be to fool us. Baby Nell has taken such a shine to you that you can't be all bad, but something ain't right, now is it?"

"Do you want that I ride off?"

She gathered the end of her apron to wipe at the sweat on her face. "I don't reckon you mean to murder us in our beds and burn down the house! I want to like an' trust people, but abody just don't dare! It's lonesome here with no neighbors near. I know how Yank Arnold don't want us. Last time Badden went to town, old Mr. Bevarts, who got us to homestead out here, warned him to watch out for Colonel Arnold's men. Said Arnold was about set to start a drive on all us nesters. Then a thing like this stuck on our gatepost!"

Rodiker didn't rest well that night. He relieved the horse's "lameness" and considered leaving at once, but decided that that wouldn't look so good. Mrs. Badden's shrewdness was disturbing.

During the night uneasiness staggered through his dozing, and every sound set him listening, as the hunted always listen. Sometime before sunup he was aroused by the feverlike dream of a posse riding down on him, and he jumped up to find that a part of what aroused him was no dream: there was the pound of hoofs and far-off yells, the nearer shriek of Mrs. Badden, the furious barking of the dog, and the bang of a gun.

Rodiker, rifle in hand, sprang to the stable door. It wasn't quite daylight. A big bunch of cows had been hazed into the yard and garden about the house. As horned shapes hurtled out of the dawn-dusk, a few ran close enough by the stable door for him to see the broad A brand. The warning tacked to the Badden gatepost was being fulfilled, and Rodiker's thoughts swirled curses on Yank Arnold.

A shotgun banged in the yard and banged again. A steer bellowed in pain. Shotgun or not, range cattle couldn't be turned by a man on foot. The bellowing and hoof thud of the cattle made him think as quickly as an echo bounces what a fool cattleman Arnold was to run weight off his own stock; there were simpler and more forceful ways of making nesters take the road out.

Rodiker's horse was saddled by the time Badden came through the wide-open stable door with a shotgun in one hand and a clenched fist trembling above his head. He was barefooted and in underwear, just as he had tumbled from his bed, and he was dry-eyed, but sobbed curses, and swore that he would kill Arnold—if it took to his dying day he would kill him!

Now he begged for Rodiker's horse and rifle because, when the cattle first broke into the yard, Mrs. Badden had rushed out with a blanket and tried to turn them from her garden, and the steers had trampled the little Badden girl and her dog, when she ran from the house to be with her mother.

As Rodiker brushed by him, leading the horse, the rawboned Badden began to struggle, trying to seize the rifle and take the horse so he could ride out and fight the men who had stampeded the cattle on him. He was crazy-mad, and swung the shotgun like a club. Rodiker fended and wrenched it from him, tossed it aside, and hit the saddle.

His glance swept through the dawn, and he knew that the cows had been driven in across the nipped barbed wire of the Badden cornfield, and he could hear men still whooping and yelling, but he couldn't see them through the dust that the hoofs had stirred in the field. Of course Arnold had ordered it done to terrify other nesters; but Rodiker hopefully thought that such a stampede as this would unite all nesters in a range war against the colonel. Arnold said he would shoot or hang rustlers, and Rodiker thought, *I'd like to hang him and all his men for this!* and meant it.

His horse went bound on bound by the house

where Mrs. Badden was crouched on the threshold with a blanket-wrapped bundle in her arms. Loose hair was over her bowed face, but she jerked up her head, flinging the hair aside, and stared wildly at him. Rodiker flashed by before her lips moved, but he felt that curses followed him.

CHAPTER 13

The cornfield was too soft for fast riding, so he headed out to get beyond the field's southwest corner and circle around beyond it to the west. He watched toward the bank of dust that was like a thin, dark fog hanging over the field in the still morning air. He didn't know how many men were out there, but not many, from the sound of the yelling; and since range cattle scatter widely in their feeding, he also knew that it had taken some days for a few men to gather and trail the herd near the Baddens for the morning raid. Also, he knew these men weren't afraid of attack and pursuit from a nester, who wouldn't have anything but work horses to ride; and maybe they hadn't intended to trample anybody to death, but they had the same as murdered a baby, and he would kill them if he could.

When he rounded the field's west corner, he saw three men in a bunch a half mile off and coming hell-for-leather, but their faces were turned back over their shoulders in a way that meant they had been surprised and were riding off.

Here beyond the cornfield the ground was untilled and nearly level, and Rodiker lifted his horse with stroke of spurs going headlong. In the full sunrise the men ahead caught sight of him and reined up hard, uncertainly milling together, but one man against three seemed to decide them, and they came on. Rodiker hadn't changed pace, but now lifted his rifle, steadying it with the hand that held the reins and, going full lope, fired over the top of the horse's head. A man went out of the saddle as if jerked by a rope about his throat.

Instantly the other men wheeled sharply, but instead of making for the open country, they put their horses over the sagging strands of barbed wire and cut right into the cornfield, as if the corn and thin dust mist would give them concealment.

Cattle were in the corn, trampling and snatching and bellowing. The sun was bright now, and the fresh dust the horsemen kicked up was like a smoke trail.

Rodiker understood why they had turned into the field; in the distance he saw a bunch of strung-out riders coming, and coming fast, over the ridge of a northwest rise. The stampeders had no way of escape except through the field itself.

Rodiker rode back the way he had come. Hard riding on solid earth would tire a horse less than plodding through plowed ground, and he meant to head the two men off if they tried to angle out of the field. But they went straight through, making for Badden's yard, perhaps intending to reach the open country beyond. The plowed field pulled the wind out of their horses. Badden's shotgun banged. Rodiker then stopped, raised in his stirrups, swung up his rifle, and, holding the sights for a guess at something above three hundred yards, fired. A horse dropped beside the Badden well.

Badden had wounded the other horse. Now the two men were afoot, and broke for the stable to hole up there. Badden's work horses were loose in the barnyard, but, even if saddled, they couldn't make much of a run—not from the four or five pursuing horsemen who had cut through the cornfield and were dashing into and around the Badden place. They piled off and took shelter anywhere they could scrouge down about the stable.

None of them had come near enough for him to see what brand they rode, but they were grim, not noisy, and under the orders of a heavy, round-shouldered man. They fired at the stable, and the men in there fired back.

Rodiker was unsure of what he might be in for by staying near these men, who had rather the air of a posse doing what seemed proper justice, and, meaning to keep pretty well out of sight, at least for a time, he rode up beside the Badden house and was still in the saddle, when a horse swept around the house and pulled down alongside of him.

His surprise was as great as Kate Arnold's, but he showed it less. She sat a sidesaddle as though she had grown there, and gasped when she reined up short.

"You!" she said, her dark eyes blazing. "You dare to sneak-hide here!" Her face wasn't pale now: it was hot with anger and had a kind of blistered red from wind and sunburn, and was tired, too, but her chin was up, and her lips curled. "After I was the fool to be more than fair with you!"

He gazed hard-eyed and doubtful, feeling that he was in for a bad time of it, and suddenly he didn't care, because it seemed that she, having watched the stampede from afar, had come to try to help the men in the stable; and he said, "The hell with you! You and every cow and man you've got!"

She swung up her hand and gripped the quirt a-dangle on her wrist, and her hand hung in mid-air, for the steadiness in his rage-filled eyes made her pause until she cried out, "I'd kill you if I could!" and the quirt swept down with a swift encircling swish across his neck and shoulder. He didn't move.

The heavy, round-shouldered man in charge of the riders was coming up afoot with a waddling hurry, and he stopped stock-still as the quirt fell; but Kate faced toward him as she cried in delirious fury:

"Marl, take this man and hang him—like you said you would!"

Rodiker thought *It's come!* and made no visible move, but tautness coiled inside him like a tight-wound spring. To rein back and draw and shoot and turn and go seemed what he would have to do, and he was ready, but the big-faced Marl said:

"God A'mighty, Miss Kate! You're dead wrong! He's not one of them! 'Twas him that headed 'em off! 'Cause of him is how we cornered 'em! I just came up to thank him!"

Kate made a faint, queer sound, her face for a moment turning dull as in a daze. Marl's puzzled eyes were laced with a net of wrinkles, and he peered at Rodiker, peered toward Kate, and pushed up his hat and rubbed at the red crease of the tight band on his forehead. Then he asked:

"How come, Miss Kate, you get such a wrong idea about him?"

She wouldn't say anything, but entreaty was in her eyes as she stared at Rodiker, and his voice was ice-hard, though he told Marl, "Wrong ideas are not hard to get. I had some myself, in thinking it was your men drove these damned cows in! The Baddens found a warning on their gate that Colonel Arnold wrote to tell them to pull out. So when—"

Kate cried, "No such thing! They never! The colonel gives his warnings face to face—not stick them on a fencepost in the dark!"

"—so when A-branded steers broke in here and

tramped the little Badden girl to death, I thought it was your men drove them in!"

Kate's voice broke whisperingly. "Child?"

He pointed toward the house. She looked around, then back at Rodiker, and was motionless for the time it takes to draw a long breath slowly. After that, she slid almost as if falling from the saddle, dropped the reins, then gathered her riding skirt about her and stumbled as she ran for the open door.

Marl's look followed until she was inside. He was heavy-set, slow-moving, perhaps slow-thinking, and scratched far back under his hat. "You a friend of the Baddens?"

"Some."

"Lucky you was here."

"I'm Jackson. The fellow that brought Miss Kate from town some nights ago."

"So you're him? The colonel, I hear, was some put out by how you run away."

"You've talked with him?"

"No, with Miss Kate."

Rodiker put his fingers to the quirt's mark on his neck, and, knowing now that Kate had not told who he was, felt much the same relief as when awakened from a dream of falling. He said, "I made her mad. She's still mad. It's always best to leave when a woman's mad. Maybe now, too, it would be best."

Marl nearly smiled. His slight nod was understanding, as he looked at the quirt's mark. "That's when she thought you was one of them. When I thought they was just rustlers, I said I'd hang 'em."

He turned and listened to the sound of guns. They weren't being fired fast or often. Marl spoke calmly.

"They'd like to kill some of us. They're waitin' for dark. Think maybe then they can slip out. I'll burn the stable first. When they come out, I'll hang 'em." He might have been talking about rabbits in a burrow and the skins he was after.

Marl swung his thick arm toward the cornfield, indicating the damage done there. "We lost a lot of cows from rustlers and nesters, too, but a thing like this—Why?"

Rodiker recalled what old Mr. Bevarts had told Badden in town and said, "Somebody wanted to make it look like your men did it."

Marl nodded. "But hell, we'd have let the corn grow, then cut the fence so cows could wander in an' eat. Put fat on 'emselves—not run it off, like in a stampede!"

"How come Miss Kate is along?"

" 'Cause I can't handle her, an' the colonel's not home!" Marl's was a worried smile. "As a little tyke, she was hard to handle when she took the bit in her teeth. Hasn't changed none by bein' back East. I guess she'll allus do like she wants. She knows how to make men let her!"

Rodiker's hand absently touched the mark on his neck, and he murmured commendation. "It's all right. She thought I was one of them! If so, hangin' was what I needed."

Marl said, "Yes," gravely, then explained. "Yesterday, a Mexican kid rode in and told her he'd seen some men bunchin' cows over this way. Rustlers, he thought. So'd she. We're havin' trouble. Lots!"

Rodiker, knowing how widely the colonel's cattle ranged, nodded and thought, *I hope you have lots more!*

"Instead of sendin' somebody, she lit out and come herself to where I was at Old Place. I scraped together a few boys an' we headed down the river. She wouldn't go home. Stayed with us all night out in the open while we were tryin' to find where they were. She sort o' fell behind this mornin' when we spread out to close in. That's why she didn't see you knock that man out of the saddle and turn the other two in here."

Marl drew a large blue handkerchief, mopped about his neck. "A child, you say?"

The flicker of Rodiker's eyelids answered. After a pause he asked, "What horses did they ride?"

Marl looked up steadily, and his deep voice was slow, almost casual. "Lazy S's. Of course fellows steal 'em and do things that give the Bevartses a bad name. Or like that Pete Croy you shot.

'Twas his own private grudge. He just happened to have borrowed a horse without askin'. Or like some years ago when Rodiker shot Craig Arnold. A Lazy S horse—but the Bevartses had nothin' to do with the murder. They never expected these horses to be seen today, no more'n the one Rodiker rode. They are pure-hearted, clean-handed, sweet-faced, fair-minded, yeah!"

Marl turned his head to spit. It was, and he meant it to be, as if he cleaned his mouth after such untrue words.

Rodiker stepped from the saddle, let the reins dangle across a forearm. Marl turned from him and walked toward the rear of the house. Rodiker dropped the reins and moved up alongside of Marl, who stood with legs spread, hands palm down on his hips, and watched toward the stable. The morning sun was bright and growing hot. The guns were stilled. Some longhorns munched in the garden, and other steers were drifting back into the corn that Badden's sweat had watered.

Badden lay in a peering huddle behind the planking of his draw well. He hadn't a hat, was still in underwear, now sweat-streaked and earth-stained. The single-barreled shotgun was poked out for quick firing. A dead horse lay sprawled between him and the stable.

Then the racket of gunfire started up. In the open air the reports were thin; black smoke puffed out, gathered into small ragged clouds, and hung low in the windless heat.

Marl's voice had a pleased rumble as he turned to Rodiker, saying, "We'll scorch their tails in a—"

Amid the bang of guns that were not close was the close-up thud of lead into flesh. Marl stumbled, his hat dropped behind him, and he fell face down as a dead weight falls, his arms outstretched, and his palms flat.

Right off another bullet went by Rodiker's head, and he spun on a heel and jumped. From the shelter of the kitchen wall he could see the hole in the side of Marl's head. When he stepped back to the horse and pulled his rifle from the scabbard, he heard a yell that was more than a yell: it was a squall of lament, piercingly rageful. Badden's voice and the words weren't distinguishable, but he fired the shotgun in futile vengefulness. Badden knew that Marl was dead.

Rodiker went to the front stoop and looked through the door toward where both women were crouched over a pallet by the wall, and one was sobbing. He pulled his hat and said:

"Miss Kate?"

She didn't move, but Mrs. Badden looked up and was staringly dry-eyed, with lips tight as a seam, and though she didn't say anything, not with words, her eyes were questioning, as in her grief she now reconsidered her first suspicions of him.

He stepped inside, hat in one hand, the rifle in the other and, bending over Kate's shoulder, looked toward the pallet where the small child's face was black with the bruises that had come with death, and his heart hurt in remembering her toddling and babbling at his heels.

"Miss Kate," he said, "Marl has been shot, and is dead."

Kate's hat hung down between her shoulders from thongs. She didn't look up, but pulled a fold of the bombazine riding skirt to her eyes, then put a hand to her throat and seemed to hold down her sobs. "Dead? This child is dead! And you say Marl?"

"Yes."

She stood up slowly, still wiping at her eyes. The quirt was on her wrist, and she dropped the weighted hem of the skirt, then staggered a little, for her knees were cramped from being on the floor.

He put an arm about her, and she yielded weakly for a moment, but only a moment; then her face lifted, and she pulled away. It was as if tears had drained weakness out of her and left her strong, because she said, "Follow me!" and holding up the front of her skirt, she went before him from the house.

He looked down at her tear-smudged face. At

first she caught her breath in hiccoughing sighs, but the hiccoughing stopped, and she said, "You take charge!" It was a command, and her dark eyes glittered with grief and anger through the undried tears.

He carefully told her, "No." His voice was gentle in saying, "I am a stranger to your men. Pick one of them."

Kate's face was wind-burned and sun-scorched; the tender complexion she had brought from back East was already ruined; her hair was a rat's nest tangle, her eyes red and swollen, but she came up on her tiptoes to be taller, and had a manner of wrathful dignity with:

"You shall take charge! I do not know the other men and I do know you! Remember that!"

He said nothing. He didn't move, not even an eyelid. There was no more expression than in a dead man's stare and as much steadiness. Her eyes turned away from under the weight of his look, and she groped for her hat, set it on her head with the pretense of caring how her mussed-up hair was arranged under the hat. When her glance again slid back to his eyes, he caught and held it, asking:

"Why haven't you told a'ready?"

"It wouldn't have been fair. Not after how you brought me home, and were nearly murdered!"

"But you will now if I don't let you blind-halter me?"

She lifted her chin, stiffened, said defiantly, "Something like that, yes!"

His sullen voice told her, "You can go straight to hell!"

Kate gasped. "Oh!" she said; then "Oh," again more quietly. She looked as serious as a small, tired child who is trying to be truthful even if unbelieved. "You've got to understand! And help. Please help me! I said I knew you, meaning I know how strong and capable you are! I wasn't trying to threaten you. Really not!" She moved a hand behind her toward the doorway. "It was our cows! I feel somehow to blame! And so helpless!"

He began to feel unproud of how he had answered her implied threat, and it had been a threat, though she denied it now.

All in a breath she was telling him, "The colonel is home and sick in bed—"

"Marl said he wasn't home."

"That's what I said to keep Marl from riding there. And I didn't tell the colonel the truth either! If he'd heard where rustlers were, he'd have got out of bed and into boots and mounted a horse if he had to be tied in the saddle. He is sick!

"When the Mexican boy told me there were rustlers over here, not a man was home but Sam, who's too heavy for fast riding. Old Johnny doesn't count. He's too stove up to kick a horse into a lope. I had to go myself. I told the colonel

I would visit overnight with Anita. Then I lit out for Old Place to find Marl. He tried to persuade me to go back but I wouldn't—couldn't!—because I'd said I'd be away all night. And I had to tell Marl the colonel wasn't home, or he'd have known if there was news of rustlers the colonel would have come himself. Marl tried to make me stay behind last night, and I wouldn't because—well—just because!"

Kate reached out and grasped his unbuttoned vest and held on, and again her words whirred, as if she could talk without pausing for breath.

"Please help me! My papa is sick—that's why I came from the East. Sam had old Johnny's wife write me. And I never wrote back that I was coming. Papa might have said no, and it was so much simpler just to come. And he is sick!

"Marl says our cattle are not only being stolen, but some of our men must be helping, and that is worrying the colonel. He likes to trust his men implicitly. Who are they, Marl says, no knowing. But it must be, otherwise cattle couldn't be stolen as they are. With the colonel sick—Oh, don't you see? And there's nobody here but you that I can trust now that Marl is dead, so won't you, please?"

Rodiker's hand, with gentle force, loosened her grasp on his vest, then he absently reached up alongside his neck, touching the welt because it burned. Now he rather liked the courageous wrath that had put it there when she thought he had thrown in with rustlers, or something of that kind; but Kate misunderstood his gesture and said:

"That shows how much I need somebody to keep me from mistakes!"

"You know how I feel about Yank Arnold."

"And I know he thinks he's right. You know he isn't. So if you help us like you can, then he will know that a man like you just couldn't have done a thing like he has thought of you!"

"And if I don't do like you want?"

Kate wasn't trying to threaten now; she showed him her small ungloved hands in a gesture that indicated helplessness, then switched her skirt, looked down and shrugged, but lifted her eyes to say, "When I haven't told yet, do you think I ever would?"

"One thing I think about you is you don't mind lyin'!"

Kate looked right at him. "Men are so stupid stubborn, however else can you make them do like they ought?"

Rodiker said, "I make no promises to you," then swung his arm toward the open doorway. "But the Baddens have been like friends. If they ain't shot, I want those fellows hung! I can get 'em out of there, but I don't like to burn a poor man's barn to chase out rats!"

CHAPTER 14

Rodiker talked to Mrs. Badden, and her round face hadn't had any expression other than the blankness of inattentive listening, but when he finished, she nodded jerkily and drew a long breath.

"Go ahead. We're ruint now and will pull out. Anyhow, I wouldn't stay—not after how she died. Seems a shameful pity this world ain't big enough for all us folks that's in it. But some are allus crowdin' other folks and hurtin' them." She looked at Kate. "We'll go away, miss, and then your cows can feed where our home was."

Kate flushed, the words hurt so much, and she set her mouth hard to keep from crying out. In the kitchen she told Rodiker, "That wasn't fair! She knows we didn't do it!"

He said, "She knows, too, you Arnolds will be glad to have them gone!"

He picked up a half-filled coal-oil can. A small piece of potato was stuck on the spout. "Take this," he said to Kate. She accepted the oilcan, then stood watching him. He searched and found a flour sack that had been washed, and after that a roll of binder twine. His "here!" was impersonal, as he put them into Kate's hand.

He used a hatchet to knock a board of straight-grained pine from the top of the homemade kitchen table, then tramped through the front room with the board and hatchet. Kate followed, her hands clumsily full and the shot-hemmed riding skirt in the way of her feet.

Outside the house he told Kate to tear the sack into inchwide strips, then he went back and said to Mrs. Badden that he wanted some cotton. She pointed to the comforter where the dead baby lay. He drew a heavy knife, opened a blade, got on his knees to rip into the comforter with as much gentleness as if careful not to awaken the child.

Again outside, he split the three-foot table top into strips almost two inches wide; these he hacked and whittled into arrow-headed shape, and made the notch for slinging about a third of the way back from the head. After that he chopped down the slender willow that had been planted before the door, trimmed off the branches, then shook the pole, trying its resilience as a fisherman tries a rod. He shortened it to a length that was suitable, then crossed to Kate's horse and cut tie thongs from her saddle. He made incisions in the thongs and looped them end to end. After tying a knot in one end, he fastened the other to the willow pole.

Rodiker squatted on his knees before Kate and had her hold the darts while he wrapped the flour sack's strips about the cotton, one after another. He pulled the piece of potato from the spout of the can and soaked the arrow-shaped darts with coal oil.

He took up the three-foot darts and, going to the kitchen corner, put a match near the middle of a dart's shaft, then he fitted the thong's knot into the notch, stepped out in the open, and let fly. The pole was stiffly springy, but it wasn't the springiness alone that sent the dart: his powerful right-handed jerk hurled it with the force of an arrow from a bow. The dart, not truly shaped, weaved in its flight, but nevertheless stuck the side of the stable some fifty yards away, then dropped to the ground. The oil-soaked rag and cotton still burned.

He threw more fire-winged darts until one landed in the haystack back of the stable. That brought a yell from the surprised Arnold man who was snugged down there to watch the stable's back door.

The haystack began to burn with the swirling fury that flames stir up even when the day is windless, and spark-filled gray smoke burst toweringly, whipped up by the fire on its flanks. The burning whisps that were sucked high overhead drifted about and died there, the ash falling like a flight of black insects.

Mrs. Badden came outside and gazed stonily until Rodiker passed her, and she said, "I don't like to hate people, but I ain't enough Christian not to be glad!"

Rodiker mounted his horse and rode out in the open. He couldn't be shot at, not accurately, through the stable's fire and smoke-filled cracks; and, anyhow, the men in there now had other things to think about than shooting at somebody.

The rear stable door faced the fired stack and nobody thought the men would emerge there, but Rodiker, making sure, rode over that way, and the flames threw a blistering heat in his face.

Soon he saw a rider coming at a furious lope down the roadway past the house, recognized him, then did not look again until the horse, as sweat wet as if he had swum a river, was pulled up abruptly alongside his own horse. Colonel Arnold, gauntly drawn of face and gray with unshaven bristles, was bolt upright in the saddle. He looked sick, but wrath was in his sunken eyes, a kind of red wrath, as if they had caught and reflected the flames.

He shouted out, "What the hell, sir, is the meaning of this!"

Rodiker looked at him steadily and hated him. Rodiker's eyes narrowed, his voice slid into a drawl, insolent and meaningful.

"W'y, Colonel, you act like you maybe didn't know your cows come in here at sunup through a cut fence over yonder with men on their tails! Your steers stomped a baby to death, ruined a corn crop and garden, and the men that drove

’em are holed up in that stable. We’re smokin’ ’em out!”

Colonel Arnold glared as if struck speechless, and Rodiker, in a lazy-sounding way, added, “Looks like you sent ’em in to drive out nesters, but you ought’ve let your foreman and Miss Kate in on the trick, because Marl got himself killed and Miss Kate—”

Colonel Arnold’s eyes were closed, and he reeled in the saddle, with one hand loosely on the horn and the other groping to find it. He had the look of a man who had been shot. Getting out of a sickbed and riding through heat, then being talked to as Rodiker had talked, hit the colonel about like a sunstroke.

Rodiker had wanted to hurt, and he had, but now he jumped from the saddle, and, reaching up, caught Yank Arnold as he sagged like a dead man in a head-down lurch. Kate came stumbling with the long skirts in a heavy flutter about her ankles and dread pulling at her eyes. Rodiker strode by her, carrying the long, lean, and now unconscious man toward the Badden house. She ran to keep up, and panted breathlessly in screaming questions above the fire’s roar, but Rodiker wouldn’t say anything.

The stable was now a hellish blaze, throwing its heat into the hot morning with the crackle and crash that flames make when they gnaw on wood. The corraled work horses plunged at a far fence corner, breaking through, and the saddle horses backed away from the increasing heat and the noise like the coming of a tempest.

They dragged their reins with necks timidly extended, fearful of the snubbing that had taught them to stand ground-hitched.

For all Rodiker knew or cared, the men who had been in the stable were by now burned to a crisp. What he had in mind was to ride off as soon as he could make his departure seem unhurried. Though having the man he hated helpless in his arms was like a wish fulfilled, Rodiker hadn't malevolence enough to gloat. He had hit with words as hard as fist blows, and they had hurt, but that small revenge seemed paltry now.

He laid the colonel down before the house where the ground was littered by splinters and shavings that had tapered the arrow-shaped darts, and Kate dropped to her knees beside her father, but Rodiker told her to fetch water.

Mrs. Badden came up and said, "Maybe he oughta be laid inside on the bed."

"The ground's good enough. He'll come to—or he won't."

Kate dropped her riding skirt, stepped out of it, and ran to bring a dipperful of water, but in her hurry hadn't thought of a towel. Rodiker took a handkerchief from his pocket for her to dip into the water. She was wetting the colonel's forehead when the men walked up—six of them, and two were prisoners.

Sweat was on the men, and sift of ashes; all were tired, dirty, unshaven. A lanky man with tobacco in his mouth looked uncertainly at Rodiker, then toward the colonel, who lay as if asleep.

Kate stood up with the water-sopped red handkerchief dripping in her hand and pointed at Rodiker.

"He's in charge!" And refusing to admit that her father had such unmanly weakness as to faint, she said, "The colonel had an accident, so now Mr. Jackson here is in charge."

Putting "Mister" before his name at once gave Rodiker increasing importance, and Arnold's men gazed tiredly and were expectant, as he stepped closer and looked at the two captured men. Their wrists were lashed behind them, their eyes sullenly insolent, their bristly faces dark with sweat, dirt, and ashes.

He asked, "Who are they?"

No one answered at once. Arnold's men eyed the prisoners, looked at Rodiker, then the man with the tobacco in his cheek said, "The Walters brothers. Got a little brand and a bad name over south. Won't talk, they say. Say take 'em into the sheriff."

Rodiker poked his thumbs into his belt, looked studyingly from one to the other of the Walters brothers; then he told them:

"Nobody gives a damn whether or not you talk. If you want to go to hell with your mouth shut, suits me! You think we'll take you in and turn you over to the sheriff, then old Jerym Bevarts'll get you loose. We know he figured that the best way to give Yank Arnold a worse name than he's got with nesters was to run a stampede of Arnold's cows in here on the Baddens, and he bully-whacked you fellows into doin' just that! I guess he picked you because you've been rustling cows and know the range hereabouts."

Rodiker quit talking to the Walters brothers and looked at the Arnold men. All were saddle-toughened, sag-hipped, and stared solemnly. The one who chewed tobacco spit without moving his eyes when he turned his head.

Rodiker said, "It's poor pay for what these Badden folks have suffered, but take these men away and hang 'em! On top of all else, they killed a baby girl!"

The Walters brothers gulped and swallowed hard as sullenness went out of their eyes and hard breath rasped their throats. Nobody made a move until the tobacco chewer said:

"You heard. Come on! It's time what's right was done in this damn' country!"

They turned and moved off in a bunch.

Colonel Arnold got to his feet. His gray hair was bedraggled from Kate's anxious sopping, and he wiped about his face as if at sweat, all the while frowning with stern and puzzled steadiness. Then he said, "Jackson!"

Rodiker faced about, and the colonel came toward him and peered with a kind of anger that had uncertainty in it. He said:

"You couldn't have done more of what I wanted if I had told you what I wanted, yet a while ago you said you thought I sent those men in here to stampede my own cattle and ruin these people."

He stopped. Rodiker waited for something more, and Kate's dark gaze hung on his face with shocked and incredulous staring that he would have said a thing like that to her father. Then the colonel's fever-filled eyes flashed as he demanded:

"Explain yourself, sir!"

Rodiker stretched his voice into a lazy-sounding drawl.

"You fly off the handle easy and make up things that ain't so—maybe so you can fly off the handle!"

Kate gasped. "Are you crazy?" She meant just that.

The colonel glared as if speechless, while Rodiker told him with quiet anger:

"I never said I thought it of you. But I did say how it could look. I wanted to show you what it's like to have folks believe what ain't so. You big rich men have everything so much your own way you never know what some folks have to put up with!"

The colonel stiffened; he seemed stunned and wondering, then looked toward Kate and quickly looked away, saying to Rodiker, "You come with me. We'll talk this over."

The colonel walked off as stiff-legged as if on stilts, and Rodiker faced about to follow, but Kate caught hold of him and jerked. He looked down, and she pressed close and rose on tiptoes to whisper fiercely, "I'll tell! So help me God, I'll tell if you say things like that about my papa!"

"Things like what?"

"That he drove those cows in here!"

"You heard what I didn't say. Ears like yours don't do abody any good! But maybe now you can feel a little of what it's like to be lied about, like I been!"

He swung around, leaving her. The colonel waited some sixty feet away, his eyes now following the mounted men, and one of the horses was carrying double as they rode slowly toward the river where there would be a tree tall enough.

Rodiker stood beside the colonel and looked at the hawklike profile. Pride was in the face, and illness too. The illness did not in any way touch Rodiker's sympathy, and he wished for a fulfillment that would knock the pride into trampled bits.

Colonel Arnold shifted his gaze studyingly at Rodiker. "Why are you so bitter toward me?"

Rodiker almost told him, but that would have meant a showdown with no chance—other than violence offered—to win, and would ruin what hope he had of putting his fingers to Cora Arnold's throat. He felt that Yank Arnold wouldn't give up until she gave him up, and now Rodiker answered bluntly with:

"I don't trust you!"

"Or any stranger?" Colonel Arnold suggested.

Rodiker nodded, adding, "Nor much of anybody else."

"From how you just spoke to me, I take it that somewhere, sometime, you have been falsely accused."

Rodiker's eyelids slowly fell and rose in affirmation.

"I've tried to be your friend, Jackson."

"I can't have friends. I'm on the dodge."

"I won't ask questions, but do you care to tell me if this man Rodiker you've spoken of is in any way to blame?"

Rodiker hesitated, unsure of just where this might end, then said cautiously, "Some."

"In that case, Jackson, why can't you trust *me?*"

"Because you've got it in for him too?"

"Yes."

"But any time you don't happen to like what I

do, you can send word to the sheriff to look me over. So it's about the same as giving you the end of the rope that's about my neck!"

The colonel stiffened but held down his temper. "I see. But no man on earth dares say I ever broke my word! I need you. With Marl dead, I am in greater need. I, too, find it hard to find somebody I can trust. The Bevartses have evidently induced some of my own men to join in rustling. They are cunning, these Bevartses! You'll find out. How did you guess it was they who sent my cattle in here?"

Rodiker's bearded smile was twisted, ironic, hard, unamused. "You're too smart a man to run meat off your own cows—'specially when you could cut a fence and let 'em fatten on the nester's corn! Anyhow, they rode Lazy S's. And will old Jerym and the sheriff be riled by the hanging of their friends?"

"No. They won't. Not openly. They won't dare. They'll say that I did right! You'll see. And will you work for me?"

He said, "Awhile," and thought, *At least till next week when Cora Arnold's here.*

Colonel Arnold lay resting in the hot shade of the Badden house. It was hard for him to breathe. Mrs. Badden brought out a corn-husk pillow for his head and a palm-leaf fan for Kate, then went back in the house.

Kate swept the fan above her father's face a few

times as he talked severely to her, then her hand fell as if the arm were broken. She sat motionless for a little while before she stood up and walked away, as if not knowing where to go or what to do; but presently she picked her riding skirt from the ground and laid it across her saddle, which Rodiker had taken from the horse he was now watering at the draw well. He had unsaddled and watered the colonel's horse too.

It was the horse, not the colonel, he cared about.

She sauntered to the well and smiled unhappily. He said, "Why don't you stay out of the sun?" but seemed to mean, *Why don't you stay away from me?*

Kate said in a disheartened voice, "I am a liar."

He let the bucket rattle down and splash heavily. "Are you braggin'?"

In a kind of scandalized mutter she added, "I lie to people that trust me."

He said, "They're the only kind abody can lie to."

"Early this morning a man came from Old Place and told that Marl and some men—with me along—lit out last night to lay for rustlers over on the flat near Badden's. So the colonel got out of bed and came. I told you he would."

Rodiker said nothing, and she went on. "You can never trust a liar. Once somebody has told you a lie—even if it's your own daughter, and you love her—you can never be sure again. And your faith has been injured. Did you know that liars were such awful persons?"

He was heaving at the windlass and said nothing.

Kate angrily slapped the fan against her fist. "He's sick. That's why he acts like I had tried to cut his throat! I wanted to keep him in bed where he belongs, and at the same time have the range taken care of as it ought to be! And now he blames *me* for all that's gone wrong!"

Kate's fingers were dirty; she smeared her face when she wiped at her eyes, and hadn't a handkerchief, and looked like a tired, unhappy little girl. She had been up all night, most of the night in the saddle; this morning she rode into the most hurtful kind of tragedy, and her father had feverishly said unkind things.

Rodiker filled the bucket the horse had drunk from and lifted the bucket to the bench. "Here, wash your face."

He untied the handkerchief about his neck, shook it open, and, though it wasn't clean, he gave it to her when she stood bending over the bucket with eyes closed, her face and fingers dripping. He said, "I want it back," and led her horse away.

He squatted on his heels with his back against the house and smoked as he gazed afar at nothing, and wondered just how much fool he was to stay on at Yank Arnold's and think it was a good place to hide out. Old Jerym would learn, and the Claytons too. But Cora Arnold was coming in a few days.

Kate came to him and held out the wet handkerchief. "I washed it, or tried to." She asked, "Will you saddle for me? The colonel is waiting till the men come back, but I am going now."

She put on her skirt and walked away. When he had saddled, she came back and said, "Papa is asleep. I didn't wake him. You tell him I was tired and went home."

CHAPTER 15

Rodiker was reshoeing his horse when Sam walked to the blacksmith shop and said, "Miss Kate want dat you come ter the house. T'ree men er ridin' up frum town-way."

"What of it?"

Sam wiped at the sweat on his black moon-shaped face. "De colonel am sick abed, an' she doan want him pestered by meddlesome town-folks lak a sher'ff askin' erbout dem Walterses."

Kate met Rodiker on the veranda. "If it is somebody from town, you tell them the colonel isn't home."

He fingered a loose button on his shabby vest as he gazed at her. "Why not the truth once in a while?"

Kate made a face at him. She was sunburned to the raw, but there was compensation in the fresh summery dress, glove-tight about the waist, and the skirt flared stiffly. Her hair was braided and coiled around her head. She was small-boned and not tall, but she was high-headed, like a thoroughbred. She said, "I won't have him bothered when he is sick."

" 'Sick' ought to be enough."

Kate shook her head. "The colonel wouldn't like that. He thinks sickness is a kind of—well—

lack of courage. He won't want anybody to know. Don't you understand?" She smiled to make the explanation more lucid.

"Did he tell you to say he is not at home?"

"He is asleep and won't know."

"The dogs will wake him. He'll ask who came."

Kate frowned with perplexed thoughtfulness as she turned about, and a starchy rustle whispered along the hem of the dress that old Johnny's young wife had labored over. Dogs were sprawled here and there and would bark. She looked toward Rodiker, and nodded assentingly.

"I never thought. I told you I am not very smart!"

He was alone on the veranda with his thumbs in his belt as three men rode at a walk around the wide lace-dripping paloverde. The dogs raced out and yapped, but no one gave them attention, and, the day being hot, they lolled out their tongues and got into the shade again. The riders came close before they pulled up, and the man with the sheriff's badge on his gray vest said, "Howdy."

Rodiker looked at him, then at Dougal Bevarts, and after that at the third man, who wore a star-pointed badge. It said "Deputy."

The sheriff was a large, red-faced, and puff-bellied man, sluggish, and rather sad-eyed, with the signs of too much whisky, habitually. "Afraid of me," the colonel had said. Rodiker could see how that might well be so, though fatty indolence probably helped the sheriff to be even-tempered and not hunt trouble. He gazed at Rodiker and asked casual-like, "You are Jackson?"

Rodiker said, "Yes."

A wide smile came on Dougal Bevarts's dark face and lingered with a look of friendliness as he said good-humoredly:

"From what I've heard, I figured you as eight feet tall and three across!"

Dougal had the Bevartses' heavy features, but an easy, devil-may-care manner distinguished him from other men of the family; though about thirty, he hadn't yet settled down, and liked to gamble.

The sheriff asked, "Colonel Arnold home?"

"But sick abed and can't see anybody."

"Now that's regrettable," said Dougal Bevarts, sounding sympathetic; but the deputy, a man with slab-sided jaws, yapped, "Conven'ent!" with such animosity that Rodiker eyed him and demanded:

"Meaning just what, you?"

The silence was heavy then. It was the silence of a small flame creeping toward an open powder keg. Rodiker's hand had dropped from the belt and hung, palm-back, on a level with the gun's low-slung butt. Words wouldn't have increased the challenge that was offered.

Rodiker heard a soft sound in the hall behind him. He knew that Kate had put herself there to peer through the door's crack and overhear, and he thought she was opening the door wide, but he wouldn't take his eyes off these men to look around.

The sheriff suddenly blurted, "God A'mighty, Jackson, we didn't come for trouble!"

"Hell, no!" said Dougal Bevarts, leaving his lips parted in a fixed grin that showed big white teeth.

Then Dougal and the sheriff, with quick movement, pulled off their hats, and the deputy politely touched his as their eyes went by Rodiker, and he knew that Kate was in the doorway. He didn't turn his head, but heard the stiff rustle of the starched skirt, and she was beside him when she said coolly, "How do you do? Won't you light down, Sheriff? The colonel is sick and can't see anyone, but he has just told me to tell you that Mr. Jackson will talk to you for him."

Dougal looked like he hoped she would remember him, but she spoke only to the sheriff; and the sheriff didn't leave the saddle, but, hat in hand out of respect to Miss Kate, he said:

"Jackson, you can tell the colonel it is this way about them Walters boys. When we heard they had been strung up, me and Joe here"—he indicated the deputy—"and some other fellows rode out. Now, ord'nar'ly, law ought to take its course. But we heard how them rustlers had shot

Marl in the back and tramped a baby to death over at the Badden place. We rode over there and got the fac's from the Baddens.

"They told how on account of the Lazy S horses that the colonel thought the Bevartses was mixed up in it. So today we come along out here with Dougal, who wants to explain that the Walterses were damn' hoss thieves an' deserved hangin'! And it sure is a fac', ain't it, that if the Bevartses had any kind of a hand in the deal they wouldn't have let the Walterses use Lazy S horses? That right, Dougal?"

"Sure is, Sheriff!" He looked more at Kate than at Rodiker in adding, "You tell Colonel Arnold from me that if he hadn't hung 'em, I would have! I figure they was trying to rustle such a big bunch of your cows that the herd got away from 'em and broke into that cornfield and killed the little baby. We've had trouble with them Walterses down our way. And Miss Kate, you tell your father from me that I'm tired of folks trying to make trouble between him and us Bevartses. Will you now, please?"

"I'll tell him," said Kate coldly.

There was some silence then until Rodiker asked, "Anything else?"

"W'y, no," said the sheriff, "but you tell the colonel, miss, that I hope he gets well right quick."

"And you tell him for me," said Dougal

smilingly, “that even if our families are not friends, I, for one, would like to be. And I mean to fix things, too, the best I can!”

They slowly neck-reined their horses about, all eyes lingering on Rodiker as they turned, because there was mystery in how this rough-looking stranger had become important to Colonel Arnold.

Colonel Arnold sat by a window with a pillow behind him and a bottle of whisky at his elbow. He had been sleeping, and now wore pants over a nightgown, and beaded mocassins were on his feet. His breathing was labored, but his head was stiffly erect with an angered hawklike look in the sunken eyes.

Rodiker pulled off his hat and stopped just inside the door. Colonel Arnold said, “Take a chair.” Kate was on a stool by her father’s side. The colonel sipped a spoonful of whisky from the glass he held, then ran his fingers through the long, thin gray hair. He said, “Smoke if you want.”

Rodiker said thanks, but didn’t make a cigarette. He laid his hat on a knee and drew his feet back alongside the chair, rubbed the beard on his chin. Kate had already told about the coming of the sheriff and Dougal Bevarts.

Colonel Arnold drew hard for breath in saying, “The Bevartses do what harm they can, then try to lie out of it. Next to cowardice, I hate a lie." His deep-set eyes were fixed on Rodiker for as long as it would take a slow man to count ten. After that, he sank heavily against the pillow and gasped in saying to Kate, "You'll have to explain about going to Woodward. I—I'm just out of breath."

Her eyes swung in a startled side glance toward Rodiker, then she stood up, passed her hand gently over her father's head, and suggested, "You are so tired. Hadn't we better go downstairs? I'll tell him there."

The colonel closed his eyes and nodded, then said, "Give him plenty of money."

Downstairs Rodiker sat on his heels before Kate's chair on the veranda and eyed the fired end of his cigarette as he heard, "When Papa said he'd send you to Woodward, I didn't dare let on in any way that you, of all people, wouldn't want to go to meet Aunt Cora."

Rodiker's eyes lifted and seemed expressionless.

"But he can't go. I am worried to death about how unwell he is. It's hard to find anybody to take Marl's place. Herebefore, he has looked after the range himself. I mean he has been like his own superintendent. Now he'll have to send instructions by men who come and go. And it worries him, for that's no way to run a ranch, and he has three ranches! The Big A, of course, is the most important. But about Cora, you won't refuse, will you?"

Rodiker's eyes dropped. He took a long time, then looked up again and said quietly, "No, I won't refuse."

Rodiker rubbed out the cigarette, tossed it aside, spoke carelessly. "Wonder why she's coming West again?"

Kate looked at him, then toward the sky; she fiddled with a ribbon bow near her throat, and after that pulled the stiff skirt lower on her knees and glanced toward Rodiker, who made aimless marks near his toes with a burnt match stick.

"That is another thing that troubles Papa. Aunt Cora is coming, she says, to arrange a settlement. Heretofore, she has left everything in his hands. Now she says she wants her share." Kate added tiredly, "It's her right, I suppose. But to break up and divide a big ranch is nearly always—well, maybe not ruinous, but injurious."

Rodiker, thinking of Dougal Bevarts's plans, said, "I s'pose so."

Kate flashed out with, "Craig was a fool ever to marry her!" Her eyes brightened angrily. "She wasn't Western! She hated it out here and complained all the time. She wanted him to sell and leave. They hadn't been married long, either. I never liked her!"

"So? Why not?"

Kate's was a mild confusion at having said

what she did, then laughed a little. The laugh was forced. "Perhaps because she complained so of my manners! I was growing up like a wild Indian! I wasn't ladylike! I think she persuaded the colonel to send me East to school! And she lied about me. What she said wasn't as bad as what I did at times, but untruths hurt!"

Rodiker said, "I wouldn't know."

He said it so matter-of-factly that the irony was hidden, but presently it burned through the silence, and Kate exclaimed, "Oh, she wouldn't have deliberately done what you are thinking, no! She told little lies. But about you—that was a mistake. You know how one cowboy looks like another a little way off!"

"A little way off, and going fast with my back to her too?"

"Yes."

"Then how the hell did she read the shoulder brand?"

And, having said that with unloud anger, he walked away.

CHAPTER 16

Rodiker followed Kate into the little room that served as an office. The safe's heavy door was partly open, and she swung it wide, pulled out an unlocked drawer. The drawer was filled with evenly stacked gold pieces.

Kate took out forty dollars and asked if it would be enough, then pushed the drawer in and gave the door a swing that didn't close it. She said, "It's never been locked that I remember. I doubt if the colonel knows the combination now."

She handed him the money, then sat at the desk and fingered among the ledgers for one of this year's date, opened it, and made an entry.

"The colonel likes figures. To me they are squirmy little devils, always playing tricks."

The item in the ledger was to "J. Jackson, for expenses to Woodward and return."

"You'll want to fix up a little," Kate told him. "Haircut, anyhow. And new clothes. She'll never believe the colonel sent you if you don't look fixed up. Aunt Cora likes handsome men, and she is a rich widow. Maybe marrying her would be one way to get even!"

Kate quickly added "I'm sorry" as she saw him glower, and her hand fluttered appeasingly, then caught at his arm. "Don't be mad, though you ought! I'm just a loose-tongued rattlebrain!"

He turned on his heel and made no reply.

Kate came out of her trancelike thoughtfulness, set the ledger in place, and went toward the veranda. The dogs were barking at a rider in skirts, but astride. She let the horse walk with headdown laziness as she looked about interestedly. The wind was up and the brim of her hat flapped, and loosened hair floated free. It was copper-colored hair. Her skirts were whipped and shaken about. She didn't bother with the skirts. The bright calico dress looked new, and was utterly unfit for a saddle. The girl paid no attention to the yapping of the dogs, and rode up close. Kate stood by a post and the girl looked steadily down at her.

Kate didn't know the girl, but she knew the brand. It was a Lazy S, and a very fine horse. The saddle was of stamped leather; it had a silver horn that wasn't rope-burned. The bridle had silver chains. At least they were bright as untarnished silver.

The Lazy S rider said, " 'Lo." Just that, with an air of unconcerned friendliness.

Kate, curious and half-amused, replied, "Why, good morning."

"Afternoon," corrected the Lazy S rider. "You're Kate Arnold?"

"And won't you light down?"

"I've heard about you nearly all my life. Used

to see you sometimes when I was little. I'm Sue Clayton."

Kate caught her breath at the effrontery of a Clayton girl riding in like this; but, after all, Kate didn't mind the effrontery—it was simply surprising. She smiled, and repeated the invitation to dismount.

Sue cocked her head in a birdlike tilt and studied the small, trim, dark-eyed Arnold girl, then stated, "You don't act snooty at all!"

"I'm glad your opinion isn't unfavorable!"

Sue regarded her searchingly, then nodded. "Sunburned some, but you are pretty."

Kate flushed, astonished and rather pleased. Sue herself was sun-browned, straight-eyed, with even features, and the naturalness of an unshy child. But she was more than a child: she was a woman, tall, full-breasted, with a manner of calm fearlessness, and she was pretty too. Kate felt a twinge that was not kindly in thinking what the older sister, Bess, must be like.

"I'm glad to meet you, Sue. Won't you light down?"

Sue said, "It's nice of you to lie like that. You ain't glad to see me. Our folks ain't friends."

Kate tried to look serious, but her eyes crinkled and laughter bubbled. "But maybe we could be friends if we got acquainted!"

Sue shook her head a little. "The colonel's a Yank. We're Texans. You're rich. We ain't—

though after Bess is married to Zig Bevarts, we'll be related to rich folks too." Sue slapped the horse's neck. "He's Zig's. This saddle too. I borrowed 'em to hunt some mules. You seen any mules a-wanderin' around up here? That's why I come."

Kate studied that, then shook her head and, knowing it wasn't why Sue had come, said, "It's a long way for mules to stray!"

"Ain't it?" Sue agreed, then drew a long breath and smiled as she sighed. "I don't lie very good, do I?"

Kate smiled back at her. "It takes practice."

"The truth is I was cur'ous about you and the ranch here, the big fine house. I borrowed Zig's outfit to hunt mules that ain't lost, and come. That's honest fac'!"

Sue watched to see if the "honest fac' " was distrusted and, assuming that it was believed, she dismounted easily and with grace in spite of the bunglesome skirts that billowed in the wind. Sue was tall, straight, in no way embarrassed by the presence of the colonel's daughter, and, having looked at Kate's trim figure, asked, "You wear a corset?"

"Why, yes. Of course."

Sue nodded acceptively, but said, "A girl like me can't wear a ladylike rig. I'd rather breathe easy than be wasp-waisted." And with no change of tone or facial expression, she went right on to ask, "Is that Jackson fellow that brought you home from town here where I could get a peek at him? I'm just cur'ous."

Kate's thoughts flew about like startled birds in a storm. She believed the girl had come for one reason and one only: to see not "that Jackson fellow," but Jack Rodiker; and, not knowing what to think, Kate thought the worst, because nearly all her life she had heard the Claytons suspected of cattle stealing, had heard often of Tex's drunkenness, and believed that the girls were not much, if any, better than low white trash. Sue had just now sounded as if bragging about her sister marrying into the Bevarts family, when once there had been talk of how loyal this sister Bess was to her outlawed sweetheart. All that was changed now. Reward money changed people. The Bevartses, as Kate had learned by gunfire, were Rodiker's enemies, and she thought this girl was here now on Zig Bevarts's fine horse and saddle, inquiring for "that Jackson fellow," to make sure he was who the Bevartses thought, and plan some trap.

Kate asked with scorn-tipped sharpness, "Have you Claytons thrown in with the Bevartses to catch him?"

"Catch who?"

"You know as well as I do!"

Sue looked at her with such profound staring that Kate saw clearly, as if it had been spoken, that Rodiker's name was in her thoughts; then Sue moved staringly nearer and said in wonderment, "You know? *You?*" Her eyes brightened menacingly from thought that became words.

"You Arnolds've trapped him here! Where is he?"

Kate answered defiantly, "Where you and the Bevartses won't find him!"

Sue thrust out both hands and closed them on Kate's neck and shook fiercely. "Where is he? You tell me or I'll kill you, you little snake-headed devil! You woman—tricked him into comin' here!"

Kate hadn't a chance to say anything now, and she pulled at the fingers which were as tight as a wet rope on her throat as Sue, with increasing fury, shook her and made fearful accusations and threats.

Rodiker saw the horse and read the brand before he came cautiously around the veranda's corner and stopped short.

Kate said to Sue, "There, you crazy fool! That's him!"

Sue looked across her shoulder, then stepped back, her arms as limp as if broken, and shook her head to clear the loose hair from her eyes.

Kate was too angered to be embarrassed, and said to Rodiker, "Come here!" Her hand moved as if throwing something to indicate the horse, when she added, "Zig Bevarts sent this

Clayton girl to make sure if you were here!"

He thought, *Not Sue!* then remembered Slim's treachery. When Sue came near and stood in wide-eyed staring within a hand's reach of him, he didn't give a sign of recognition. She knew him, of course; and also knew him for the bearded man she had talked with in the twilight on the Santsander, and now she asked with hurt puzzlement, "Why didn't you tell me?"

He said quietly, "Ask Slim."

" 'Twas Slim sent me!" She was closer now, and her eyes glowed angrily. "Ronnie's been put in jail for horse stealin' an'—"

"Who put him there?"

"—Slim sent me to tell you it's a trap for to catch you when you try to get him out!" She hurried the words. "Slim said some folks think you are back, and had the sheriff grab Ronnie for to bait the trap. There's a guard ever' night. Slim's one and Bill Brody too! I hate him! How Slim knew you were here he wouldn't say, not even to me, who he tells ever'thing to! But somehow he did know that you are that Jackson fellow, and here at old Yank Arnold's!"

"Does Bess know?"

"Bess know what? That you're here? I don't guess so. But ain't you got sense enough to forget Bess? Though if she did know, she wouldn't tell on you!"

Sue, as if reminded, turned toward Kate and asked Rodiker:

"How it come you trust *her* more than me? You didn't let me know that night we met, but her—she knows!"

He pulled out a handkerchief and wiped at Sue's cheek as he said, "She guessed. That's all."

"That's all?" Sue gasped, absently taking the handkerchief from him. "All! When Yank Arnold'll make any man rich that kills you?" Sue whirled about to face Kate. There was only one conceivable explanation, and Sue angrily accused her. "You're in love with him!"

Rodiker said, "Hell!"

Kate's dark eyes flashed. The jealousy in Sue's voice was unmistakable and challenging. Kate almost said "Yes!" and wanted to say it, but instead told Sue:

"I don't believe he did what people say and—"

How Kate would have explained there was no knowing, because Sue broke in. "And *I* don't care what he's done or not done! I love him! I've loved him from the time I was big enough to know one boy from another! When I love a man he's mine! You understand? I'd've took him away from Bess, if I had to shoot her! Or you too!"

Sue's jealousy had sensed a rival, and that was her way to give warning, backed by a fury look.

Kate, with scorn-edged quietness, inquired, "And the man has nothing to say about it?"

"Not if I want him, he ain't!"

After that no one spoke for a while. The wind whooped as it shuffled gravel and twisted the paloverde's fringed drapery. The horse, with ears forward, put its nose down to the nose of an inquiring pup.

When Rodiker asked, "But what of Ronnie?" Sue misunderstood and said, "He's just a kid, and sweet, but he knows I used him only to practice on. I told him so!"

"No, no. I mean, who accused him?"

"Bill Brody!"

"And he's still working for the Bevartses?"

"Not reg'lar, no. He's got a two-bit-sized ranch of his own over south and a beef contract to feed Indians, I hear."

"And the sheriff arrested Ronnie on Brody's say-so?"

"His dep'ty did. That long-nosed Joe Roberts. I sent word I'd claw his eyes out—him an' Bill Brody's both! I never could un'erstand why the Lord didn't put Bill Brody in a snake's shape, like he belongs! And are you goin' to stay on here at Yank Arnold's?"

In asking that of Rodiker, she turned suspiciously toward Kate and watched her as he said, "For the time being."

Sue shook her head in studying bewilderment.

"It beats me!" Then she told Kate, "You dirty-trick him, an' I'll tear all your clothes off and stake you 'Pachy style on an anthill!"

"Just you don't tell he's here!" said Kate.

"Us Claytons don't tell tales. Not even to each other we don't! We're Texans!"

Rodiker helped her into the saddle. She tucked her skirts high about her legs as she said, "Ain't you goin' to kiss me?"

When Sue had loped out of sight, Kate watched Rodiker's solemnness. He stood with thumbs in his belt and his eyes fixed afar, and the set of the jaw muscles was distinguishable under the beard. His thought was of Slim and the warning, and he believed it, but there was no lessening of the hurt hate for the man who had been his best friend.

Kate's eyes were not laughing, though she smiled tauntingly to say, "She goes after a man headlong and swinging a wide loop—the same as after a steer! I always thought you used bait and coaxed and appealed to his chivalry. That's how they teach you in a ladies' school back East!"

Rodiker's eyes turned slowly. "She's just a fool kid."

Kate's smile went away. She put both hands to her gaping waist. "And is Bess Clayton marrying Zig?"

"If she wants. I mean if he wants her!"

As he walked away her eyes followed from under a tight frown. When he was out of sight, she shook her head a little, drew a long breath, and let it go with a sighlike sound, then shrugged a shoulder. After that her small sharp teeth came together, and Kate told herself. *Sue Clayton won't get him! Not away from me!*

CHAPTER 17

Old Johnny limped through the starlight, leading one of the colonel's favorite horses, a high-headed, lean-legged black gelding. He told Rodiker:

"Miss Kate said fur you to have him. He's purt' near a house pet. You treat 'im easy now. Hand-raised an' dog-gentle. When you leave 'im in a stable at Moheela, you tell 'em to grain 'im, an' none of that musty ol' hay of theirn!

"And I don't envy you none meetin' that Miz Cora Arnold! Bet the colonel's glad to git outa goin'! He never liked her."

Rodiker's "No?" was softly inquiring.

"Hell no! She's sulky as a wet hen in a thunderstorm."

"He *never* liked her?"

"Not from the first sight of her."

"How do you know?"

"I fit all through the War as his ord'ly. I can read him like a big-print book!"

Rodiker cinched the saddle, let his hand slide along the horse's neck. "Did you ever hear her tell about how her husband was killed?"

"All I heard tell was that right after the killin', she went tearin' home from the piñons in the buggy. The team run away with her, but it run home. She was tur'ble scairt, natur'ly. Fellers went out after Craig's body, and a couple headed this way to tell the colonel. Craig was shot in the back."

"Funny he'd turn his back to a man on a Bevarts' horse, don't you think?"

"I reckon. An' you can do me a big favor, if you will. My stomik is upset these days, an' from time to time I needa smidge. Will you bring a bottle?"

Rodiker rode off. The black was a pacer, alert and eager, as easy-gaited as a rocking chair, and Rodiker sat with head up, brooding. Wariness kept him alert, but his thoughts clustered about Ronnie. One thing sure, the forethoughtful and farseeing old Jerym had guessed wrong. *I'd let him stay till hell freezes!* Rodiker told himself, meaning that if Ronnie broke jail he would be outlawed too. *Just a kid, younger than I was!*

Bill Brody's was a name that hurt, not so much as Slim's but it also now had the significance of betrayal. *No trusting anybody!*

Then he thought of Sue. "Just a kid," was maybe true, but not the whole truth; grown up, she still had the same frank passion as when she had fought against having her arms pulled from his neck. And pretty; pretty as Bess, or prettier. But there was Judas-blood in the Claytons, and no matter how much Slim might try to redeem himself, he had done what wasn't forgivable.

He rode into Apache Flat and looked toward where he had shot Pete Croy out of the saddle, and beyond that place he had overtaken Slim. He went by the spot where the buggy stopped, and remembered Kate's being tricked into the belief that he, Rodiker, had led the murderers.

Farseein' the Bevartses. Which reminded him again of Colonel Arnold's guess that he, presumably "Jackson" by name, was also an outlaw, but an enemy of Rodiker's. *It's all right to be an outlaw if Yank Arnold can use you!* So far Arnold had been too sick to make much use of the outlaw. *I'll make him sicker soon!*

As he rode up the grade and again saw the light burning late at Whitman's his thoughts once more gathered ununderstandingly around Kate. In spite of swift recurrent doubts, he trusted her, and had a perplexed wonderment that he did. Her admission of childish admiration for him was a favoring influence because he, too, had always remembered the colonel's pretty child whose pained ankle made her faint—or so he had thought. That she had schemed coquettishly seemed amusing now, though his vibrant wariness wouldn't let him forget that she was tricky with lies and could be dangerous. She had scorched his neck with a quirt and ordered him hanged when she thought he had run Arnold cattle in on the Baddens. He admired her for that.

He didn't pause at Whitman's. People there

would mention to others that he had been by, and if word got about, he might be laid for again. He also rode wide of Moheela, not leaving the horse stabled there, as old Johnny expected, then using the stage as the colonel had instructed.

After rounding Moheela he returned to the stage road where he pulled the horse into a walk, taking it easy, for he knew that he could make it to Woodward by midmorning and not rattle a spur.

At sunup he looked down from the red hills and saw Woodward, still some two hours away. It lay all spraddled out like a lot of toy blocks on a rumpled carpet that was mostly buff-colored. The town was larger now than when he had been in with beef drives, and, drawing nearer, he saw the checkered effect of city blocks and the jackstraw outline of the stockyards and the track side's stilt-legged water tower which lowered its hollow beak to puffing engines.

Outside the town he dismounted, pulled on his shirt, and concealed his revolver by hanging it under his arm, then fastening the holster's end thongs about his waist. He stowed the belt in a saddlebag. The rifle was still in its scabbard, but would be left at the stable.

He hadn't a watch, but knew the time was near ten o'clock when he dismounted in the livery stable's wide runway.

A fat man with a straw in his mouth sauntered

up and said, "Howdy," taking notice of Rodiker's hard looks and the splendid Arnold-branded horse that was a long way from home.

Rodiker said, "Colonel Arnold sent me to meet some woman relation of his due on the afternoon train. She's fussy, I hear, so I want to hire a pole buggy instead of going back by stage."

The fat man chewed his straw. "Colonel Arnold, heh? Who's the relation?"

"Sister-'n-law."

"She comin' back? Well now, ordinary I'd want a pretty good deposit, but for the colonel 'tain't nec'sary." He looked Rodiker up and down and grinned. "At first I wasn't sure of you. You didn't look the kind of man to be on that kind of horse! Not spruce enough."

"I'll be spruce by traintime," Rodiker told him, and walked away, thinking some of what the colonel would say about hiring a buggy here to return all the way to the ranch. *By the time I get back with that woman, I won't care what he says!*

Rodiker went to the Ace restaurant for breakfast. He had flapjacks, an inch-thick steak that was scorched outside, raw within—the way he wanted it—and three cups of coffee and three spoonfuls of sugar to each cup.

After that he felt pretty good, relaxed and sleepy. He smoked a cigarette at the table, and decided that he had better spruce up. Cora Arnold might not want to go in the buggy with somebody who looked like a ruffian.

In the general store he bought a pair of new pants, an iron-cloth blue shirt, some underwear, and socks. The boots he wore were as good as money could buy, but he laid down twelve dollars for a new black hat. He didn't like its newness, although his weather-darkened band helped take off some of the unworn look, and he would work over the hat with punches, pulls, and by sitting on it.

The heavy breakfast made him thirsty, and on the way to a barbershop he stopped for a bottle of beer. One wasn't enough.

At the barbershop he took a bath and changed clothes, then waited his turn at the chair. He said, "Haircut, and take off the rough edges of these whiskers."

The little barber absently said, "You bet!" as he flirted with a lady in a yellow hat who smirked in sidling by.

Rodiker closed his eyes, stretched his legs, relaxed, but was pleasantly drowsy and let himself drift. When he opened his eyes, the barber was stropping the razor and talking politics with a couple of fellows. Rodiker moved his hand to the side of his face, then sat up abruptly; one cheek was as smooth as his palm and chalk-white; the other side of his face was untouched. If he had done what he felt like, he would have knocked the barber through the window, but there was no way now of changing things.

The barber asked perkily, "Feel better, won't it, to have all the wool sheared?"

"But the skin's white. Whiter than a scared girl's face!"

The little barber tittered. "That's what fools all fellows that shave their beards. But I got skin stain—it's really hair dye! That'll fix you up till you get good and brown again."

When he had been "fixed up," as the little barber called it, Rodiker thought he looked like one of big Sam's near relatives. It wasn't that dark, but the barber, in a flutter of artistic effort, for the stain on Rodiker's cheeks had been given a deeper shade than the tan on his forehead, darkened the forehead. The darkened forehead then made the cheeks appear lighter, so they were again rubbed with cotton dipped in hair dye.

Rodiker moved out on the street, with his fingers feeling inquiringly from one side of his face to the other, and he paused repeatedly to peer at his reflection in store windows. Presently he felt a little amused satisfaction in the thought, *At least now I don't look like that fellow Jackson the Bevartses are laying for!* All that was left to mark him as "Jackson" was the old brown vest, now very shabby in contrast with his new duds.

In a store that sold hand-me-downs he asked if he could buy a vest without a suit, and the pale, sickly clerk studied, as if trying to decide on Rodiker's nationality, then said that he had some fancy vests that came without suits. From an assortment of a half-dozen Rodiker reluctantly chose one. He changed his tobacco, papers, nubbin of a pencil, and the envelope containing old Jerym's "agreement" into the pockets of a brightly beaded buckskin, which was the only one of the lot big enough to fit. For that he paid six dollars, being glad it was secondhand and showed wear, having been taken in as part payment on a new outfit.

The train was due a little after 2 P.M., but long before that time Rodiker sat on his heels with his back to the red boards of the station and listened to the enigmatic chittering of the telegraph.

The train whistled at the edge of town, and came plumed with smoke around the curve. The station agent, wearing black sleeve protectors that reached to his elbows, ran out with flimsy fluttering in his hand as the train rolled bumpily to a stop and the engine panted with long-drawn breathing. Heads were stuck from windows, watching people get on and off. Roped trunks tumbled from the baggage car, and all the while the bell tolled as slowly as a church bell at a funeral. Presently the conductor's "All 'bo-ard!" rose above the greetings and partings, and the train began to chuff-chuff-chuff away. The conductor swung aboard the last car as casually as if stepping onto his own back porch.

A dozen passengers left the train, mostly men, and all the women had escorts. Rodiker had never been nearer to Cora Arnold than years before, when he had peered at her through Tex Clayton's 'dobe doorway; and now there wasn't any woman standing about alone and looking for someone to greet her. He was sure she hadn't come, but walked over to the trunks and read the tags, finding Cora Arnold's name.

A short man in a high celluloid collar, swallow-tail coat, and brown derby, came up and with glib ease asked, "Are you by any chance from the Arnold ranch? Mrs. Arnold's waiting over there."

The drummer led Rodiker to the shaded side of the station, where Cora Arnold sat on the drummer's up-ended sample case with her own traveling bag at her small feet.

She didn't rise, but looked steadily at Rodiker's dark face as he stood hat in hand, and he wouldn't have known her—not from the vague memory he had of what she looked like. She wasn't sullen or, as old Johnny put it, "sulky"; and she was larger then Rodiker remembered, much bigger, but not fat, and still had a prettiness that was slightly startling. Her eyes were blue as turquoise, with the hard glaze of turquoise that has been polished; her face was a bleached white and now powdered. The features were as even as if chiseled. The hat was a dark blue, almost black, and he hadn't remembered that her thick hair was red, but it was now. She held a folded parasol in gloved hands and wore a tan alpaca coat that covered her from throat to feet, and the coat was stained with soot, and had fine cinders in the creases.

When she had looked him over with much the appraisal of a slave buyer, Cora Arnold asked, "What is your name?" Her voice had a low, silky huskiness, not unpleasant, but strange.

"They call me Joe."

She smiled quickly. "And sometimes 'José'?"

"*Si*, señora."

Cora Arnold's smile had lingered, and she told him quite coolly, "You are very handsome, José!"

The little drummer's laugh was a kind of snort. He blurted, "You do beat all!" and sounded displeased. Then he tipped his hat and clapped it on his head again with, "G'-by, Mrs. Arnold. If I can have my case—"

She stood up. He lifted his heavy sample case and with petulant abruptness turned away and started off. He had missed the hotel carry-all; it was uphill and a long way to the hotel. On the train she had offered invitation and given promises, or so he had believed.

Cora Arnold stared up at Rodiker, as she inquired about the colonel, not looking so sorry that he was ill as she said she was. Then she asked with a hint of playfulness, "You know, don't you, José, that you are working as much for me as for him?"

He wasn't rattled, but she thought he was, and smiled at the hard set of his face, never dreaming that he said to himself, *She's within arm's reach!* and she didn't see that his hands were knotted into fists.

She said, "I like your vest," and fingered the edge of it. Perfume that set his nerves a-tingle came into his face. "Black and red beads. Very artistic," and, lifting her eyes, added, "Spaniards are, aren't they? How tall you are! And is the colonel all alone at the ranch?"

"His daughter is home."

"That brat!" The words flashed on the instant and with temper, but she peered at his unchanging face and smiled. "Perhaps you like her?"

"I am just a hired man, señora."

"It sounds nice to be called 'señora!' And what are we going to do? It's too late for the Moheela stage, isn't it? Anyhow, I wouldn't go today. I'll stay at the hotel tonight. I'm tired. You'll have to find a cab. Or don't they have cabs in this miserable country? And there are my trunks."

When he told her that he had a buggy, and they could start this evening and drive through the night, avoiding the heat of the day, she laughed at him. "Ah, that would be pleasant, but miss my sleep? There was no Pullman west of Kansas City, and I didn't shut my eyes last night. I feel

I've been drawn through a knothole, and must look it, too, don't I?"

Rodiker found a dray and helped the man with the trunks. He sat on a trunk, and Cora Arnold sat on the seat under the striped umbrella as they drove to the Claymore Hotel.

He helped her from the seat, and she at once took off the alpaca, gave herself a little shake, smoothed the dress about her hips, straightened, and walked ahead of him into the hotel. Her dark skirt was below ankle length, but didn't drag, and her corseted curves stood out with applelike fullness. Men watched, and she knew it, and she cared as a showgirl cares when on the stage.

A porter followed her upstairs, and Rodiker turned to go into the hotel bar, but Dougal Bevarts lurked at one side of the bar's doorway, his eyes following her on the stairs, so Rodiker, without a pause, went on to the street door.

He soon was telling the stableman that the buggy wouldn't be used until tomorrow. The stableman looked him over and said approvingly, "Danged if you ain't spruced up! Don't look like the same feller, and I'd never a-took you for a Mexican—not with that beard on! Have you heard the news?"

"Not particularly, no."

"You know about the Rod'kers, or, at least, Jack?"

"I've heard things, yes."

"W'y, you know, I reckon, 'twas Jack shot Miz Arnold's husband a few years back. The ol' colonel's been after him ever since."

"But what now?"

"A brother of Jack's was caught hoss stealin' lately. Just a kid, so they locked 'im up instead of hangin' the pup. Last night somebody broke him outa jail! Shot up Slim Clayton, who was on guard. Dougal Bevarts rode in a while ago and he says there's some talk that it was Jack Rodiker himself that got the kid out! You people out to the colonel's better watch sharp. It's said Jack Rod'ker has swore to kill him too. Bad lot, them Rod'kers."

CHAPTER 18

Rodiker avoided Dougal Bevarts by staying away from the Claymore, and went to a rooming house where he sat for hours on the side of the bed. His thoughts were cool and steady, but decision evaded him. Ronnie was an outlaw now. In spite of Cora Arnold, that was mostly in his thoughts. Now his mother would suffer as if she held hot coals in her palms, and the once-broad back of his high-shouldered father would bend a little more. *Who got him out?* It couldn't even be guessed at. Nobody who was trying to help Ronnie would have shot Slim, yet somebody had.

Although he had been sleepless the previous night, it was near dawn when he turned in, and he slept until well past noon. Then he stood before the mirror with rather the feeling that he didn't know himself, as he ran a hand over his dark cheeks. When he had dressed, the beaded buckskin vest made him feel outlandish; it was ornate and flashy, and he hadn't a liking for trappings of the kind.

He went into an empty restaurant. Bluebottle flies hummed against the warm windows, and a hefty waitress came from the kitchen. She had freckled arms and a wide freckled face, and grinned at him across the table as he sat down. "Lots of excitement, ain't they?"

"I've been asleep."

"W'y, ain't you heard Dougal Bevarts married Cora Arnold this mornin'? They left for Moheela a while ago. She looked mighty purty as they drove by with a spankin' pair. 'Magine her marryin' Dougal Bevarts! That sure is romance, ain't it?"

Rodiker pushed back his chair, rising.

The fat stableman was a-quiver. "I wondered where you was! I told Bevarts straight out he couldn't have the buggy, because I was savin' it for Cora Arnold, and he said that's who he wanted it for!"

Rodiker saddled, strapped on his revolver, examined the rifle, making sure the magazine was full and a cartridge lay under the hammer. The bridal buggy left at noon.

The stableman was all for Colonel Arnold and called it a damn' shame that the Bevartses would now grab off half the Arnold property. He said, "An' Dougal must've planned for trouble, 'cause he had two men with him here in town, and when he drove out with her they tagged along. One's called Mack. Don't know the other. Both rode Lazy S's."

The first miles from town were up-grade toward the lumpy red rocks that often had the sunset glow of fresh blood. Dougal Bevarts wouldn't have any fear of being chased, but probably would push the team hard, being that kind of man. He had come to town with more purpose than Rodiker suspected, and had carried out that purpose.

An hour later Rodiker turned into a barren yard before a small adobe that the weather had gnawed to near ruin. Ragged tots huddled in the doorway to peer, and a ponderous Indian woman waddled through them. Yes, the buggy and horsemen had stopped; they used water from the well without asking, and had driven on without thanks. There were two men on horseback with the buggy.

Some miles beyond, Rodiker came to a roadhouse that was back from the road and lay under deep, bluff-cast shadows, thought it wasn't yet sundown. Old outbuildings straggled off and sagged in disrepair, and were followed part way by a broken fence of upright sticks that had once guarded a garden. Dougal Bevarts wouldn't stop with his bride, not at this unclean place, but three horses were at the hitching rack, and it was on one of these horses that Dougal had ridden to Arnold's with the sheriff. Rodiker couldn't read the brand from the road, but he could recognize a horse he had seen as readily as he remembered a man he had once taken notice of.

He turned from the road and moved along at a walk, with his hat shading his eyes, and his eyes struck here and there, searching for signs. All three horses at the bark-stripped rack were

Lazy S's. Dougal's was the best, and carried a finer rig than either of the others.

Rodiker dropped the reins when he left the saddle, and without a pause started for the door, where a chunky man looked out.

The chunky man shouted back over his shoulder, "Hey, Mack! Here's that José!" Then he stood aside as Rodiker entered, but spoke jeeringly. "Hiya, Mex! Lookin' for somebody? Couldn't be a lady you've lost, could it?"

Rodiker's swirling glance took in the room: it was dim, not large, with a low ceiling and a pine-board bar from window to dirty window across one end. The floor was hard-packed earth.

Two more men were in the room; one was behind the bar, and, by the vague light of the dusty window, his round face looked fatly swollen and sullen under the flat-crowned black hat. His hair was Indian dark and coarse, covering his ears, and he wore a dirty buckskin vest from which much of the bead design had dripped away from broken threads.

The man called Mack was on the drinking side of the bar, and stared at Rodiker, and wasn't amused by his partner's joshing. "A Spaniard named José," Cora Arnold had told Dougal Bevarts; and this was the man, and Mack didn't know him, but uneasily sensed something familiar.

The jocular man said, "Was you scairt to show up at the weddin'?"

Rodiker's thumb went over his shoulder, indicating the horses outside as he asked, "Where's Bevarts?"

The question had a jerk to it, and the jocular man threw away his good humor, put on a scowl, stuck his fists on his hips, and demanded loudly, "Can you tie that? Yank Arnold's greaser talking like—"

Rodiker hit him. The blow flashed up from the hip, and wasn't a fist, for he struck the fellow's throat with thumb and fingers spread, knocking breath out of his windpipe as his head rocked back, then the fingers closed, chokingly. The fellow tugged at Rodiker's grasp, but couldn't break it, and Rodiker banged his head rapidly against the 'dobe wall as if using the head for a knocker.

For a long moment Mack stood in dazed glaring as he watched his husky companion being batted as a man might bang a dummy about, but something in Rodiker's size and strength and quickness jarred up delayed recognition with the shout of "Jackson!"

At a glance Rodiker had known him for one of Zig's companions in the barroom fight, and was ready. He flung the beaten man away, letting him fall as a drunken man topples, then spun about with his revolver hip-high, cocked, and pointed. But Mack was already dropping with a limber-kneed sag when his fingers slipped from the partly drawn gun, and broken glass clattered on the rock-hard floor.

The sullen half-breed leaned heavily on the bar to look over and down, then straightened up and spoke softly.

"Eef I know you so queek to draw, I let heem be shot, but—" He shrugged a shoulder. The round, fatly swollen face hadn't a flicker of change as he asked, "You hav' dreenk?"

From somewhere he brought out a bottle of good liquor, and, wordlessly, they drank together from tin cups.

The half-breed gave his name as Enzo. He didn't know anything about Bevarts having passed in a buggy with a bride. These men, with an extra horse, had stopped a little while ago. They laughed about how a big jolt had been handed Colonel Arnold.

Enzo said stolidly, "I do not esk queestions." Then he commented, "Harry Hand there, he weel not be so funnee for a long time, uh?" In as muffled monotone as a bumblebee's drone, he explained that this was his brother-in-law's place, and the brother-in-law had taken the family to a funeral, so he, Enzo, was in charge for today.

"Me," said Enzo proudly, "I am a blacksmeeth. Ho!" He showed the swollen muscle of his doubled-up right arm.

Rodiker covered his impatience with attentive

listening, and heard Enzo say, as if regretful, "You are not Mex'can then?"

After that he asked, "Thees man Jackson?" The unreadable black eyes rested on Rodiker's hair-dyed face.

"He works for Colonel Arnold, and the Bevartses don't like him."

"He is your friend?"

Rodiker smiled, nodded.

Enzo said, "You, huh?"

"Yes."

The inscrutable eyes carefully studied Rodiker, then Enzo grunted, peered over the bar at the men on the floor, who were stirring as drunks do when awakening with headaches. He rounded the bar, stooped from one to the other, taking a gun from each, then returned and, putting the guns out of sight, rested his elbows on the bar and said placidly, "Now I bet you they be good. They Beel Brody's men. I do not like Beel Brody now."

Rodiker asked why, but Enzo didn't reply to that. He dropped his voice and spoke softly. "Thees Colonel Arnold, do you theenk he ud pay good to know how he lose cows?"

"Ride over and talk with him."

"You talk to heem. Say to look good in Los Muertos Canyon, but go careful!" It had grown darker than twilight, but Rodiker saw the enigmatic shrug as the half-breed asked, "Maybe he pay sometheeng, eh?"

"I'll tell him all you've said."

"G'-by," said Enzo.

"*Adios*," said Rodiker, leaving.

Night was near, but that wouldn't mean darkness—not under the translucent purple of the star-bright sky. He had lost time, and hadn't learned anything except that Dougal Bevarts, having left his horse in the care of the two men, had driven on. He wondered some that Enzo had taken his part, but nevertheless guessed that the half-breed was pretty much of a scoundrel and could look out for himself when the two Bevarts'—or rather Bill Brody's—men lifted their broken heads. The evasive way he had referred to Los Muertos, wanting money, suggested to Rodiker that the stolid half-breed was selling out somebody; but as the chance of getting money was slight, he perhaps was doing it for spite.

Rodiker hadn't any doubts about Bill Brody being a rustler in cahoots with the Bevartses. Perhaps old Jerym had trusted him enough to confide that Rodiker was back in the country, and had suggested using Ronnie to bait the trap. Old Jerym must feel bewildered at thinking Rodiker (no matter if under the name of "Jackson") was now high in Colonel Arnold's favor. Jerym himself may have urged the hasty marriage to secure property enough to bolster his bank in case Arnold should make known why Rodiker had been summoned back into the Santsander.

When I catch that buggy I'll ask questions of them both! He told himself.

An empty high-wheeled freight wagon creaked and jolted as the eight mules dozed along, and the bearded freighter whoa-ed up with a careless pull of line as Rodiker, hand half-raised in the sign of friendliness, hailed him.

"Yep," said the freighter. He'd pulled out for a buggy three-four miles back afore the Redburn crossin'. Hadn't rek'nized Doug Bevarts, but might've been him. Was a woman with him.

Asked if there was fresh news about the jail break, he put a hand to his beard, holding it back as he leaned to spit. "Don't rightly know, but I heared Bill Brody's offerin' a small-size reward. Slim Clayton ain't bad hurt much. Just shot in the laig. I was out to the Claytons. Swopped some mules." With a burst of feeling: "That Rodiker kid never no more stole one of Bill Brody's horses than I stole the chunk that's missin' out of the moon!"

"Why are you so sure?"

"Hell afire, them Rodikers are hones' folks!"

"How about Jack?"

"He jes' shot a cantankerous Yankee!"

"In the back, they say!"

The freighter demanded, "Who the hell air you?"

"Name is Jackson, and I work for Colonel Arnold!"

“Hope you burn in hell with me shovelin’ the coal!” the freighter shouted, then he yelled at his mules, and they went jolting on.

Rodiker hurried on, now sure of the chase. When he splashed into the ankle-deep spread of the Santsander at Redburn Crossing, he let the horse drink, then took it easy on the upgrade. Moheela was less than fifteen crooked miles ahead, and the buggy team tired, and the newly married couple might like the cozy slowness of the team’s tiredness.

It wasn’t long before he expected to see the buggy when he rounded each succeeding curve, and at times he paused, listening, but there was no sound of hoof-throb or harness-jangle in the stillness. He rode faster, uneasy at the thought that Bevarts may have labored the team on, as if aware of being pursued. When Moheela’s few lights lay ahead at the foot of a descending curve, he met another empty freight wagon.

No, the freighter said, he hadn’t seen any buggy and team; hadn’t seen a soul since pulling out of Moheela. When Rodiker explained that he had tried to overtake Dougal Bevarts to give him a message, the freighter said:

“W’y, maybe he turned off there at Redburn’s to go to Calisto. It’s a deuce-sized ranch Dougal’s got. I hauled in there onct about a year ago. If you’d watched the road for wheel tracks, you could have told.”

When the freighter's wagon rumbled on, Rodiker dismounted, pulled the saddle, letting the horse breathe easily, then turned the blankets when he resaddled, and rode at a walk. He had never heard of Calisto, and wouldn't turn back to ride in the dark through country he didn't know, not when the buggy had gone so many miles from him.

He told himself that he'd somehow soon get to Mrs. Dougal Bevarts, and she would tell him things.

CHAPTER 19

The dogs knew the horse, and didn't bark when Rodiker reached the ranch before sunup. He turned the horse loose in the corral and made his way to the bunkhouse, pulled his boots at the doorway, and went quietly to his blankets, where he lay on his back with hands folded under his head. He was dog-tired, but sleepless. His thoughts were still being woven and unraveled, much of the time about Ronnie, but he couldn't shut out Cora Arnold.

When the straw boss sang out, the bunkhouse was still dark, though the sky was dawn-streaked. Men stirred and grumbled meaningless complaints. Rodiker hadn't closed his eyes. He didn't get up for the breakfast call.

The black horse indicated that he was back, and soon Colonel Arnold sent Sam to ask where Cora Arnold was.

When he first had a good look at Rodiker, Sam opened his mouth wide, then closed it noiselessly, but retained a popeyed stare, wondering at the change from an unkempt beard to the smooth-faced dark hue.

Rodiker said tonelessly, "I'm a dude now," and felt of his cheeks, again needing a shave.

"Huccome Miz Arnold ain't wid you?"

"The lady had other ideas."

He stamped into his boots, slipped on the vest, made a cigarette. Sam eyed the brightly beaded vest and beamed approval.

"Dat sho' am a styl'sh garment, Mist' Jackson."

Rodiker's palm rasped his beard. "I'll trade it for a shave."

The big Negro's grin widened like a split watermelon. "You jes' funnin'."

Rodiker emptied his pockets, folding and sticking old Jerym's agreement into a boot top, then tossed the vest to Sam.

"Try it for size."

"You is earnes'?"

Sam proudly slipped on the vest. It was big, but not big enough to meet in front of his bear-shaped body, which didn't much matter, and he beamed at himself in the piece of looking glass on the shelf by the door.

"Even Steven," said Rodiker.

Sam went to the bunkhouse kitchen, borrowed the cook's razor, and returned with hot water and yellow soap. Rodiker sat on a backless chair with a flour sack tucked under his chin, and had the carefullest shave of his life. After that Sam brought a pint tin cup of stale black coffee, and admired himself in the looking glass, while Rodiker smoked thoughtfully.

"Sam, between friends, what do you think of Cora Arnold?"

Sam, under the influence of Rodiker's gift, looked about cautiously before he confided, "She jes' white trash in fine cloz!"

Rodiker murmured encouragingly, "I'll go along."

"I neber say dat to nobody b'foh, and I'll say I neber said it 'f you say I has!"

"Fair enough. But what gave you the idea?"

"I seen her onct lovin' up a fella from town. She seen me see her, an' she come later an' say, 'You dirt' black nigger, doan' you dare say boo erbout me!' "

"Who was she making up to?"

"Dunno. Jes' a young fella in city duds dat come wid visitin' folks. I kep' my mouf shet, kaze if a white lady call you a liar, you is!"

"She ever try to make up to the colonel?"

"He'd a-tuk her head off! He's a gent'mun, suh! An' his own brudder's wife?" The big Negro's eyes clouded wrathfully. "Huccome you talk lak dat erbout the colonel?"

Rodiker met no one in the house and went up the stairs. The door was open and the colonel, dressed except for boots and hat, sat in a chair without pillows and stared from a window. He turned and frowned toward Rodiker as if at a stranger, then the frown relaxed and, ignoring the changed appearance, he asked matter-of-factly:

"Where is Mrs. Arnold?"

Rodiker was still in the doorway, his thumbs in

the front of his belt, and the straight back gave him a high-shouldered look. He said quietly:

"She married Dougal Bevarts in Woodward."

Rodiker had braced himself for wrath, but silence followed. Colonel Arnold didn't move, and not even a muscle twitched as he gazed at Rodiker. He seemed still listening to the words that had been spoken. A dog near the colonel's chair stirred and bitingly nosed for fleas, and when he sprawled flat again, a pin's fall could have been heard.

Then the colonel turned in his chair, lifted a cigar-box lid, took up a cigar, and studied it, now on one side, now on the other. At last he bit the end of the cigar, spat, put it in his mouth, and bit down hard. After that he pulled slowly at one side of his mustache, then looked up to say with military brusqueness:

"Come in. Sit down. Let's hear."

Rodiker took off his hat and went to a chair near the table, where he sat bolt upright and spoke quietly.

"I rode into Woodward and met her at the train. It was too late for the stage back. I offered to bring her in a buggy, but she wanted to stay overnight at the hotel. I went to a rooming house and slept until about noon. In a restaurant I heard they'd married and gone. I came on back."

The colonel again didn't move for a long time, then silently offered the box of cigars. Rodiker shook his head. "Thanks," he said, and pulled papers and tobacco from his shirt pocket. When he struck a match he first offered it as a light for the colonel's cigar, but Colonel Arnold said, "Thanks," and shook his head.

As he put the flame to his cigarette, he saw that the colonel was smiling; it was a cold, tight smile, and bitter, but so meaningful that Rodiker forgot the match until fire nipped his fingers. He dropped the burning stick and put a foot on it.

Presently the colonel asked, "Anything else?"

"Not much. But Bevarts must have had it all planned ahead, and was ready for trouble, because two men were with him, and rode part-way back. I saw Lazy S horses at a roadhouse, and stopped to inquire, though the buggy had gone on. There was a set-to. When my beard come off, my face was so pale the barber put hair dye on it, and these fellows mistook me for a Mexican. A half-breed who called himself Enzo took up for me, and the Bevarts men quieted down.

"This Enzo asked would you pay for information on how you lost cows. He mentioned Los Muertos Canyon. I said I'd tell you."

"I've never seen him to know him, but Enzo has the name of a bad breed, and probably does know first hand how I've lost cattle. Los Muertos is off my range, but we'll ride down there one of these days and look around. You didn't get much sleep last night."

"I dozed in the saddle."

The colonel nodded and put the tips of his fingers carefully together, seemed making sure they were placed just as he wanted them, then removed the cigar and examined the end he had chewed. He continued to look at it as he said:

"I surmise that Dougal Bevarts went back East to court her and learn just how much of the Arnold property is hers. That is why she decided to come West again and demand an accounting. I suppose that Dougal and old Jerym have figured that the marriage ought to put their shaky holdings back on their feet, including that bank. I would give half of what I own to smash old Jerym!"

He spoke with such vehemence that he was again breathless, and now his chest heaved as he gasped, like a man tired by running.

A commotion started among the dogs in the yard, and the hound that had been by the colonel's feet got up and went scrambling out of the room and down the stairs to learn the cause.

The colonel showed no interest at all, but soon Kate, in a fantastic getup, came, followed by two men who made a mild chatter with spurred boots and scrape of chairs when told to take seats. They sat down and gazed with awkward admiration at Kate, who wore a loose, swaying dress of as many colors as a shattered rainbow, and there was the glittering jangle of bright metal and cheap jewelry about her. She had heard what to expect of Rodiker's appearance from Sam, and now showed no surprise, though she looked at him with interest until the colonel said, almost at once:

"Your aunt Cora has married Dougal Bevarts."

Kate cried, "Oh!" as if struck hard from behind, then turned on Rodiker and told him, "I don't believe it!" But she did, and asked, "How on earth?" After that she whirled toward her father. "Does that mean—will the Bevartses get—Oh, does it?"

Colonel Arnold plucked at the tuft on his lower lip as his eyes slanted toward a far corner of the ceiling. "Would I give up my brother's property to men who hired him murdered?"

Kate's glance turned uneasily toward Rodiker as she left the room, but he didn't see, and sat stiffly taut until introduced to the two men.

Neither was old, and both had the sunburned leathery skin and bulging thigh muscles of horsemen. It was a tribute to the former range boss, Marl, that the colonel was using the two of them to do his work.

One was a bronzed man, his clipped hair being white enough to look gray, and the china-blue eyes were sheltered behind perpetually narrowed lids. His thick shoulders were egg-round, and his neck dropped. His name was Tom Small.

Frank Pierce was thinner, darker, straighter,

with a way of staring suspiciously. His mouth was crooked and tight; bad temper seemed to lie within him like hot coals under ashes. Rodiker took note that he was left-handed, wore a hand-stamped belt and holster, and had girl-leg spurs.

Both knew of Rodiker as "that man Jackson," who had licked Zig Bevarts and friends in a town fight, had shot Pete Croy when Pete and others tried to dry-gulch him, had ordered the Walters brothers hanged after turning them into Badden's barn and smoking them out. So it appeared that this mysterious stranger was all of a sudden some kind of right-hand man to the colonel.

After handshakes, Frank Pierce said, "The talk is, mister, that you are a range detective."

Rodiker impassively answered, "A range detective that says so wouldn't be much use, would he?"

Frank Pierce stared before he replied, not pleasantly, "We're all Arnold men! It's like you didn't trust us."

Rodiker said, "I draw wages to do as I'm told. I've not been told to tell anybody what I do."

Tom Small rubbed both palms on his knees and nodded. Frank Pierce kept staring at Rodiker as if at somebody he didn't like, but met unyielding eyes, and so looked away. The colonel watched, but made no comment, then offered cigars.

The two foremen talked business under the shadow of cigar smoke, and Rodiker listened.

Tom Small said somehow cows kept drifting south. Frank Pierce said fiercely that line riders needed hauling over the coals. There was talk of grass and water, and about pushing the herds to higher ground for summer feed. Rustling was going on, and Frank Pierce said he'd like to get his hands on anybody that dared touch an Arnold cow with a hot iron. The colonel didn't mention Enzo or Los Muertos Canyon, though the canyon was nearest to San Miguel Ranch, where Pierce was in charge.

With business over, the conversation got around to Ronnie's escape from jail. Frank Pierce said, "I don't see how it could've been any friend of them Rodikers done it, 'cause they and the Claytons are close as hand in glove. Slim's known as that Jack Rodiker's best friend."

Tom Small commented with slow thoughtfulness, "That seems so right it spoils the report that Rodiker himself is back and got his brother out."

Frank Pierce grinned. "Wisht he was back, Colonel! I'd sure like some of that reward of yours. It still stands?"

"And will until he's hung!" said the colonel.

Tom Small was untalkative; now he blinked a few times, shook his head, rubbed his palms on his knees, then took the cigar stub from his mouth, and said carefully, "I'm not a very smart feller. But Bill Brody is a Bevarts man and a friend of the Claytons, so even if that Ronnie kid stole one of his horses, why would Bill Brody have him drug to the hoosegow?"

Nobody commented, and Tom Small sucked again on his dead cigar butt.

When they had gone, Colonel Arnold was breathing hard and looked tired. He sternly said, "Damn this thing of being less than half a man!" and sat on a couch that was overlaid with Indian blankets. He lay back wearily, but couldn't get his breath, and sat up again erectly. He said, "Don't misjudge Frank Pierce by his bad temper. He has worked for me since he was a boy and he is brave—loyal too."

Rodiker sat solemnly silent, scarcely listening, as he remembered how the colonel had said Cora Bevarts would not get any of his brother's property.

After a time the colonel said, "I have some plans for you, but they will wait." He asked Rodiker for the whisky that was out of sight on a shelf, then drank no more than a thimbleful, and gave the bottle back without comment for Rodiker to return to the shelf.

"Do you think Rodiker is back in the Santsander?"

"Wouldn't surprise me none."

"That means the Bevartses are trying to use him against me, and will do what they can to protect him. Don't you think?"

Rodiker said, "Sounds logical."

"Ask Kate to come, will you?"

Kate was in the kitchen talking with old Johnny's good-looking, pleasant wife, and wasn't wearing the gypsy dress. She rubbed her peeling nose and told him:

"After Sam showed me that vest, I thought I'd fix up too. But after I learned about Cora today, I didn't feel like playing I was queen of the gypsies. And you've made Sam perfectly worthless! A while ago he was strutting around out there and talking to himself. And old Johnny's drunk as a hoot owl, so did you bring him some medicine for his 'stomik'?"

"It was in a saddlebag, but—"

"If you buried it ten feet deep, be all the same to him!"

It was something more than an hour later that Kate ran with stumbling haste to the corral where Rodiker was scratching between a colt's ears, and called:

"Oh, come! Papa's downstairs and can't breathe, and Sam—I don't know where, damn him!"

He climbed the logs and jumped down beside her, but she stood perfectly still and almost trancelike as she said:

"It's Aunt Cora marrying like that! I've always hated her!"

Colonel Arnold was downstairs at the office desk with a hand to his throat, and his sunken eyes had a dull, perplexed staring as he asked brokenly, "What is the matter with me? I can't—can't get my breath!"

Kate told Rodiker, "Upstairs, please!"

He stopped and lifted the colonel, who let one arm fall laxly over Rodiker's shoulder, but held a long brown envelope in the other hand. There was no weight to his body; all the tall erectness was skin and bone, and he gasped like a man who is suffocating.

Kate said, "He would come down here to look for—"

Then she broke off and ran ahead on the stairs and, anxious but unflustered, waited at the top.

Rodiker helped her undress the colonel and put him to bed.

CHAPTER 20

That night Rodiker pulled off his boots, making ready to turn in, but a noisy crib game was going in the bunkhouse, so he stepped outside with a cigarette to think things over and saw a shadow move furtively at a corner of the kitchen.

The cook was among the crib players. Rodiker flipped his cigarette upward, carelessly letting it fall and splash sparks. That, he knew, would keep the prowler from peeking again for a long minute or two, then he went on sock-covered tiptoes into the unlighted kitchen and, looking through the back door, saw the shadow shape pressed close against the kitchen wall and peering around the corner. He couldn't tell whether or not the man had a gun in his hand, but said, "Get 'em up."

Hands flew overhead as the man turned, and Rodiker stepped from the dark doorway to move nearer. That brought him into the starlight, and the kid gulped, "Jack!"

Rodiker at once reached out and jerked the boy to him, looked quickly into Ronnie's wide-eyed face, and said, "Go to the stable!" and gave a shove. "I'll meet you there!"

Ronnie crouched as he started off, and Rodiker's long-reaching hand fell on him again and straightened him up:

"Walk like a man! Don't hurry! Never look on the dodge!"

Ronnie tried, but with a tired, hobbling scrape of boots, and he glanced back often in crossing the open starlit space.

Rodiker went into the bunkhouse and put on his boots. The crib players were having a boisterous time. He came in and left unnoticed.

At the stable Rodiker at once lit a lantern and hung it near the door. Ronnie backed into shadows and protested, "But somebody'll see!"

"And be seen if they come. And won't think anything is up, not with a light going on. Never act scared!"

"Well, I am!" said Ronnie.

Rodiker gazed at the tired, gaunt, worn-out kid, then led him toward the rear of the stable, beyond reach of the lantern. He asked, "How'd you know to find me?"

"Slim."

Rodiker's curse blasted Slim. "Who shot him?"

"He shot himself."

"Good!"

"I'm hungry, Jack. I'm starved! I never stole Brody's horse. He loaned it to me. He said, 'Here, you ride him for a week or two. Do him good.' Honest, Jack. You don't believe me?"

Rodiker's face had a hard, unrevealing set as his eyes narrowed down on the kid's face. "Of course I believe you. But about Slim?"

"He shot himself so I could get away, and—"

"Himself? You mean on purpose?"

The kid nodded, then took off his hat and ran fingers through his hair, and looked up anxiously.

"He said you'd understand. Said for me to come to you and tell you why he done it. He said he wouldn't let old Jerym trap you like was planned. First he offered me his gun to shoot him in the leg or arm, but I wouldn't. He said he couldn't let me just walk off because then ever'body would suspicion him of lettin' me go, so he said he had to be shot. Didn't need to be bad hurt, he said, but he'd have to have a bullet in him someplace."

"The ornery fool!" Rodiker murmured, not bitterly.

"The only chance he had was when Bill Brody—they kept watch together at night—went up town for a drink. Slim planned it out, and told me to ride off on his horse up the river, then turn him loose, and he'd go home. He said nobody'd look for me over near Yank Arnold's any more'n they'd look for you here. He said you called yourself 'Jackson,' and had fooled old Arnold into thinking you was ace-high! I'm hungry, Jack. I come on foot from the river, and haven't et since supper in jail last night."

Deep shadows lay about them. Rodiker sat on his heels and gazed blankly at his brother, now on the dodge; and Slim had put him there, but with the loyalest of intentions possible.

"Where'd he shoot himself?"

"In the leg. Halfway above the knee. He said he'd miss the bone. I seen him, then skedaddled."

"I'll be damned!" Rodiker muttered.

Ronnie squatted down and rubbed his toes. His feet hurt. He had walked miles on high heels, and his feet were so swollen he couldn't pull off his boots. He had tried earlier this evening, after he got to the water trough and drank all he could hold. He had wanted to soak his feet.

"Jack?"

"Un-hunh?"

"How come you are here at Arnold's?"

"It's safest."

"He'd kill you!"

"He's sick. I carried him up to bed this afternoon when he couldn't walk."

"Why didn't you choke 'im?"

He thought, *I didn't want to,* and wondered at the thought. Of course he had no liking for Yank Arnold, but, somehow, the feeling was slipping away that Yank Arnold had joined up with that Cora woman to put the blame on him. She'd maybe fooled Yank Arnold.

He told Ronnie, "You don't hurt helpless folks."

"Slim said for me to say to you that nobody knows you're back but him and old Jerym. He said Jerym had hinted some to Bill Brody to get him to rig the trap, and there's talk around about you. He says Jerym is scairt to death of you. Why?"

Rodiker shook his head, not replying. Now that Cora Arnold had married into the family, old Jerym wouldn't be so scared. There would be money enough to hold the shaky Bevarts credit on its legs.

"Jack?"

"What?"

"Can I get something to eat?"

In the bunkhouse kitchen there would be bread, and cold boiled potatoes ready for breakfast frying, and some canned stuff, all of which was food in a way, but not the right kind for a starved kid brother, and, if detected getting it, there would be questions, suspicions, talk.

Rodiker asked, "Can you lie good?"

"I don't know. I never could fool Maw, and she larruped me when I tried."

"All right, this lie is that you don't know who shot Slim. Next, you got lost and straggled in here, because you had to have water and was hungry. And I caught you. You don't know me, but you 'fessed up to being the Rodiker kid, because you never stole Bill Brody's horse. He loaned it to you. Now come on."

Rodiker shoved the kid ahead of him into the kitchen.

Old Johnny was huddled by the stove, shivering with teeth a-chatter as he sipped hot coffee. The night was warm, but the whisky had pulled all the marrow heat out of his old bones, and he had the "ager," as he called his hangover shakes.

His good-looking wife was placidly about her work, and smiled with childlike quickness at Rodiker, then gazed in kindly surprise at Ronnie, who looked like a kid tramp.

Supper was long over, but Rodiker said, "If it's not too much trouble, fix this boy up with something to eat. Anything filling. And kid, go out to the pump and wash up. White people live here."

The only lighted lamp downstairs was in the kitchen, and Rodiker, as if half-blinded, made his way to the stairs, then more readily on up to the open door of the colonel's bedroom. Sam sat glowering near the foot of the bed, not wearing his gaudy vest. Kate sat on the bed, holding her father's hand, and the colonel, with easier breathing, kept his head on the banked-up pillows as he looked toward the doorway.

Rodiker said, "I just found that Rodiker kid wandering around here, tired and hungry. I'd say he's lyin' when he says he don't know who shot Slim Clayton. He says Bill Brody told him to take the horse and ride him for a week or two, then had the kid put in jail for horse stealin'. He says the talk is that his outlaw brother is back in the Santsander, and Bevarts and Brody used him—the kid, that is—as bait to draw the outlaw to the jail. We've got the kid ourselves now, and maybe we can use him for bait to draw Rodiker."

A little frown had tightened Kate's forehead as if she were trying to read too small print, then astonishment fluttered over her face. She wanted to laugh, but was fear-chilled, too, and though shadowy smiles trembled and went quickly away, his quiet audacity made her solemn.

Sam had jumped up bulkily, and his heavy voice rolled in incoherent mutters about the Bevartses and Rodikers being up to devilment. His mumbling had such an uncanny feeling of invoking curses that Kate told him sharply, "Be quiet!" Sam stared at her as if awakening, shut up, and sat down, working his fingers together, as if showing how worms squirm.

The colonel gazed thoughtfully at the ceiling as he asked, "Do you think Rodiker got him out?"

"And shot his best friend to do it? Though from what I've heard of the fellow, perhaps so!"

"Good Lord!" Kate exclaimed, then pressed a palm to her mouth.

Sam's rolling rumble announced, "Nobody kain' tell me he doan' know whar he come to when he done come heah. He am a spy, dat what he am! Spy!"

Kate said, "Since we've caught him, who cares? Where is he now?"

Rodiker told her, "In the kitchen being fed. If he don't eat like he's starved, I'll agree with Sam that he is a spy. If he does, he's just a hungry kid that's in trouble."

Sam nodded, pleased by what seemed agreement with his own idea, and was more pleased when Kate said, "Sam, go down and watch him eat. That way we'll know."

"Then bring him up here," said Colonel Arnold.

Kate's eyes widened as she heard Rodiker say with easy carelessness, "No need for me to wait, Colonel. You know more about questioning folks than I do." With that he left.

Sam pushed the sullen half-grown kid into the room, then threw up his palms and shook his head. "Eat? He done et us outa termorrow mornin' brekfus'!" He scowled at Ronnie. "What foh you come prowlin' 'round heah?"

Kate pointed toward a chair. "Let the boy sit where the colonel can talk to him."

Ronnie looked at her, but was sullenly expressionless. He sat in the chair Sam placed, stared between his knees, and wouldn't answer when Colonel Arnold asked, "How did you happen to come here?"

Then Sam blustered, "You bettah talk, you had! I sho' lak to break youah worfless neck!"

"Sam, please!" Kate pointed toward a chair, and Sam went to it.

Again the kid looked staringly at her, and his voice was low. "You are Miss Kate?"

"Yes. Why?"

"Nothin'."

"And you are Ronnie. I saw you a long, long time ago and remembered." She was untruthful, but sounded kindly, and coaxed, "Tell the colonel why you were put in jail and how you got out, won't you, Ronnie? Please."

The colonel lay with a hand raised to his thin gray hair and watched the Rodiker boy in puzzled thoughtfulness: a good-looking lad with hard-set jaw and strong face, he was colt-awkward and gangling, but had big bones, and when he lifted his eyes they were steel-blue and straight.

Ronnie said defiantly, "You all wouldn't b'lieve me."

Kate's voice was kindly. "Perhaps we will, Ronnie."

"No more," said Ronnie, glaring at Colonel Arnold, "than you'd believe Jack. He never killed Craig Arnold. I know he didn't. I tell you, I know it!"

"Heah, you! Dat no way ter talk to—"

"Be quiet!" said Kate. "Go on, Ronnie."

Ronnie's mouth was closed tight until the colonel asked, "And how do you know he didn't?"

"He told our maw he didn't. We don't lie to Maw. First place, she knows if we do! Next place—Aw, what's the good of talkin' to you! You keep offerin' money for people to kill him, an' if he wanted, he could've killed *you* long ago! An' ought've done it too!" Sam's big hands fidgeted into fists and he growled. Kate said, "Ronnie!" sounding shocked, and was. The colonel said nothing. Ronnie glared sullenly, then looked down between his knees. The colonel's fingers moved with slow twisting among his long gray hair, and he looked inquiringly at Kate, but she was studying her fingernails, and thought the colonel must hear the pounding of her heart.

Then the colonel spoke matter-of-factly. "You've said things that interest me, Ronnie. Why doesn't your brother want to kill me? In his place, I think I would."

Ronnie blurted, "That's 'cause you're not the man he is!"

Sam rose out of his chair. "I'll choke you foh dat!"

"Sit down," said the colonel. "This boy is saying what he believes. That's honest."

Sam growled, "But it ain't truff!"

The colonel moved on the pillows, looked at the ceiling, put his fingertips together, said, "I won't ask who did get you out of jail, but do Brody and the Bevartses think it was your brother?"

It was then that Kate suddenly held her hand to her throat as if afraid to breathe. All at once it seemed to her that Ronnie looked so much like his brother that anybody would notice the resemblance, but she tried to reassure herself by thinking it was only because she knew the relationship that it seemed so obvious.

Ronnie sullenly said, “Dunno.”

“You realize that you are being hunted?”

“I know.”

“The last place you would be looked for is here, don’t you think?”

“Yes.”

“And you didn’t steal Bill Brody’s horse?”

“No.”

“You want to keep out of people’s sight for a time?”

“Guess I do.”

“You can stay here. Nobody is going to guard you. You can leave when you want to.”

CHAPTER 21

"Folks comin', Colonel, suh." Sam flung his arm vaguely. "I seen um frum the porch. In buggy an' horseback. Dey comin' lak frum town."

Colonel Arnold roused himself thoughtfully, and sat with hand to chin. Soon he said, "And are not unexpected."

From the upstairs porch Rodiker saw that a mile or more away the dust was swaying off the road like smoke in a breeze, and he made out a covered vehicle and also two men on horseback.

Colonel Arnold dressed, even to spurred boots and a black string tie, and he was waiting downstairs in the dining room when Rodiker went out to meet the callers.

Kate, from an upstairs window, looked down and said disappointedly. "Cora's not with them!"

The barefoot Ronnie pressed close beside her and spoke with bitterness. "Them damn' Bevartses!" A horseman came alongside the surrey, and Ronnie sucked in his breath. "That's Bill Brody!"

Rodiker knew him at a glance, but remained motionless beside the veranda post, though his quick thoughts told him, *He'll know me!*

Zig was horseback, too, and from the saddle peered toward Rodiker, at first not quite certain that this dark beardless man was "Jackson."

Bill Brody swung off and dropped the reins. A chunky man with no angles, he had grown heavier since Rodiker had worked under him. Rodiker thought that in build Bill Brody now looked enough like a Bevarts to be one of the family.

A young colored man had driven the surrey, and cramped it for his passengers, but old Jerym didn't get out right away. He sat heavily, shoulders hunched, head drooping on his crooked neck, eyes fixed on Rodiker. Then he opened his nearly toothless mouth and lifted a hand in greeting. "W'y, howdy, Mr. Jackson!"

Jerym got out of the surrey backward, moving with heavy slowness, then said to the other man on the back seat, "Light down, Judge."

Rodiker thought, *The whole pack is fat as hogs!*—and in a country of lean, hard men.

The judge took off his duster, laid it on a seat, and was in his shirt sleeves, until he removed a Prince Albert from the front seat and the lump-faced Zig helped him on with it.

Jerym said, "Jackson, this is Judge Langdon. We come for a little talk with the colonel."

"He's ready."

"Then kindly show us in, sir," said the judge with full-mouthed resonance.

Rodiker didn't move as he looked toward Zig, then toward Bill Brody, who was coming from the hitching rack where he had given the Negro boy a hand with the horses. "All you?"

"All," said the judge, looking dignified.

Bill Brody walked up and started to say something to Rodiker, but the words stuck in his throat, and his eyes changed as he staringly settled back on his heels. Rodiker read his mind: Brody was thinking: *This fellow is Jack Rodiker, only he can't be Rodiker—not doing the helpful things he's doin' for Yank Arnold! Here is the last place on earth Rodiker would be, yet I'd swear he is Jack Rodiker.*

Brody said, "Who the hell are you?"

"Ask Mr. Bevarts!"

Old Jerym hastily scratched his thick nose with an ink-stained forefinger, then his head bobbed up and down. "Yes, Bill, he's an all right fellow. I know 'im. Known 'im for a long time. We all come peac'bly, Mr. Jackson."

Rodiker led the way through the hall and into the room where Colonel Arnold sat at the dining table. Rodiker stepped to one side of the door and remained there after the men filed in.

As they came in Colonel Arnold stood up with knuckles on the table. He greeted no one, and was as tautly stern as if presiding at a court-martial.

"Take seats, gentlemen." He tried to control his breathing, but it was labored. Rodiker thought these fellows would misguess that the way he was breathing was nervousness.

Zig sat heavily in a chair that was against the wall. His face had the swollen tightness of an over-stuffed sausage, and he moved his feet, scratched, shifted in the chair, and his small brow-shadowed eyes looked nervously here and there.

Bill Brody sat close to where Rodiker stood, and kept looking at him with as much of a frown as if studying a puzzle.

Old Jerym rumpled an Indian blanket that was used for a rug as he plodded to a soft, worn couch beside the window. He paused and carefully straightened the rug with push of toe, then sat on the couch and seemed to beam on the colonel.

Langdon coughed, reached under the tail of his coat for a handkerchief, turned toward Rodiker as if not liking the presence of such a sentrylike figure, but sat down at the table where Colonel Arnold remained standing, erect, high-headed, with eyes flashing. The long, thin hair had been brushed back over his head and the gray mustache waxed so that it stood out instead of falling about the corners of his mouth.

"Colonel, you have no doubt learned by now," Langdon began, as if addressing a crowd, "that Cora Arnold, the relict of your deceased brother, has given her hand in marriage to Dougal Bevarts, who has empowered me to arrange for the—"

Colonel Arnold's knuckles rapped the table.

"That is enough!" He drew from his coat pocket the long brown envelope that he had held in his hand when Rodiker carried him upstairs, and, removing a paper, said, "Read this!"

Old Jerym stopped beaming and sat with apprehensive hunch of shoulders, his deep eyes watching Arnold. Zig left his chair to peer over Langdon's shoulder, and Brody stopped looking at Rodiker to glare toward the colonel, as Judge Langdon's red face became nearly white, then flushed as red as a turkey gobbler's wattle. He shouted, "Why ain't you ever recorded this?"

Zig sidled off and said angry things in a low voice to old Jerym, who blinked, tightened his mouth until the hooked nose came almost as low as his chin, and Rodiker thought he looked like an angry buzzard.

Langdon handed the paper back across the table and said, with sorrowful shake of head, "You've fooled folks! You ain't played fair, Colonel!"

"More than fair, sir! You know it is a common practice among ranchmen who are partners for each to leave his share to the other. This is to prevent the property from being broken up and loss incurred through forced settlement with heirs. The surviving partner, of course, shares honestly with the other's family. As long as Cora Arnold showed no disposition to require a settlement and left the management in my hands, there was no need to record it. But now

I shall record it. And as long as she is the wife of Dougal Bevarts, she will never receive another dollar!" He added quietly, "That is all, gentlemen."

Zig, the first to leave, stamped out, taking long steps. Only Bill Brody had his head up. The judge mopped at his sweaty forehead, and old Jerym shuffled with eyes downcast.

The colonel stood erect until the last man had filed through the door, then collapsed. Rodiker heard the fall, and turned back. The colonel lay on the floor, and blood was running over the gray hair from where his head had struck against a corner of the chair seat behind him.

Rodiker knelt for a close look and said, "Dead?" He stayed knees down with brooding thoughtfulness for a little while, and thrust his hands under the colonel's body, lifting it. Then he arose, turned about, and started for the door that opened into the hall.

Bill Brody was there with old Jerym behind him. Bill Brody's gun was leveled. He grinned evilly. "Hands up, Rodiker!"

Rodiker's arms were half-extended, and the colonel lay on them. "He's dead. Nobody'll pay that reward now, Brody!"

Jerym's was a gleeful cackle. "I'll pay it, Bill! Just let me get some papers off—" He shuffled up close, and then and there would have gone through the colonel's pockets, but Bill Brody pushed him out of the way with jolt of shoulder, and ordered:

"Get that gun off'n him!"

Jerym padded around behind Rodiker and pulled the gun from its holster, and kept saying, "Put 'im down! Down! Drop 'im!"

Rodiker turned his back on them as he said, "He's too much man to be dropped like a dead dog!" and went toward the worn couch by the window. The muscles of his back squirmed tensely, bracing themselves for the bullet that might come, but he was unhurriedly quiet, and, being disarmed, felt sure that Brody would want the distinction of having taken him alive.

Brody followed close behind, but old Jerym went with joggling haste to the other side of the couch so he could at once get into the colonel's pockets.

Rodiker laid the body on the couch, straightened, put his hands overhead, and faced about. Bill Brody's gun was within less than a foot of Rodiker's belly, and Brody gloated.

"This is a pleas—"

That is as far as he got. Rodiker's whole body pivoted on his right foot as his down-swinging arm struck Brody's gun. He hit hard, meaning to knock the gun from Brody's hand, but he didn't, and the off-balance gun fired into the wall. Then Rodiker's fist swung up against Brody's jaw, and Brody went down with the thump of an overturned barrel. Rodiker jumped for him, but the loose rug slid under his feet, and he came down flat and spraddled out. Cat-quick, he rolled over with his feet drawn under him, and a backward look showed old Jerym grabbing for the revolver he had laid at his feet when he stooped and used both hands to search Colonel Arnold's pockets.

Bill Brody seemed a little stunned. Jerym was now the more dangerous, and Rodiker, reaching afar as he rose, caught up a lamp from its stand and hurled it. The china shade and chimney shattered on Jerym's head, and before he could do so much as shake his head, Rodiker jumped across the couch, knocked him down, and seized the gun.

Bill Brody fired from a knee, and the bullet broke a windowpane alongside of Rodiker's head. Then the two blasts from the gun Rodiker held made only one roaring echo against the walls of the room, so fast were they fired. He crouched low below the swirl of thick black powder smoke, and saw Bill Brody huddling face down like a very tired man. Two-bits would have covered the holes in his heart.

Jerym's face looked like dirty dough as he stammered, "B-B-Bill knew—knew—knew you!"

"Which is why I haven't killed you for telling!"

The sound of gunfire had caught Judge Langdon between changing his Prince Albert for the duster. He rushed in, coatless and with his mouth open. Zig came too. Sam burst in, and the colored lad with whom he had been talking. Then Kate, her dark eyes as wide as fear could stretch them. Old Johnny's wife stood timidly in the kitchen doorway, and it was she who pointed to the couch and hysterically cried, "The colonel! He's been shot!"

Kate ran to her father, and found breath struggling in his throat. He hadn't been shot, but she called to Johnny's wife for water and a towel, then at once turned back her dress and wiped at the blood on his face with a lace-fringed petticoat.

Jerym was in a chair at the end of the table, and rested as heavily on his forearms and looked as cravenly helpless as if Sam's curses had broken his bones.

Rodiker said to him, "Speak up! Tell how you and Brody sneaked back in here, meaning to take the paper from the colonel at the point of a gun!"

Jerym heard, and peered slantwise with head lowered, but didn't say anything. He was shaking as if palsied.

So Rodiker said to Langdon, "But it's still on the floor over there under the table where the colonel dropped it. When you get to town, tell what happened. Folks will believe a judge."

"Er—r—ex-judge. The title—former justice of

the peace, so—er—courtesy. But I'll tell—tell just how it was."

Rodiker thought, *Probably not!* He said, "I'll hear if you don't." He eyed Zig. "That goes for you too!" Then he asked Zig, "Just how'd you know so soon that I was working for Colonel Arnold?"

Zig was surly with, "That night you threatened the Claytons, Bess told me."

"So? I see!" He didn't see at all, but covered over the mystification; then he turned to old Jerym.

"Us Arnolds are tired of tricky thieves and liars. Liars like this Bill Brody. We may not like the Rodikers, but we play fair. That kid never stole Brody's horse. It was a put-up job. When you get to town you tell the sheriff so—so that kid can go home."

Rodiker stood by the post on the veranda to watch them leave. Sam was giving the colored boy a hand in placing Bill Brody's body on the surrey floorboards between seats. Ex-judge Langdon put on his duster, and came near to offer his hand. "You did nobly in defending the colonel from Brody, sir!"

Rodiker thought, *So that's how it's going to be told!* He said, "I take the colonel's wages. And you can send a doctor out from town. Tell him to come fast."

When the judge stepped away, old Jerym, who

had started to climb to his seat, took his foot off the surrey's step, looked about, hesitated, then shuffled over to Rodiker. "I can't buck you an' the colonel too." Jerym looked sad and humble, gave his head a woeful shake, turned his crooked neck a little to make sure no one was near behind him, asked, "The colonel knows who you are, don't he?"

Rodiker said, "And that you Bevartses murdered his brother!"

But it didn't jar old Jerym in the least; he even seemed unoffended, and shook his head, saying, "No. No." Then he turned and shuffled back to the surrey.

CHAPTER 22

The thin young doctor said the colonel must stay in bed. His heart was bad! no chance for improvement without rest, and he must not be agitated. The dizzy spells and shortness of breath were from the heart. He must not leave the bed to eat or even wash his face.

Kate's was a brave smiling face until she got to her room, then she cried. The door was ajar, and Ronnie heard her. He pushed at the door and came in, awkward and helpless, but bursting with sympathy, and Kate put her arms about him and held on until she was through crying. The kid did look a lot like his brother.

The young doctor stood by the buggy before he headed back to town, and in talking with Rodiker mentioned that Slim Clayton hadn't a chance. The bullet wound itself wouldn't have been dangerous if cared for, but the leg, badly powder-burned, was now infected. The Claytons hadn't had a doctor at first. Old Tex said that during the War men got well from far worse than Slim without a doctor. Too late now for even amputation. Blood poisoning. So Slim just lay in pain, waiting to die. Pills put him to sleep, and when he awoke his young sister played the fiddle for him.

"I like that girl," said the young doctor.

"So do I," Rodiker replied.

Old Johnny had hauled freight to the ranch at the Bend, and had been away when Jerym's party came. As soon as he was back the next day, Rodiker asked him to return with the wagon and bring Mrs. Badden to help care for the colonel. He was tired and crotchety; anyhow he didn't like orders from anybody but the colonel, so he got on his high horse and said he wouldn't. "You ain't runnin' our ranch!"

Rodiker didn't want to quarrel with the old fellow, and Johnny swelled up at having told the dangerous "Jackson" where to head in. But Mrs. Johnny told Kate, and Kate lit into him with a tongue lashing that hurt worse than a blacksnake.

"He *is* running this ranch!" said Kate. "And all the other ranches too! The colonel said for him to!" Which wasn't true, but was how Kate wanted it to be.

When she finished, the rheumatism was scared out of old Johnny's creaking joints, and he was soon on his way with the wagon and a letter for Mrs. Badden.

And Kate told Rodiker, "You *are* in charge! The colonel said so."

"He never told me."

"He told me. And do you want to worry and bother him, asking questions, when you know he has to be quiet and not disturbed?"

"The men don't know me, and won't want to take orders."

"You give them," said Kate. "They'll take them—the way you can give them! That's why you are in charge!"

"He wouldn't want an outlaw running—"

She interrupted scornfully. "Marl was an outlaw!" He wasn't of course, but Rodiker believed her.

Kate's warning of "Don't try to talk to Papa" wasn't needed when Rodiker saw him propped high on pillows. He gasped as if dying. Sam hovered at the foot of the bed with his eyes dripping, as he twisted his mouth in soundless grief. The colonel's deep-set eyes were more sunken, and the proud, hard directness had faded. There was no strength at all to the voice that thanked Rodiker with, "I knew you were a good man." His eyes closed tiredly.

Rodiker left the room on tiptoes.

He went to the stable and put a saddle on the kept-up horse, and thought of the Claytons as he rode through the pasture and brought in a couple of horses, one of them his own.

Hatred of Slim had gone away, and the hurt remained, but not the blame, for when old devil Jerym got his hooks in you, you moved the way he pulled. Slim had done the best he knew to make up for the treachery. He thought kindly of Bess, too: she had stuck to what she said she would, and hadn't betrayed him. *I got to where I was feeling wrong about the Claytons!* He saw now that in making up that story about him being an Arnold man, Bess had somehow dodged Zig's suspicions, and it was because Zig retold the story to Moheela's marshal that Kate thought he worked for her father, and got him to bring her to the ranch.

That night Ronnie climbed his brother's bare-back horse. Rodiker rode with him until they reached the river, then said:

"You go on home. Nobody'll bother you from now on, but don't tell anybody, only our own folks, where I've been."

"Where you goin'?"

"To tell Slim good-by."

"Jack, you ain't pullin' out of the country again?"

"No, but Slim is."

Rodiker rode down the Santsander's hard sand and slowly climbed the shadow-blackened zigzag trail up the bluff behind the Clayton stable. The white mare's bell tinkled when she stirred.

He left his horse at the side of the corral. A light was in the kitchen, but first he looked around front. No horse was there.

He had never knocked on a Clayton door, and didn't now; he felt that he ought to sing out to let them know somebody had come, but he didn't.

It was dark in the front room. The adobe was

a rambling old place, and he went on through the lighted kitchen and out to the back veranda, then along that clear to the end room, which was Slim's.

The door was open, and a small, dim tin lamp was on a narrow homemade table by the bunk. A water pitcher with a cracked lip, a glass, a pillbox, and the makins were there. Slim's thinner-than-ever face was upturned and his eyes were closed. There wasn't any covering on him but a gray nightgown, and it was pulled up off one leg that was partly boil-red, partly black-and-blue, and swollen to twice its size, looking monstrous.

Sue wasn't really fiddling, but sat in a straight chair with her head down and the loose hair falling forward over her face.

He stood there, not wanting to awaken Slim, not wanting to startle Sue, but she sensed his presence, or seemed to, when she lifted her head, and unhurriedly brushed the hair aside from her eyes. She wasn't startled, not even surprised, and her eyes had a hopeless empty stare.

When he said, "Sue?" in a way that asked what was the matter, she arose and went slowly to the door.

"If you come to kill him, it's too late. He needed it, he said, and I guess he did, for he told me about dry-gulchin' you. And now I'm 'shamed of ever bein' his sister!"

"Slim was all right!"

But she didn't hear, or so it seemed, such was the hurt and shame she felt. She said, "He died a while ago. He wanted to. I purt' near want to die from just bein' an ornery, no-good, white-trash Clayton!"

No trace of tears, and nothing of anger, and no pleading either; but she kept her head up and dully looked right at him. He put his arms about her, and there wasn't any response. She merely yielded with head downcast, and her hair fell forward again, as if to veil her face.

"Where's Tex?"

"Off drunk, I guess. We're just white trash."

"Bess?"

"Off spoonin' with some fella. Any fella, I guess."

"But Zig?"

"They fussed." Tonelessly, "I want to be dead too."

"Ann?"

"She's been gone for years. Is a gambler's woman. Up in Denver." Sue again pushed the hair to one side of her face. "We are no good, I tell you!"

She quietly pulled away from him. "Don't you know better'n to come here? Us Clayton'sud sell Jesus for less'n Judas did!"

Rodiker took off his hat to go close and look down at Slim's waxen face, thinner now because pain and remorse had eaten on him. Then he pulled the blanket up over the ugly leg and clear over Slim's face too.

Sue stood with arms dangling and looked on as if she weren't really watching. Only a kid, he thought, but she had a woman's size and grief, and the sorrow in her was like sickness.

He asked, "Didn't Slim tell you about Ronnie too?"

She nodded indifferently. "Doin' what you ought don't make what you oughtn't've done right."

"Tex know?"

"About Slim? No. He jus' told me. Told how he'd laid for you. In my whole life—outside my no-good family—I never loved nobody but you." Then somberly, with level eyes, "Now I'd spit and despise a man that'ud take up with a girl from a white-trash family like me!"

The sound of trotting horses came nearer through the stillness, and, even before they stopped at the house, Rodiker left the room to look around the corner and toward the road. He saw the peg-legged Tex lurch hurriedly from the buggy, where a saddled mule was tied behind. Then Rodiker recognized the thin young doctor who, pill bag in hand, was following.

Tex passed close by Rodiker with no more than a quick "Howdy," not knowing or caring who he was, and stumped into the small room, and the doctor went in too. When Tex saw the drawn-up blanket he was hard hit, and stumbled against the wall, resting there, and he stared as a lost man does when wondering about the way out.

The doctor lifted the blanket from Slim's face, and a moment later replaced it gently. Then he turned toward Sue and saw Rodiker in the doorway. He said, "Why, it's Mr. Jackson!" in a surprised way, wondering at the presence of an Arnold man in the Clayton home.

Tex then fixed his look on the tall man at the dim-lit doorway, and after a moment said, "Jackson?" in a puzzled ununderstanding way, because in two blinks of an eye he knew this tall, dark-faced man was Jack Rodiker.

The doctor explained rather uneasily, "Colonel Arnold's man. You've heard of him. He—he—Bill Brody, you know!"

Rodiker said to Tex, "When the doctor visited the colonel, he told me how Slim was, so I come to say good-by, but I ought've started sooner."

When the doctor had gone, Tex led his saddled mule toward the stable, and Rodiker went along, but nothing much was said until they returned to the kitchen.

Tex took off his hat and sat in a chair with the wooden leg outstretched. Then he asked Rodiker to reach down the jug on a shelf behind the door. The gallon stone jug was about half full. Rodiker gave him a glass and the jug, but shook his head at the invitation to drink too.

"Not that stuff," said Rodiker.

Tex gulped a half glass of white "likker," wiped his mouth on his arm, poured more in the glass, and, warmed by the liquor, reproached Rodiker with:

"I'd nevuh b'lieved yuh'd join up with Yank Arnold." Tex shook his head sadly, then drank some more. "You been like mah own son, purt' near."

Sue came in slowly. The long faded Mother Hubbard reached her toes in straight lines, making her erectness appear tall. She pushed her copper-colored hair back over her shoulders and stared at Tex as she told him, "You are the best daddy that ever lived. Even drunk, you are. But drunk, you ain't got a lick of sense, Tex, and you know it! So here—"

She lifted the glass from his hand and emptied it with a toss out of the door, then she took up the jug by a finger through the handle and walked on into the darkness of the next room.

Tex watched the doorway after she was out of sight, then he picked up the glass she had replaced on the table and drained the last drop into his mouth. He put the glass down and told Rodiker, "They're all good girls, but Sue's the beatenest!" Tex heaved a long sigh. "I don't want that any of mah girls had been boys, but I wisht I had mo' boys. Who do you reckon did shoot Slim thataway?"

Rodiker shook his head, not saying anything. If Slim hadn't wanted his father to know the why and wherefore of the self-shooting, he wouldn't tell.

Presently, after much thoughtfulness, Tex looked up with something sly at the back of his mind and suggested, "Jack, yuh've got an awful good chanct to git even with ol' Yank."

Rodiker scowled and spoke impatiently, but without anger. "Tex, you and your folks are my friends, though I guess you are pretty much of a rascal, seeing you've been thick with old Jerym all these years. You won't break off. You can't. You go to bed and stay there. I'm going after rustlers, and I don't want to catch you among them."

"Yuh ain't takin' up for Yank like that, are yuh?"

"I'm in the saddle, Tex! And it happens that I don't believe—like I used to think—that Yank Arnold lied about me. He just believed somebody else's lies. He's took enough likin' to me that I'm running his ranch. All his ranches! I mean to make him know I'm not a man who'd do what he's been made to think! So right after Slim is buried, you go to bed and stay there!"

Tex looked at him and said nothing. He looked

away, and thoughtfully mopped his head with a bandanna, then stared into the next room's darkness.

"I wish Sue hadn't carried off that jug."

CHAPTER 23

Rodiker sat on his heels in the shade of the kitchen, and Kate stood with arms behind her and shoulders to the wall, as she listened to him explain why he didn't think that he could accomplish very much.

"I'm too much stranger for men to believe me when I say I am range boss. I know I wouldn't believe it of a man I didn't know."

She stared thoughtfully and far away, admitted, "You may be right." After a time she said soberly, "Before you leave for Old Place come back by. I'll fix that. You'll see!"

When he rode back, she was waiting on the veranda, and her dark eyes sparkled as she tripped out into the sun and held up an envelope. "Read it! I wrote it, and Papa signed it!"

Rodiker read: "Be it known to all men, I herewith appoint Joe Jackson as my superintendent, with full authority. Ben V. Arnold."

He slowly refolded the paper into its envelope and said, "I'd have thought the colonel was too smart and careful to give anybody that much say-so."

The sparkle went out of her eyes. She nodded soberly and said, "You must do things!" For a long moment she seemed almost uneasy, then laughed a little. "Nothing risked, nothing gained!"

He crossed the crooked Santsander, eying cows and sparse grass with frequent lift of eye to the timber-fringed upland, thinking of feed and strays, wondering about moving herds, and when he saw a nester's clearing in the distance, he suspected the family of putting Arnold beef into the skillet, putting Arnold hides underground.

He saw a rider coming, not fast, but with purposeful directness. Rodiker waited under the shade. The man came up and said, "Howdy," without friendliness. He was lean-waisted, with a double row of cartridges in a wide belt and a rifle in a battered scabbard, and was hard-eyed under straight eyebrows. His saddle was a double-rig, short-skirted with a roll cantle. After some conversation he gave his name as Clary, and said that he had been hired that spring. When the roundup was over he had been put to riding line up here.

Rodiker said to himself, *You are on the dodge. That gun-quick look in your eyes says so. No cowboy rides with a rifle if he is not out hunting—or being hunted! You are from up North. The Cheyenne saddle says so. You like the loneliness of riding line because not many people ever see you.*

He said to Clary, "There may soon be a little trouble with some rustlers. I am picking fellows who haven't been in this country long because they won't be likely to find themselves shooting at friends. I don't want anybody along that don't want to be along. So if you want, I'll have Tom Small send somebody else up here, then you can go straight to the home ranch and say I sent you to wait."

Rodiker reached Old Place before sundown. He had a talk with Tom Small, the sunburned, slow-spoken cowboy, and the next morning a man was sent over to take Clary's place in the line camp.

Small called up a young fellow, new-come from Texas. His name was Steve; he looked good-humored, but underfed, and was as awkward on foot as a new-born calf. After some talk, Steve set out for the home ranch.

Rodiker went on over to the Bend, which was mostly a hay ranch with some fenced-in Herefords, and the foreman regarded Rodiker with respect after seeing the colonel's signature. Besides, Badden had told about how the Walters brothers had been cornered, burned out, hanged.

The old foreman talked about rustling. "No rustler don't hardly dare ship a steer that's been brand-changed, because inspectors'll nail it at the stockyards, if their eyes ain't blurred with likker. Mostly they ain't. Old Jerym, he is smart. He's got himself some kind of new wrinkle, if he's gettin' away with cows under Frank Pierce's nose. Frank is hot-headed, but he is a good cowman, or the colonel wouldn't ever have put him in charge over south there.

"Now 'f I was you, I'd find out who has got the contract to furnish beef to the Reservation over south. It has to be delivered on the hoof, and maybe the Injun agent ain't partiklar about what marks are on the hide. Sure thing, the Injuns don't care."

Rodiker was dead tired that night when he used the nubbin of a pencil and ruled tablet to write a letter to Colonel Arnold. He sat in the foreman's room with a coal-oil lamp that smoked and dripped sweat, but what he wrote was to the point.

"Our cows can't be stole like they are without somebody we are paying wages helps. I have picked two men who are new-come to the range and won't have friends. I am going to do some scouting around to be sure, then you'll hear from me. Your friend."

A shiver ran down his back, because he had almost signed it "Jack Rodiker."

He gave the letter to the foreman to send to the colonel, then borrowed a horse, put his own on a lead rope, and headed out.

When he reached the Reservation two days later, he was stopped at the entrance by a cavalryman on foot, who wore woolen blues and looked as if he had melted down after putting them on. An old sergeant with crooked legs came from the guardhouse and pointed afar to where he could find the Indian agent, Mr. David.

Mr. David let Rodiker into a room that was kept dim against the heat. He was fat and had stomach trouble, which nothing but whisky and bitters helped. Rodiker didn't look like the superintendent of a big cattle outfit, but Mr. David wasn't doubtful. He had been two years in this damn' country and was willing to believe anything. He said that beef was supplied by the Associated Ranchers. Being filled with whisky and bitters, and not answerable to anybody but such political friends as had appointed him, he said that he thought the sooner the damned Indians died off, the better it would be, but while they lived they had to be fed.

Rodiker pretended that he knew about the Associated Ranchers. After Mr. David, with quavering fingers, drew the brand he felt that he did know a good deal. When the cattle were brought in, the Indians excitedly killed some of them and ate the flesh uncooked. What wasn't killed was pastured, but the pasture was poor, and the cows wandered. At this point Mr. David winked heavily.

"Un'erstan'?"

Rodiker nodded. Cows that "wandered" could be resold time and again. The half-starved Indians had cause to be excited when the beef drive came.

The cattle were branded by the Associated's AR. Bill Brody was in charge, and receipted for the money, payment being made in gold. Mr. David understood that it was dispersed by the Cattlemen's Bank of Moheela among the members of the Associated Ranchers.

Mr. David said there weren't any hides about that he knew of. The Indians might have some in process of tanning, but most were sent to Woodward as soon as possible. "The smell, you know?"

When Rodiker reached Woodward, he again looked so much like a saddle tramp that the livery-stableman said, "Colonel Arnold must sure work you hard."

He rode to the edge of town where the Coal, Grain, and Hide Company had a storage shed, and, after examining piles of board-stiff hides, he found what he expected. This was proof. The skinned hide showed if a brand had been changed.

It was late afternoon. He ate a steak, then stepped into the saddle again with the lead horse following, and, near dark, he reached the roadhouse where he had seen Dougal Bevarts's horse and men. The high bluff's shadows fell like black curtains that shut out the evening's glow. Three or four Mexicans were loafing in the dim room, and eyed Rodiker with distrust, but the big fellow behind the bar, though probably as distrustful as the others, smiled in a way that showed strong white teeth.

Rodiker leaned on the bar and said softly, "My name is Jackson. Some days ago your wife's brother helped me out here when there was a little trouble. He asked me to take a message for him. I am back with the answer."

The big fellow at once set out a cup and a bottle of *good* whisky, then went into the kitchen. Presently he asked Rodiker to come. Enzo's sister stared solemnly. Her heavy face was without expression in saying that she did not know where Enzo was. He had been away for days. As she talked she held a lamp in her hand and raised it shoulder high.

The lamplight clearly revealed Rodiker's face, and the stolid Enzo came through the back door. "Soh, eet is you, my freend!" They shook hands. The sister placidly replaced the tin lamp on the table. She didn't say anything, but the brother-in-law laughed and brought in a bottle of good whisky. Then Enzo and Rodiker stepped out into the bluff shadows.

Enzo said, "An' is eet you that keel Beel Brody?"

It was with Bill Brody that Enzo had had trouble that turned him against the layout, and Rodiker promised that Colonel Arnold would pay one hundred dollars for Enzo's information and help. The half-breed said that wasn't much.

Rodiker told him it was a hell of a lot, since Colonel Arnold would no longer be an enemy.

"So what do you say?"

"I say yees, señor."

They presently set out together, and Rodiker learned many things about how Arnold cattle were stolen and sold. Enzo, the blacksmith, was an expert with the running iron.

When Rodiker turned off to head for the San Miguel Ranch, Enzo warned, "Frank Pierce keel you queek as he stomp a cockaroach, eef he guess what you know!" Enzo then rode on with a note to Colonel Arnold in his pocket.

The stars said it was about halfway between midnight and dawn when Rodiker reached the Santsander, and, having had little sleep that wasn't saddle-dozing for some nights now, he fed the horse grain out of the saddlebag, then with a saddle for a pillow lay down.

At dawn he came out of a dream cussin' old Tex for being caught with the rustlers in Los Muertos Canyon, and, as he saddled, wondered just what would be the right thing to do if he did catch him.

As he rode cross-country, he saw some cows, not many, and went out of his way time and again to look at the brand. He reached San Miguel before noon, and, from a canvas hammock slung on a pole alongside the kitchen, the cook unwelcomingly eyed Rodiker. The cook was a big fellow, but old, raw-boned, with a mustache that straggled and a sickly sallow face. When he rose out of the hammock for a better look at Rodiker, he picked up a long butcher knife from the box beside the hammock and stuck it in the front of his belt.

"Where's everybody?"

The cook drawled with toneless earnestness, "In hell, I hope." The horses were A-branded, so he asked, "You wanta eat?"

When Rodiker learned that nobody would be in until suppertime he said not to start a fire in the stove, but to give him a steak, and he'd cook it outside.

Not a word was spoken between them until Rodiker finished, put out the fire, washed his plate, returned it to the kitchen, then handed the cook the authorization signed by Colonel Arnold.

The cook read it. "You the Jackson that shot Bill Brody?" Then in a manner of deliberate surprise, "You must be an honest man!"

"Colonel Arnold must think so."

"He thinks lots that ain't so!"

"As, for instance?"

"Look," said the cook, returning the note and drawing his butcher knife, then sensitively feeling the edge with a thumb, "don't you know purt' near ever' man in this part of the country is Bill Brody's friend?"

"I'm listenin'."

"And I ain't talkin'!"

With that he lay back in his hammock and closed his eyes.

Rodiker took what was left of the good whisky from his saddlebag and invited, “Care for a nip?”

By the time the bottle was empty, the cook was drunk. He said Bill Brody and Frank Pierce were hand-in-glove, and that now Frank Pierce, knowing the colonel was sick and expecting him to die, was more reckless than ever. The cook was tearfully vituperative, because Frank Pierce even killed Arnold beef for the men to eat, when ever’body knew that you never et your own beef if a neighbor’s cow was within easy ridin’!

CHAPTER 24

Late in the afternoon three riders came jogging, and Rodiker stood at the front of the bunkhouse as they passed on their way to the stable. They came from the stable and cussed when they found the cook drunkenly asleep. A fat, pimply young fellow with fuzz-covered face demanded of Rodiker, "You give him likker?"

"We had some drinks."

"Wait till Frank Pierce finds out!"

Rodiker sat on his heels, smoked, fingered little marks in the dust, and said nothing. The pimply youth talked big about how girls liked him, and the other boy, with a scabby cold sore on his mouth, said, "Yeah," but the older man sat apart and stared thoughtfully down his nose. The nose looked as though it had been broken and not reset carefully.

When Frank Pierce rode in, the pimply youth hurried to the stable to say that the cook was drunk and a stranger was squatting before the bunkhouse door. And Pierce came striding with swing of bat-wing chaps and rattle of girl-leg spurs. Temper was on his face, because strangers were unwelcome, but when he recognized Rodiker, the temper turned to sarcasm with, "Well, if it ain't the range detective!" That gave all the men warning against Rodiker's nosiness, and the man with the broken nose looked with sidelong uneasiness.

Pierce added jeeringly, "I see you got the cook drunk. Did he tell you anything bad about us, Mr. Detective?"

The two young hands grinned. "Detective" was a worrisome word, but Frank Pierce was handling things. He wasn't Rodiker's size, not nearly, but was telling him off, and Rodiker seemed trying to evade trouble by not noticing the unwelcome. He merely said:

"Before we talk more, here is something for you to look at," then handed over the paper the colonel had signed.

Pierce squinted as if reading slowly. The pimply youth looked over his shoulder, then let go an excited squawk. "Jackson?" His bugged-out eyes swung to Rodiker. " 'Twas you shot Bill Brody!"

The man with the broken nose moved his feet nervously, angling a stare that searched Rodiker from boot toes to hat crown, and edged back watchfully.

Frank Pierce was a hard man, and quick-thinking. He slapped the paper with the back of his hand, demanded, "How do I know the colonel signed this? I sure ain't going to accept it until I know some more about *you!*" He tossed the letter to the ground and stuck out his chin a little and frowned, as his hand dropped alongside his leg within a finger's twitch of his gun butt.

The older man looked solemnly ill at ease, but the young fellows' jaws sagged in eager grinning. Here was a showdown. The pimply one tittered mockingly as Rodiker stooped for his letter at Frank Pierce's feet. But instead of picking up the letter, Rodiker's hand darted out, caught Pierce's left wrist, jerked him close, and, clapping a hand to Pierce's neck, shook him violently, and kept on shaking him just about as a pit bull shakes a rat.

It happened with such swiftness and was so astonishing that nobody made a move. There was something that seemed contemptuous in the way that Rodiker didn't strike Pierce at all, but, when he had shaken him into a kind of drunken dizziness, Rodiker suddenly heaved him upside down in a way that made the revolver fall from the holster. Then he flung Pierce some ten-fifteen feet away, as if tossing out old clothes that happened to have a man in them. Pierce wasn't so much smaller that that seemed easy to do. He had been made to look ridiculous, and Rodiker looked from face to face and said:

"Now maybe he knows enough more about me!"

Next he told them to go to the kitchen and fix themselves something to eat if they wanted. They walked off with backward glances, some toward Rodiker, who had unarmed a dangerous man by shaking the gun out of its holster, and some toward Frank Pierce, who was just about as ruined as if Rodiker had broken his neck. He'd never live down what had been done to him.

Frank Pierce was sitting up, but wouldn't look at anybody. When the other men were out of sight, he got to his feet and kept his eyes down as he came limpingly toward Rodiker and picked up his hat, then he reached toward his gun. But Rodiker told him:

"Leave it lay."

Pierce's eyes blazed. "I'm leavin'!"

"But not alone!"

It was sundown now. Rodiker walked to him and again took hold of Frank Pierce's neck, telling him, "Put your hands together behind you and keep them there!"

He did. Rodiker drew a handkerchief and tied the wrists, then loosened the chaps and had Pierce step out of them. After that he said, "Come along!" and left the gun on the ground, as if even Frank Pierce's weapon was not worthy of notice.

In passing the kitchen, Rodiker saw shapes moving about the lamp in trying to put stuff together to eat. The cook lay on the ground where he had been dumped from the hammock.

Rodiker put Frank Pierce's saddle on a horse, but used a lead rope instead of a bridle. When Pierce was being helped into the saddle, he gave

Rodiker a vicious kick with a girl-leg spur, and was told, "You won't feel so mean pretty soon." Then he hobbled Pierce's feet under the horse's belly.

After that, Rodiker opened the corral gate and turned out every horse, which meant that the men here would be all afoot, since range horses are not to be taken with a pan of oats and coaxing words. Nobody could slip away and carry word of who had come and what had happened.

He rode off the back way, and soon put the horses into a trot. Pierce's hands were tied behind him, his feet were hobbled so that he couldn't ease the jolts by rising on the balls of his feet, and it was as though his teeth were being jarred out of his head by the malletlike pounding of the saddle that hit the end of his spine with every bounce. Pierce was a tough man, bad-tempered and now infuriated; he cursed wickedly, making threats. There wasn't any reply, and the trot continued.

Rodiker rode into the shadows where trees and brush lined the river. He took the rope off the lead horse and put the noose about Pierce's neck, then tossed the rope over a low limb and made the end fast to the tree's trunk. He unhobbled Pierce's feet. When the untied horse got tired of standing, and walked away, Pierce would be dragged from the saddle and left dangling by the neck. And now he began to beg. The sounds he made were slobbery.

It was dark under the tree. Rodiker made a cigarette and lit it. The flame showed that his face was hard-set and cold-eyed. He said, “Pierce, if you tell me things, I won’t hang you. But if you don’t tell me what I want to know by the time I have finished this smoke, I’m leaving you just as you are.”

The next morning big Sam heard horses lope in, and looked down from the upstairs porch in the pre-dawn light with wonder, as Rodiker left the saddle and called up, “Wake the colonel, Sam. I’m bringing news—and a rustler!”

He unbound Pierce and dragged him from the saddle. Pierce couldn’t, or wouldn’t stand, so Rodiker flung him across a shoulder and went into the house, up the stairs, and into the room where Sam had just turned up the lamp that was kept burning all night on the bedside stand. Sam opened his mouth noiselessly, and left it open, when Rodiker dropped Pierce into a chair, and Pierce sat there with head down and back bent, his hands tied behind him.

Colonel Arnold scrouged over on an elbow, his deep eyes bright and questioning. Rodiker motioned wearily.

“I brought him in ’cause I didn’t think you’d believe me if I said what he said!”

The colonel’s fingers moved slowly through the tangle of thin, long gray hair, and he gazed at Pierce, not speaking, then looked intently at Rodiker, who asked, "Did Enzo get here?"

"Yes," said the colonel. Just that, and somehow as if strangely uncertain of what to think. There was some silence before the colonel said, "Frank?" and his voice had a hurt sound, but also it asked Frank Pierce to explain, and seemed to imply that he didn't at all want to believe anything against him. But Frank Pierce wouldn't say anything, or even look up, so the colonel's eyes lifted questioningly to Rodiker.

And Rodiker told him, "According to Pierce, you wouldn't work your wagons with the Lazy S, so for years nearly every rep you sent went cahoots to keep a false tally, and your cows grew up as Lazy S's. Fact is, he says, you haven't nearly as many cows as your books show.

"Jerym all along has been stealing calves under your nose, but a couple years back, with Bill Brody's help, and such other fellows as Pierce here, they began stealing your beef. Like I wrote in that letter Enzo brought, it's your steers that go to the Reservation. Knowing how much you trust Pierce, I wanted him to tell you his own self, so we stayed in the saddle most of the night to get here. Now I want to hurry back to San Miguel. We'll go into Los Muertos Canyon and see what's there, though Pierce says a herd is ready to be moved to the Reservation."

Colonel Arnold was breathing hard and slow.

He fingered the tuft of beard and stared at Pierce. When he asked how it happened Pierce had been willing to talk, Rodiker said:

"I showed him that order of yours putting me in charge of your ranches. He as much as said I could go to hell. So we went off by ourselves and talked the matter over. Then he agreed to come and tell you too."

Colonel Arnold held out his hand. "Let me see that order."

It had been crumpled, and was dirty. The colonel turned it slightly for a better light, read it at a glance, but continued to study the writing, then turned the paper over and back again. For a long minute or two he didn't move, but looked toward the ceiling, then he refolded the paper carefully and extended it to Rodiker.

"Yes, that is right. Keep it."

Then the colonel said, "Sam, tell Miss Kate I want to see her at once."

"W'y, sah, Colonel, she lit out foh town las' night!"

"Town?"

"Dat's what she say. Ter git the doctor, she say. She feared you am erbout ter be worse, she say. Dat's what she say."

" 'About to be worse'?" the colonel repeated, and studyingly added, "I understand. But why didn't you tell me?"

"I 'lowed she done tol' you, sah."

The colonel drew a long, tired breath and lay heavily on his pillows, his eyes on Rodiker. "No," he said quietly, "I am not about to be worse. I am improved. In spite of Frank Pierce, I feel much better. You promised Enzo a hundred dollars. I'll pay him. The other men, Steve and Clary, are still here too. The letter Enzo brought asked me to send them to you at San Miguel, but I didn't. I didn't fully understand that message but now—yes, you *are* superintendent and in full charge. Go ahead with whatever you plan!"

It was while Rodiker sat half-dozing in the kitchen, where the sweet-faced Mrs. Johnny prepared breakfast, that Sam stopped to say, "The colonel sho' did ac' lak he was erbout to be worse when that Enzo come an' give him dat letter ob youahs. It 'peared lak he done forget dat he made you boss, lak I jes' heared him say you is. I s'pose as how he was upset frum the comin' of dat no-good Bevarts woman."

"Cora Arnold?"

"As uster be. She ain't none ob our relation no mo'. She didn't uster be red-haided lak she is now. She was drove out by the liver' boy, an' didn't get invited to come even indoors. The colonel, he wouldn't see her. He send Miss Kate to say dat he won't eber see her."

An hour later the hard-eyed Clary came up to Rodiker and said, "All set!" Behind him the gangling Steve grinned shyly, and Enzo stolidly said, "Soh. You are not a liar!"

Rodiker's eyes were questioning, and Clary told him, "When Enzo rode in here and said you said for us to come to San Miguel, the colonel said for us to stay right here. He said that he, not you, was running his ranch!"

Steve nodded, showing a grin that tickled both ears, and a quick smile crossed Clary's thin mouth in adding:

"But just now he had us all up and said he wanted to correct any wrong ideas we'd maybe got about you. He said whatever you said was what we was to do as long as we took his wages!"

The dark Enzo shrugged, showed his palms, dropped his hands, made a face. "But he is not smart, that colonel. He has send a'ready for the sher'f to come queek. Poh! An' the sher'f weel turn Frank Peerce lose, sure theeng, you weel see, I bet you! He knows I tol' you about heem, so he weel hunt me. When I keel heem, men weel say I am a damn' half-breed and must be hung! Ho, well, I haf not been hung before!"

Rodiker lit a cigarette, eyed the half-breed thoughtfully, then shook his head and watched the smoke ring he blew until it drifted into shapelessness. He said, "Pierce won't hunt you."

They set out.

About noon they turned to the river, pulled the saddles, let the horses drink and roll. The men sat on their heels and smoked, watching the horses rest, and Rodiker guessed that all of them had sometimes kicked up some dust to ride in front of, for, though Steve didn't have the outlaw's look, he had grinned in saying, "It oughta be again' the law for sheriffs to cross state lines."

It was past midafternoon, and hot, with heat waves rippling against the edges of the stable and corral, when they reached San Miguel, coming in at a walk.

The fat pimply youth, whose name was Carl, and the other fellow, called Sodo, were waiting before the stable. Rodiker looked them up and down from the saddle and didn't say anything. Carl's pimply face was as greasy as if it had been smeared with lard, and there were scratches like cat-claw marks on his cheek. The scratches were still fresh enough to bleed, and Carl dabbed at his cheek with a red handkerchief. Sodo's shirt was ripped, and his white shoulder scratched. The smell of fear was on them, and fear was in their eyes. They talked fast, both at once, to the men who swung from saddles and somberly heard that the older, crook-nosed man who had been stranded here with them had killed the cook, caught a horse, and rode off.

"We had a fight with him," said Carl, pointing at his cheek.

Enzo stolidly looked at Rodiker, and Clary looked at him with a sharp questioning glance, but Rodiker said nothing, though he, too, knew they were lying, for no man catches a range horse on foot.

Carl said, "You all go look there in the kitchen. You'll see the cook! We'll put up your horses for you."

Steve, less than his companions, had sensed something wrong, but he drawled, "Now just how the hell did that fella catch a horse?"

"W'y—w'y—" Sodo began with a kind of stuttering haste and blank expression.

"A horse come in for water," said Carl, wiping hard at the sweat that oozed through the grease film on his face. He reached out for the reins of Steve's horse, and his voice had an urgent whine. "Here, mister, let me put him up for you, and you go look at the cook."

Something was wrong, badly wrong. This Carl and Sodo had the look of hiding guilt; there was desperation under the fidgetiness that tried to seem friendly and to get their hands on these saddled horses.

Steve said, "Dead men have a lot of patience about folks comin' to look at 'em." He clucked to his horse, waggled the reins, and with pigeon-toed awkwardness started for the wide-open stable door. No one else had spoken. Rodiker's eyes burned on Carl's face; Enzo's was a wooden-Indian look, and Clary, with an outlaw's keenness for signs, stabbed restless glances at one, then the other. The horse hadn't followed inside the doorway before Steve's yell came back.

"What's a woman doin' here?"

"Woman?" said Enzo softly. Clary said nothing, but knew "woman" was somehow the awaited disclosure. Rodiker, with anger arising, demanded, "Woman? What woman?" Then all turned about and looked toward Steve as he came from the stable with a woman's sidesaddle in his hand.

Rodiker saw it, and whirled with his gun hip-level, and would have spoken, but there weren't any words, for Enzo shot the fat, pimply Carl and the sore-mouthed Sodo too. He fired from the waist with a fanned hammer striking so fast that both men were still on their feet when Enzo, coolly sure of himself, opened the gate to prod out the empty shells, but his steady look watched them go to the ground.

"That," said Enzo with a droning slowness, as he now stared toward the sidesaddle, "is the leetle señorita's!" which was what Rodiker had known too. Enzo added calmly, "I, myself, I put eet on her horse when she want to ride away queek an' not hav' the colonel know!" Then Enzo looked down at the two bodies. "So slow, they do as well to reach for guns weeth their feet!"

The others hurried searchingly into the stable, but Rodiker jumped for the saddle and gouged with spurs as he rode furiously the fifty yards to the bunkhouse, where he hit the ground with skittering slide of heels before the horse stopped, and he ran to the door.

Kate, hogtied and gagged, with clothes more than half torn from her, lay on the floor. She had been pushed under a bunk, and a blanket draped over the bunk's side, so as to keep her out of sight, but she had squirmed and wriggled until she was out on the floor where she would be seen by men she knew were riding in.

Today when she came, the older man with the crooked nose borrowed her horse to round up some horses into the corral, but he had headed straight out over the road toward Los Muertos to tell about Frank Pierce. And soon the two young scoundrels lost their heads. They killed the old cook who tried to knife them with the long butcher's blade when they wouldn't leave the girl alone.

The cook was scarcely dead before they saw the four men in the distance, and they knew that no matter who these four men were, whether the colonel's riders or little ranchers looking for strays or even Bevarts's cattle thieves, they would kill other men who had tried to rape a woman. Their only chance of escape was to gag and conceal the girl, then get hold of the saddle horses. They had forgotten that the woman's sidesaddle had been left by the stable door.

Kate's clothes were in rags, or nearly so, but

she wouldn't, just wouldn't, she said, put on any shirt that might be found in a war bag here. However clean, she felt it would be filthy. So Steve cut holes in a washed flour sack, and she slipped that on. Clary brought water and held the basin while she, leaning from the bunk's side, washed her face. Then Enzo, hat in hand, offered freshly made coffee. The stolid half-breed might be a blacksmith, but he was as much at ease as if all of his life he had waited on fine ladies.

Rodiker sat nearby on a backless chair, and his face was as tight as sun-dried rawhide; there was anger in him, puzzlement, too, and some worry because, while the men with labor of pick and shovel buried the old cook in a manner befitting a worthy man, Kate had told Rodiker to leave the country, get out, go! To bring that warning was why she had fled from home, and, after staying all night in town, came to San Miguel. She learned through Enzo that he would be here.

What she had been through today had shattered her self-control and made her sound frantic in telling that the colonel knew he was Jack Rodiker.

"He guessed it first from how much your brother looks like you."

It had amazed and troubled the colonel. "When you shot Bill Brody he knew you were his friend. He liked you from the first, and he trusted you in spite of everything—Craig and all—and wanted to believe he had misjudged and wronged you terribly. But when reports came in that you claimed to be his superintendent, he thought you were—"

"But I am superintendent," said Rodiker wonderingly. "You know it and—"

"No, no! And right away the colonel thought that you—because he's hunted you and vowed to have you hanged!—were out to get even with him while he's sick, to rob him, and do anything mean to hurt him!"

Puzzlement plowed wrinkles in Rodiker's forehead. "But when you gave me that—"

Kate begged, "He must never know! He'll hate me! He'll think I betrayed him! I got him to sign a blank sheet. He thought it was to be an order for a freighter's load from town! Please! Please give it to me. Won't you, please? I oughtn't have done it, but—please!"

Rodiker said quietly, "No, I won't," and gazed at her with brooding steadiness and some distrust and a vague kind of anger. In what seemed a desperate attempt to evade any blame for her part, Kate was urging him again into an outlaw's flight, and that was so unlike what he had grown to think of her that he was as hurt as if deceived, and, stubbornly, he would not say that her father had studied the forgery and then affirmed its authority.

• • •

The next morning Rodiker rode off alone, and that night stayed in the camp of two line riders. He told them to turn back all Arnold cows that were drifting toward Los Muertos, adding:

"Shoot anybody you see driving them! And keep Lazy S's off our range!"

"There'll be trouble."

"If that's what you boys don't want, I'll give an order for your wages now!"

When he returned to San Miguel, he found a Mexican friend of Enzo's hobbled to a chair in the kitchen and cheerfully playing cards with his captor.

The fellow had been sent as a spy to learn what was going on here. The crooked-nosed man had brought word of Frank Pierce being manhandled and carried off, and the men with a herd in the canyon were uneasy. Enzo knew the spy from working together and hadn't any grudge, but now was working for Rodiker, so, at a gun's point, he invited his friend to stay, and entertained him with monte.

That was how Rodiker learned that a herd was being hurried from the canyon for delivery to the Reservation: a hundred and seventy cows, and every cow a botch-branded Arnold. The Associated Ranchers formerly mixed other brands with the herd, but after how Colonel Arnold had mistreated Dougal's wife, this seemed one way of evening up. So Zig Bevarts had explained to the men handling the running iron. Bill Brody usually took the herd in; the Mexican didn't know who was in charge now, but thought it was Zig or Dougal Bevarts.

Kate had received devoted attention from Enzo, Clary, and especially the shy Steve; and also from each she learned that the colonel had indubitably put Rodiker in charge. That confused her, but she believed them. It confused her because she had seen her father's wrath when men first told him this "Jackson" claimed to be superintendent, and the colonel had been amazed and convinced that "Jackson" was Rodiker and bold enough to hide out right at his home ranch.

When Rodiker came to her, she was wearing a blue satin shirt that the men swore came from the cook's war bag, and she could still use the weighted riding skirt for a garment, so she looked very well and felt in good spirits too.

Kate was at the bunkhouse table with a tin cup half full of coffee, and there was a trace of liveliness in her dark eyes as she demanded, "Why didn't you tell me you had seen my father after I left?"

Rodiker hooked his thumbs in his belt and stood tall and unbending as he told her calmly, "Forging that letter you said he signed was bad enough. But wanting me to cut and run and be outlawed again for something I didn't do—no! And Steve is taking you home."

With that, he put on his hat, swung about, and left the bunkhouse, but he was troubled then, and for long afterward, as to whether or not the little liar had lied. Of course he knew that she had, but such was his liking for her, and her pull on him, that he tried to hoodwink himself by figuring some way to feel that perhaps she wasn't wholly untruthful.

CHAPTER 25

After riding most of the night, it was still starlight when they entered the Cathedrals for a jagged climb up and down that would bring them out beyond Los Muertos. They went single file.

It was chill in the mountain shadows, and slow-going on the narrow trail that curved sharply with black depth below and bulky darkness overhead blotting out the sky. The slow chop chop of the head-down horses was the only sound, and reverberant in the stillness. An old Indian trail, Enzo called it. Rodiker surmised that white horse thieves had often gone this way, but not cattle: the trail in many places was too precipitous and narrow for clumsy hoofs. Daylight came without bringing much light down through the red pinnacles and weather-shaped domes. They rode with slow, untiring doggedness, and at times in the uplands found the trail divided like an unraveled rope, but Enzo never hesitated.

They came down the red buttresses in the dusk and found scum-covered water among the boulders in the bed of a stream that flowed out of Los Muertos. The horses drank. In another hour they would know if the herd had left the canyon.

They found the trail freshly cut with hoofs. Enzo dropped to his knees and sniffed like a dog above the trampled dust. He brushed his pants when he stood up, and said they had passed three or four hours ago.

Enzo went ahead and climbed a rise off the trail. Even if the trail was padded with dust that would muffle the horses' feet, the sky was too star-bright to go trotting forward at the risk of being seen from afar. He came back and shook his head, not having been able to see a camp fire or bedded cattle, but the country was lumpy, and in the starlight cactus and rocks and bedded cattle at a distance would be much alike.

Again, later, Enzo scouted ahead on foot at a down-grade turn. He came back, and with finger to lips whispered, "No talk out loud!" Sound carried afar in the thin, dry stillness. His noiseless whisper told that the camp fire was just around the bend, farther on the cattle were bedded down, one man was riding guard. How many other men he didn't know, but he did know that usually not more than three or four took the beef into the Reservation.

"Hell, let's tear into 'em!" said the restless Clary, forgetting to whisper.

Rodiker said, "No," not forgetting, and was thoughtful. "We don't want to chase scared cattle. No gunfire if we can help it." After a pause he decided. "We'll take them in ourselves. The Indians need their meat. The colonel can use some cash money. You fellows get some sleep. I'll keep watch. We'll jump them around midnight."

Rodiker, lying like a lizard on top of a rock, saw the herd's lone guard come in near midnight and shake his relief into wakefulness, then flop and draw his boots before the relief man had poured himself a cup of coffee from the pot on the coals.

Rodiker awakened Enzo and Clary. He said, "No shooting. Let them get away first. We want the cows."

Rodiker went forward, knees down or belly-creeping, and tried to stay lined up behind yucca or cactus, and to avoid rattling pebbles. A handkerchief was loosely wrapped about the action of his rifle to keep out sand in case it was laid flat on the ground. The quiet scrunch of Clary's movement was some thirty feet to the left, the quieter movement of Enzo on the right, and he knew that they, too, watched the horseman beyond the camp as he rode around the bunch of bedded cows.

Rodiker was some fifty yards from the sleeping men when a dog barked. That was as unexpected as a thunder clap. He kept on barking. Rodiker crouched motionless behind the thorn-tipped spray of yucca leaves and saw a man sit up and heard him say, "What the hell?" Another sleepily called, "Sic 'em, Tig!" The dog dashed forward, barking furiously, then retreated.

"It's sure somethin'!" somebody guessed.

"Coyote?"

"Coyote, hell! He don't act like that from them. Hey, Zig, tell Mack to come back in and ride over there an' see!"

A chunky shape stood up, the outline blurred by night vagueness, and with hands cupped to mouth, called, "Mack? Ride back down this way an' look what's botherin' Tig!" The dog barked and barked.

The horseman turned back from his clockwise circling of the bedded cattle, and when near the camp said, "What is it, Tig? Come on, feller. We'll chase the spooks."

Then Mack trotted by the camp, following the dog that bounded ahead, barking savagely. The dog made straight for Rodiker, who squatted low and motionless behind the yucca. Then the dog stopped and, as if not wanting to fight in the Spanish bayonet, veered and charged toward Enzo. The horseman pulled down, his eyes following the dog, and an amazed curse exploded as he saw Enzo rise up as the dead might come from an unsuspected grave.

The horseman was broadside and nearly within arm's reach of Rodiker's yucca as, with eyes on Enzo, he drew his gun. Rodiker rose with ghostly swiftness and silence to swing the rifle barrel clublike. The blow was quick as lightning's glint and weighted with fury, and the horseman's revolver dropped from a broken arm. Before the falling gun reached the ground Rodiker's long arm caught the bit chains, powerfully holding the terrified horse when Mack kicked spurs into its flanks and yanked at the reins.

Rodiker said, "Out of that saddle, or I'll shoot you out."

Mack, recognizing him, went out all in a heap, with as much of a flop as if he had been shot.

Rodiker swung the horse's head around until his left hand, with the reins between his fingers, was on the horn, then with a stirrup step and swing of leg he was in the saddle, and held the rifle overhead as he rode straight for the camp. Not a shot was fired. The dog was howling, having been cracked over the nose by Enzo's gun barrel. And Rodiker's shout of, "Come on in, fellows!" had the assured sound of calling up a dozen men.

He rode to where Zig Bevarts and two other men had their hands on guns and were puzzled, frightened, too, for it seemed they were surrounded. Rodiker casually held the rifle shoulder-high as he pulled the horse down and told them, "Start shootin'—or get your hands up!"

That bluffed them—that and the far-echoing whoop Enzo let out, followed at once by Clary's loud, quick-witted, "If you hear a shot, boys, open up on 'em!" Enzo and Clary could be seen coming in slowly, and some cactus probably looked like other men, too, moving in. Hands went up in resentful slowness.

The bull-necked Zig said, "Outnumbered like that, we haven't a chance!"

"Right! No chance at all, so line up, hands up, and stay still!"

They obeyed, facing Rodiker; then he rode behind them and repeated, "Stay still!"

Presently four disarmed and disgusted men sat on the ground; their hands were bound behind them, their ankles tied. Mack was among them. He had come in holding his broken arm; it was hopeless to try to get away on foot. His handkerchief was used as a sling about his neck for the broken arm, his good arm was tied behind him. Harry Hand spit curses. Zig was sullenly shamed. Mack swore at the half-breed as at a traitor, but Enzo seemed deaf. The half-breed built up the camp fire and rummaged among the provisions that had been brought along on a pack mule and set about cooking a good meal.

By the camp fire's blaze Rodiker eyed them, one man in particular, recognizing him as that Joe Roberts who, wearing a deputy's badge, had accompanied Dougal Bevarts and the sheriff when they came to see the colonel. No badge was in sight now, but Rodiker went to him, turned over the vest, and there it was, pinned out of sight.

"I'd be ashamed too!" said Rodiker, and walked away.

An hour later he told Clary. "We'll be back sometime tomorrow night."

Clary showed his teeth, grinning. "Do you want 'em alive?"

"Enough so to be able to tell folks while the sheriff's listenin' how it's been!"

Rodiker turned and gazed in the firelight at Zig's upturned lumpish face and said softly, "We're taking Zig along. Maybe he'll try to escape!"

Zig shuddered then. Later he begged with a whine and a whimper in his heavy voice when he was helped to a horse that hadn't a bridle, and the saddle was loosely cinched. His hands were free but his feet were hobbled. He'd have to sit quietly and let the horse go slow. If the saddle turned he would be tied head down under the horse's belly and be kicked to death or have his brains pounded out on the ground. A few hours of that and Zig would be willing to blab.

The cows got to their feet in unstartled slowness. There was click of horns, an inquiring bawl here and there, the sluggish swing of heads, and Enzo booted a rump or two with a toe as he sang, "Hoo—ee—eye—O!" not unmusically. The straggling line followed a broad-shouldered steer, and the bunch was on the move.

Rodiker rode drag with Zig beside him. Zig tried to talk, to explain, to beg, and hadn't any reply at all until some hours after sunrise when the Reservation was in sight below the bench. Then Rodiker told him, "If I thought you'd tell the truth about your own folks, I'd take pains no accident happened to you. But you'll promise anything, then back out."

Zig hoarsely said, " 'Fore God, I won't!"

"You'll tell the agent down there how it's been? He'd like to know."

When they came to the edge of the bench, the Reservation with buildings and corrals and wide village of cone-shaped tepees lay below as clearly as a child's blocks on a carpet. Rodiker cut Zig's hobbles, let him tighten the cinches and have a bridle.

Cavalrymen under a sergeant rode out with soft jangle of accoutrement to meet the herd, and the herd was tallied into a large corral while Mr. David, the agent, stood on a platform with sweat running down his cheeks.

Mr. David's stomach, always squeamishly delicate in spite of whisky and bitters, was seriously affected by Zig Bevarts's eager and explicit admissions. Zig privately demanded that Mr. David detain him, saying frankly that he was afraid Rodiker would kill him, then swear he had tried to escape.

In the presence of curious army officers, Rodiker instructed Mr. David in the way of brand blotters by having a hide fresh from a steer spread, green side up, for his inspection, and everyone could see how a hot iron had added an R's bend and leg to the old, deeply scarred A.

Rodiker, in Colonel Arnold's name, received payment at the quartermaster's office where the Indian money was safeguarded. The amount was $2,120. He gave Enzo the promised one hundred dollars and took a receipt marked with an X that was witnessed by the quartermaster's clerk.

As they rode toward the bench Enzo asked, "You pay me off?"

"As promised."

"I no work for you now?"

Rodiker turned in the saddle. "You'd better be working for me. I don't like rustlers that are out of work."

Enzo shrugged, showed his palms. "Soh? Long as I work for you I cannot steal that gold, eh? Eet'ud not be what you call hones'?"

"Hell, you're too much Indian to steal a hair out of my horse's tail. Whoa-up!"

Rodiker left the saddle, unstrapped the bags, lifted them over the horn of Enzo's saddle, strapped them on, then grinned as he stepped back. "Now let's see you steal 'em!"

It was dark long before they reached the bench, but the dark meant coolness, and a light wind drifted from the Cathedrals. They rode in silence, Rodiker being asleep in the saddle. How long he slept, no knowing, but he awakened the instant his horse stopped, and found Enzo's hand on the reins.

"Sometheeng I do not like," Enzo muttered as he hunched forward, peering. "We leave theese trail an' go wide!"

They turned their horses and hadn't gone fifty feet off the trail before guns from on ahead blazed at them—two guns, separated by the width of the trail and a hundred yards away. The men there opened up as soon as they saw Enzo and Rodiker were not riding into the ambush.

Rodiker said to himself, *They've killed Clary!* as he pulled the rifle and reined back to let Enzo get farther away from him so the dry-gulchers would have a divided target. Enzo returned the fire, but Rodiker didn't, not liking to shoot blindly, and he hadn't much fear of being hit by revolvers in the night at such distance. He judged that only two men were firing. They would be the deputy Joe and Harry Hand, who had laid in ambush.

Enzo, leading in a wide circle, was well ahead when Rodiker flung up his arms and threw himself from the saddle, taking the rifle with him. The ground was hard; he hit a rock that nearly broke his back, but that was better than flopping onto yucca or into cactus, and he heard Harry Hand's voice. "I got 'im, Joe! I got 'im!" It was a jubilant shriek.

Rodiker didn't raise his head as he squirmed

and crawled quickly to get away from where he had landed, and he heard the pound of Enzo's horse becoming fainter. He thought, *If they're smart enough to catch my horse and go away, I'll be the same as barefoot and lost!* But he knew they wouldn't—men never do when they kill from a grudge. They aways want a close look, and these fellows would empty his pockets, thinking of the beef drive's payment.

He could hear them talking as they came his way in stumbling hurry, and he guessed that they had come up to their ambush along the trail without horses. Horses out here might whinny or be spotted from afar.

Rodiker lay face down, motionless, even holding his breath as they went by near where he was. Then he rolled over, stood up, and said, "Hands up!" They whirled and faced the glint of a shoulder-high rifle. Deputy Joe flung up his hand, but Harry Hand was still carrying his revolver, and he fired. The revolver's report mingled with the rifle's blast and Harry Hand went into a spinning stagger and dropped, being hit in the right shoulder, high up where the bone's knob fits in the shoulder socket.

Rodiker, leading his horse, marched them into camp. There he found Clary. He had been shot in the back. After Mack had had his arm broken and went out of the saddle he had picked up his gun from the ground and put it down inside his waistband under the shirt. Nobody had noticed it when he came in holding his broken arm. Today Clary had untied Mack's arm to let him eat.

Rodiker said to Mack, "That adds murder to cow stealing." Rodiker put his prisoners on horseback and started. About noon the next day they reached the Reservation. A doctor looked at the wounded men. Rodiker was taken to the commanding officer, a grizzled cavalry colonel. He had never met Colonel Ben Arnold, but knew of him. The commanding officer thought it quite right for the Army to assist in making sure that rascals who had imposed their thievery on an agency of the United States Government be placed in the hands of the proper civilians for punishment. Four troopers and a corporal were detailed to accompany Rodiker to Moheela. When he asked about Zig Bevarts, no one knew where he was. Mr. David had apparently suffered so acutely from his queasy stomach that he neglected to arrange for Bevarts's detention.

CHAPTER 26

A hot wind blew as the ambulance, with its escort of troopers and string of horses, jogged into Moheela about midafternoon and raised dust in Main Street.

Rodiker stepped from saddle to sidewalk, then into the unattended sheriff's office. Cigar butts were on the floor, and the blown grit scrunched underfoot. The corporal put a trooper in front of the door to keep back people who came clattering over the sidewalk. Rodiker, sure that the sheriff would be called from a nearby bar, swung a chair from before the desk, then saw the back door open and close as a man ran toward him.

The man was angularly tall, with sleeves rolled up. The sleeves were dirty, the fingers ink-smudged. He wore an eyeshade that had been shaped from cardboard, but jerked it off as he said:

"I'm Purcell, editor of the *News*. What's up?"

Rodiker looked at him. Purcell's hair stuck out in all directions like a windblown straw stack, his eyes were black as shoe buttons, and as bright. He explained, "My printshop is just 'cross the alley here. What's up *now?*" There wasn't any reply, and Purcell dashed on to the street door and looked out, then returned as if perhaps he could read what he wanted to know from Rodiker's face. He couldn't.

"Don't you understand, I'm editor of the newspaper!"

Rodiker said, "The Army's caught Bevartses stealing our cows to fill their beef contract. I'm Colonel Arnold's range boss."

Purcell gulped. "Caught? Army? Ho!" Then he swore and half laughed, but groaned too. His "You'll never prove it!" sounded like he hoped Rodiker would say, "Oh yes, we will!" Rodiker said, "It's already proved. Where's the sheriff?"

"Sick abed. Went to bed when Frank Pierce busted out of jail. You've got Joe Roberts out there. He's deputy sheriff, and you mean him too?" Then Purcell laughed like a man who suffers from being over-tickled in the ribs.

Rodiker drew tobacco and papers. Purcell said, "What a week! And I go to press tonight! Usually a dogfight is news, but this week—That Arnold girl, she disappeared off somewhere, and the old colonel came to town on a mattress! But he went home with her yesterday—still on a mattress. And he's withdrawn that offer on Jack Rodiker. After all these years of vowing up and down to see him hung."

Rodiker's fingers paused at the cigarette. Then he rolled the tobacco, licked the paper. The match flame trembled at the tip of the cigarette. *After all these years!* He felt weak.

The town marshal showed his badge at the door, and was admitted by the stiff-necked trooper. Loose-jointed and slope-shouldered, with galluses holding up his pants, and his long mustache now in a flutter, he greeted Rodiker as "Jackson," and asked questions, but Purcell, with the manner of being Rodiker's confidant, did most of the answering.

Rodiker pulled off his hat and wiped about his forehead and neck. *After all these years!* He seemed shaking inside, as if badly scared, and felt the heat now though he hadn't before.

The sheriff had been fetched from his house in a buggy. He wore a fresh shirt under the old vest where the star was pinned. His face was whisky-red, his body bloated, his eyes blood-shot and sad. He sat down, took off his hat, and smoothed the wet, freshly combed hair as he looked unhappily at Rodiker.

"I been sick," the sheriff explained. He gazed staringly at the marshal, staringly at Purcell, then took a cigar from his vest and bit off the end, but shook his head when the marshal offered a match.

Still-backed troopers brought in Mack and Harry Hand and Joe Roberts. They walked head down with clumsy stumble. The sheriff drew a long breath. "W'y, what all is the matter, boys?" He knew what was the matter, but asked it anyhow, just as if he didn't. The sheriff then pulled a long sigh, let it go, looked at Rodiker.

"Now just what is the complaint you've got agin these fellows?"

Rodiker said, "Cattle stealing, murder, and—"

He didn't finish. There was stir and clang of voices at the door, where the ramrod-still trooper barred the way. The sheriff turned slowly to look, then said, "Purcell, tell 'em to let Jerym an' them with him come in."

A half-dozen citizens crowded through with Jerym and Dougal. Jerym's broad shoulders looked more humped than ever, and his head was low on his twisted neck, but his eyes peered up under the shaggy brows. He shuffled his feet tiredly on the grit-covered floor, and when he came near Rodiker, spoke pleasantly.

"Howdy do, Mister—uh—Jackson, ain't it? Now what is the complaint against my—uh—friends?"

"For one thing, rustling. The proof's at the Reservation. Green hides. Also Zig's confession!"

Silence came and dragged itself like a smothering blanket over the room as old Jerym studied. He appeared surprised and hard hit as his nearly toothless mouth tightened under the hooked nose. "Le's hear some more," he said.

"Bill Brody had the beef contract, he used Arnold cows, and put the money in your bank. When Brody couldn't do the job any longer, Zig took charge and—"

Jerym's astonishment was great. "You mean Bill Brody pulled the wool over my eyes like that! I allus thought he was an honest man. He was in charge of my ranch for years and years, and never a thing was wrong! And Zig, you say, confessed? Confessed to what? That fool boy of mine don't know enough about my affairs to 'confess' anything, even if something's wrong, which it ain't!"

Rodiker held down his exasperation, said coldly, "Zig and these men here were caught with Arnold cows. Zig confessed to the Indian agent, so—"

"Then, mister," said Jerym, as he showed a trembling fist, "Zig'll just have to take his own medicine. Whether he's my own flesh an' blood or not makes no difference! I hope you skin 'im alive!"

A low murmur of sympathetic admiration moved on men's mouths, and pitying eyes watched old Jerym collapse into a chair.

Then Dougal Bevarts said, "Mister, like maybe you've already guessed, Zig is not much good!" He looked a little proud of Zig's not being much good, and put his hands into his trousers pockets, spread the coat, showing the gambler's vest with bright flowers painted over the satin and a gold toothpick dangling from a loop of the gold chain.

Jerym said to the prisoners, "Zig just took you boys in!" To the sheriff: "W'y, you know Joe

Roberts here wouldn't be mixed up in anything he had an idee wasn't honest! Mack and Harry, they are good boys. I'd go bail for 'em any time. It's all Zig's fault. Yes'r, that damn' Bill Brody must've got my boy mixed up in cattle stealin'!" To Rodiker: "Mister, anything I can do to help catch that ornery, no-good whelp, I'll do it! I'm through tryin' to make a man outa him. He's got to take his medicine!"

Then old Jerym got up and went out with an unsteady shuffle, and the townsmen who stood about felt sorry for him: he was sure fair and honest. Murmurs of commendation followed him.

Rodiker was dead tired; he hadn't had a good sleep for a week. He was grimy, unshaven, and bitterly disgusted. For the time being at least, old Jerym had outwitted him. Jerym's slyness made him hard to grasp and hold. He had baffled Colonel Arnold for years, and now made Rodiker feel a little helpless.

He watched the corporal and troopers swing about and leave town, and that increased his feeling of being alone and baffled, even though the sheriff had confirmed the editor's statement that Colonel Arnold's reward for Jack Rodiker was withdrawn.

"I don't know why. He wouldn't say. Just said I'd find out soon enough. Sick man, the colonel. I'm sick too. An' you know I can't stick them boys with broken arms in jail. They need a doctor. As for Joe Roberts, like Jerym said, he just got took in. I'll put a guard over 'em, though, just to show the colonel I want to be fair."

"Who let Frank Pierce out of jail?"

"Don't know. Somebody sawed off the padlock. I got to go back to bed."

Rodiker sat alone after the sheriff left. Enzo knew and could tell things—but Enzo was a half-breed, and not to be believed against the word of a fine old man like Jerym. Anyhow, it was doubtful that Enzo would ever be seen again, not with that gold in his saddlebags. *He wouldn't have stole from me, but after he thought I was killed—it wouldn't be stealing then, not for him!* But it was doubtful if Enzo had ever had closer contact with Jerym than through Bill Brody. *Too bad now that Bill Brody's dead.*

Then Rodiker thought of Tex Clayton, who knew and could tell. *I'll have to have a talk with Tex. Good stiff talk!*

As he walked down the street he reflected that it now looked as though he had been too skittish about being recognized. This afternoon he had seen men he knew, and he hadn't been recognized. Of course he had changed, had grown and hardened, and was now stubble-faced, dirty, begrimed, but more likely the fact that he was known as Colonel Arnold's top man kept people who ought to have recognized him from even dreaming he could also be Jack Rodiker. Anyone but old devil Jerym, who already knew. *He'll have to do something—or try! He knows I'll get him in the end. Knows I've purt' near got him now.*

He washed up with water dipped out of a barrel in the back room of the barbershop, then was shaved, but didn't doze in the chair. He might have, but the old barber said:

"I wonder what all will be in the paper tomorrow. You Arnolds won't get favored. Purcell owes Jerym money. A mortgage sort of hobbles a man's ability to express himself."

It was after dark when Rodiker walked into the printshop. A lamp at the back was suspended by wires and threw a cone of light over a small square table, the top of which was stone. Purcell had a mallet in one hand and a block of wood in the other, and he pounded the wood as he moved it about over the face of the type locked in a metal form on the table.

Purcell said, "Well, howdy."

Rodiker said, "I want to put a piece in your paper."

"Too late. Here's the last form. I'm ready to go to press."

Rodiker didn't seem to understand. He repeated, "I want to put a piece in the paper."

"What kind of piece?"

"Depends. What have you already wrote about the rustler I brought in?"

Purcell pushed up his cardboard eyeshade and tried to sound firm. "I wrote what was said about them. An editor knows only what he is told."

"I didn't say much. Jerym did most of the talking. You favor the Bevartses over us Arnolds?"

"See here. I am the editor. I can't have people telling me what to print and what not to print. I try to print the facts."

Rodiker said, "Maybe you don't know the facts. I'll give them to you."

"You'd give only your side and—"

"A fact has got only one side. And it is a fact that old Jerym has got a lot of people in the Santsander buffaloed. It is time the truth about him is made known. I'll tell it to you, and you put it in your paper, will you?"

Purcell was in a hurry, impatient but polite. This tall superintendent of Colonel Arnold had cool eyes and the steadiness of a man who intends to have his way, and Purcell liked him, but he didn't like the stubbornness that wouldn't understand how a newspaper was run. So Purcell took up a pencil, and from the floor picked a piece of galley proof that his inky fingers smudged as he laid it on the stone, and so made ready to pretend to take notes. This was the easiest way to satisfy importunate news-givers.

Rodiker hooked his thumbs in his belt, looked

earnest, and spoke quietly. "First, put it down that Jerym Bevarts is an old copperhead."

Purcell's pretense wasn't equal to that. He flinched, looked up, and said, "I can't print things like that. It's libel."

"It's a fact," said Rodiker unyieldingly. "I want it in."

Purcell shrugged and scribbled.

"Next, for years he has had a rustling bunch. On the spring roundups he'd fixed it with Colonel Arnold's rep so that our calves would be branded Lazy S's and a false tally kept."

Purcell exclaimed, "Jumped-up Judas, Mr. Jackson! I can't print anything like that! Not about anybody!"

Rodiker's quietness was unchanging. "But it's a fact. Frank Pierce told me. For years he helped the Bevartses do it. I took Pierce to Colonel Arnold, and he told the colonel the same thing. I don't know for a fact that some Bevarts man broke the jail lock and let him out, so we can't say that's how it was. But the other part I do know. You got it down?"

"Why—er—yes," said Purcell, making meaningless jots.

"Next, you put down that old Jerym organized what he called the Associated Ranchers, who are nothing but rustlers. That was so they could take the big Arnold A and turn it into an AR—like this."

Rodiker used the pencil and illustrated. Purcell shuddered, but kept his mouth shut as Rodiker explained. "Through Bill Brody's name, Jerym got the beef contract for the Reservation. He filled it mostly with change-branded Arnold cows. Bill Brody usually took them in. Then money was paid to him, and he put it in Jerym's bank here. That is a fact, Mr. David, the Indian agent, told me."

"Yes, yes," said Purcell, making wild scribbles that he couldn't read, had no intention of reading.

"Now," said Rodiker, "we come to something else important. Jerym sent for Jack Rodiker to come back into this country, and he come. Jerym wanted him to hold up his Cattleman Bank here. The reason is that the bank is purt' near broke, and Jerym wants a good excuse for all the money being gone so people won't blame him for stealing it."

Purcell's editorial honesty flared, and he slammed down the pencil. "I don't believe it."

Rodiker was unruffled, even mild. He nodded. "I didn't hardly think you would, but it's a fact." He drew a dirty, sweat-stained envelope from his hip pocket and removed the paper he had extorted from Jerym.

Purcel mumblingly read, " 'I, Jerym Bevarts, having sent for Jack Rodiker, hereby promise him two thousand dollars to raid my bank because it is so near broke it has to fail, and I want to make people think it was Rodiker, and not me, that got away with the money!' "

It was on bank paper, the writing and signature were Jerym's. Purcell looked up in amazement. "How'd a smart man like old Jerym ever write a thing like this?"

"I'd say that Rodiker persuaded him to put his proposition in writing."

Purcell said, "I see it now! Jack Rodiker turned this over to you people, and in exchange Colonel Arnold withdrew his reward on him! A thing like this will ruin old Jerym. That's what you Arnolds want!"

"It's what we Arnolds want," Rodiker admitted quietly. "Only it ain't a fact that Colonel Arnold made that kind of a deal with Rodiker, so don't put that in your paper."

Purcell said, "All right, yes, of course. I'll fix everything. You'll see when the paper comes out in the morning."

Rodiker looked about, reached for a chair, and brought it nearer. "I am aiming to stay on here till the paper comes out."

Purcell didn't stagger. He caught hold of the stone and steadied himself. The scribbled-on galley proof fell to the floor, and Purcell's black eyes were dimmed with a kind of film, as he looked heavenward and seemed prayerful. Then he explained pleadingly:

"I can't print things like that. I don't like the

Bevartses. Jerym is a damned old hypocrite, but I can't print it. Don't you see, I just don' dare print things like that!"

Rodiker scrutinized the shaken man for a full minute, then matter-of-factly said, "Jerym buys or scares people. You're not his friend. Yet you won't print facts about him. A coward is always the friend of a scoundrel. This is no time for you to straddle a fence, so you tell me—do you want to be on the side of us Arnolds, or do you throw in with the Bevartses?"

Purcell said, "I'll be murdered sure!" But he set his "facts" directly from the case. He was a fast compositor, though at first his fingers trembled and a lot of type went into the stick upside down.

When the form was locked and placed on the Old Washington press bed, Purcell ran the press, and Rodiker inked for him, and so didn't see the head until the first page was printed.

JERYM BEVARTS IS RUSTLER
SWINDLER AND HORSE THIEF!

Rodiker protested. "I never told you he was a horse thief. That is going too far."

CHAPTER 27

Rodiker left the saddle and looked eastward. The sun wasn't up, but was coming from behind a red blaze that was as bright as if the world were on fire. He hadn't had any sleep, coming directly from the printshop to the Claytons for his talk with old Tex.

Bess Clayton ran to the door, then tiredly said, "You" without welcome and with reproach. Sleep was still in her eyes, that or the weariness of having cried until they looked sleep-swollen. Her brown corn-silk hair wasn't brushed, and she was barefoot.

He asked if they'd heard any news from town yesterday, and she dully said they had, and nothing more. She was pretty, but she wasn't tidy now, and she was unfriendly. When he asked, "You know, don't you, Colonel Arnold's taken off that reward?" Bess said listlessly, yes, she knew. She said, "You ought to be 'shamed, doing things that made you friends with old Yank Arnold." Her eyes had such a hurt look, were so dull and pain-saddened that he asked, "What's all the matter?"

"Matter?" She shrugged a shoulder. "Zig knows now that I knew you that night when you came here and hit him. The Bevartses and Claytons are friends, too, you know. Or were! You'd better go back to your Arnolds and stay there."

"I come to see Tex."

Bess stepped back. "He's still in bed. Only don't stay long. I mean don't stay here long. We don't want you. Be best if you didn't stop at all!" She turned her back on him and walked away.

Tex had heard voices and was sitting up, and scratched his breast through an undershirt that had lost its buttons. He didn't look well; the flesh of his face sagged, and his heartiness was gone, but the warmth of his welcome was pleasing, though he seemed anxious too. His eyes were wide and staring.

Rodiker stood by the bed. "Tex, the Bevartses are through!" He drew a folded paper from his hip pocket, but didn't at once open it. "You've been mixed up with old Jerym for years. I want to know all you can tell me. I'll see that Colonel Arnold don't hold it against you. I mean, won't do anything to get even."

Tex stared at Rodiker for a long time, then shook his head. He said, "I'm s'prised you'd ask a thing like that of me." He looked down and put the fingers of both hands into his hair and shook his head again. "No, Jack, I can't. I don't go back on friends." He raised his eyes. "I ain't mad or nuthin', but I sho' do wish yuh'd go."

"You mean we're not friends now?"

Tex shook his head worriedly. "I don't mean a thing like that at all. On'y I wish yuh'd go away."

"The Bevartses are licked, Tex!"

"But Jerym's been a frien' to me. He's seen to it that I had money when I wouldn't've if he hadn't. An' I am sho' pleasured that yuh are in the clear, boy. I like you. I allus did. But I won't tell even you things agin mah frien's. No mo' than any of us Claytons'ud go to Yank Arnold when we knew where you was!"

A smile barely touched Rodiker's mouth. "And I was mighty glad not to find you over at Los Muertos!"

Tex nodded soberly. "That's how it is with frien's. But I wish you'd go away. Go now."

"Did you send Jerym word that I knew about Los Muertos?"

Tex evaded the question with a forced grin as he said, "Sue hid my laig. She heard you give me warnin'. She didn't give it back till yest'day when she heard you was back in town." He pointed toward the wooden leg on the floor by the bed. Then: "That girl loves you, Jack. She loves yuh mo'n Bess ever did. She on'y a yung'un still, Sue is, but a mighty big an' fine woman is a-growin' up inside of her."

"I'm sure," said Rodiker, and laid the open paper on the bed before Tex.

He said, "Eh?" and leaned forward, then blurted oaths in uneasy astonishment, his eyes wide and bugged out. As he read his lips moved.

Rodiker turned toward the door. It was Sue. Her face was shiny from soap and water, her loose hair was tied at the back of her head by a blue ribbon, and the hem of the faded clean calico dress brushed the earthen floor. Unsmilingly she crossed the room, going straight to Rodiker, and rose on tiptoes to kiss him, and he stooped a little and put an arm about her, then was jarred to his heels by the warmth from her lips. The harum-scarum kid was woman grown, and solemn too. She lay against his arm and looked at him and didn't smile, asking:

"That girl got Yank Arnold to take his reward off you?"

"I don't think so. When Ronnie was there, the colonel guessed from how much we looked alike. Then things like what happened to Bill Brody made him know I never killed his brother. So the colonel's being honest enough to try to make things up to me."

Sue said, "That's what you think. She loves you, and talked the colonel over." Then steadily: "I love you too. I always have. But you know about us now. We're no good an' poor at that! So go away. Go now, I mean! Right now!"

She pulled from him and pointed toward the door. Her eyes followed her own gesture, and she cried out, then at once she swirled about and backed against Rodiker with her arms spread protectively as she faced the doorway.

Frank Pierce, on tiptoes, was at the door, and his gun was leveled hip high. Zig Bevarts was behind him in a stealthy posture, also with a drawn gun. Pierce's thin face gleamed with an evil temper that was pleased. He warned, "Don't move, or I'll kill her too."

Rodiker believed him, and was caught hands down and helpless; nevertheless, now he realized how very loyal and friendly the Claytons had been in telling him to go away, to go at once, meaning, *Go before men who hate you creep out of their hiding place and find you here!*

Tex at once flung the paper aside and swung his leg and stump over the bedside as he roared, "Put down them guns! This is mah home an' he's mah frien', too, goddamn yuh souls!"

Zig Bevarts laughed, or rather sneered. " 'Twas here he hit me when I wasn't lookin'!" The lumpish face glistened greasily as he leveled out his gun at arm's length, taking aim at Rodiker's head above Sue's shoulder. "Put your hands up, or I sure will!" he threatened.

Sue's "Don't" was furious, and she rose to tiptoes trying to cover Rodiker. Zig told him: "You duck down behind, and I'll shoot right through her! Get them hands up!"

Rodiker's hands went up, shoulder high and palm out.

Frank Pierce was saying savagely, " 'F I'd wanted to kill you, I'd have done it before now. But you've learned me tricks I didn't know, an' I'm gonna hang you like you purt' near hung me!"

Rodiker said, "You heard him, Sue. They'll not shoot now. Get away!"

"I won't!" Her arms were still outstretched, and she kept her back to him protectively. She said, "You men come here as friends of Tex to hide. We sheltered you. He's a friend too. We'll shelter him or die tryin'!"

"By God, that's right!" Tex roared, and jumped one-leggedly from the bed. He waved a fist. "I let you hide out here, an' you—"

Zig yelled, "Shut up, you old buzzard!"

Rodiker said, "Sue, you keep me helpless!"

Frank Pierce shouted, "Go round her after him, Zig! Put a gun to his back, an' bring him from behind the woman's skirt!" Then jeered, "A fittin' place for the likes of him to hide!"

Zig started. Tex held to the bed and stooped for his pegleg. He caught it by the peg, and swung it clublike at Zig's head. Rodiker was on edge for any chance to move, and now left-handedly struck Sue's shoulder, shoving her aside as he thrust out his foot. Sue tripped and fell as if knocked down. Zig dodged the heavy pegleg and shot Tex, then Frank Pierce fired with startled jerk at Rodiker, whose gun smoked over its holster.

The sound of guns pounded the walls with the reverberance of long-drawn thunderclaps, and black smoke burst out as if from busted bladders, gustily filling the room. Rodiker stood flat-footed, forearm steadyingly against his hip, and he aimed with twist of body, firing fast through the smoke.

Frank Pierce had gone down with the grunt of a man knocked breathless by a blow in the belly, but he was tough and strong with hate, and got dizzily to his knees and used both hands on the butt. Even then, he weaved as he fired. Old Tex roared curses and floundered, trying to rise one-leggedly. Zig fired as a scared man does, his finger yanking at the trigger, and when he was knocked back against the wall, he stood upright in the smoke fog long enough to seem unhurt. Rodiker shot twice more before Zig fell. Any of the three slugs in him was death-dealing. And when Frank Pierce sprawled forward and lay quiet, Rodiker's gun was empty, the five shots having been fired in less time than a man could draw a full breath.

Bess came fearfully to the door, and Sue said, "Bring water!" Rodiker lifted Tex onto the bed, and Tex yelled, "I want likker!" He made a bluster about being only scratched, but the black pucker, no bigger than a mouse's ear, under his right breast meant internal bleeding. He coughed hard, and the spume was blood-colored, and he soon quieted, as if very tired.

A freighter had stopped to do some trading. Rodiker had him saddle one of Tex's mules and go the three miles to town for the doctor. "And tell the sheriff too!" said Rodiker.

The young doctor came with his buggy horses on the run. He gaped at the fresh gouges in the bedroom's 'dobe walls as Tex, weak and cheerful, bragged that he had taught Jack Rodiker to use a gun. It wasn't so, but he probably believed it. Sue wiped his lips and told him to shush.

A few minutes later the doctor dragged his feet a little when he came out to where Rodiker was sitting on his heels at the edge of the back veranda. A stone's throw away two bodies lay under a blanket. The doctor didn't say anything at first, but tried to squat on his heels by Rodiker's side, and had to use his hands to steady himself, then was too cramped. He stood up.

"I didn't tell them. I couldn't!"

"Tex?"

"Tex."

Rodiker threw away his dead cigarette, then slowly arose. His face was haggardly worn, hard-set, and his eyes had a faraway vagueness. The doctor ventured, "You must be greatly relieved that the colonel has put so much trust in you after—uh, you know—the reward and all."

Rodiker walked away, not replying.

Road dust showed that people were coming from town, and he waited out front. The sheriff was on horseback. A half-dozen men were with him, and they didn't ride fast. One of the men was Dougal Bevarts, glum of face but in fine clothes, with slick black boots and small shiny spurs. Another was Enzo, and his heavy face had no more expression than a cigar-store Indian.

The sheriff dismounted wearily, dropped the reins, and came to Rodiker. He looked sick, but interest flicked in his sad, blood-shot eyes. "So you are Jack Rodiker?"

Men pressed encirclingly close to stare and listen, but Dougal wasn't among them. Without a glance he went directly to the house.

The sheriff spoke tiredly. "Jerym tells me you got that letter out of him at the point of a gun."

"I did, but what it says is so."

"Jerym says it ain't, not a word of it." Then the sheriff bit at a cigar, spat, asked, "Was it with a gun, too, you made Purcell get out that paper?"

Rodiker glanced carefully into the faces about him; they had a listening tenseness, narrow-eyed and frown-drawn. He said, "I gave him facts, and I asked did he want to throw in with the Bevartses or be with us Arnolds."

The sheriff put a match to the cigar, puffed, removed the cigar, and looked at the fired end. He said inquiringly, "I can't figger how Colonel Arnold ever come to put you in charge of his affairs. Not after all these years of tryin' to get you hung." Rodiker didn't say anything. The sheriff then suggested, "Was it maybe a deal for you to play hell with the Bevartses, like you've done?" Rodiker still didn't say anything, so the sheriff told him, "Murder is murder, you know, even if the reward is dropped."

Rodiker asked, "Are you thinking about arresting me?"

"No," the sheriff droned. "No, I ain't. Not now."

"An' had better not be!" said a man close by, looking hard at the sheriff.

Another man spoke up hotly. "That bank hadn't better fail. Last week I put nine hunert dollars in it from beef I'd sold in Kans' City. If I don't get it back I'll nail Jerym's hide to my stable door!"

The sheriff moved on with flat-footed slowness, and men followed him into the house.

Then Enzo came closer and said stolidly, "Rodiker, soh! No wonder I feel strong you are a freend! I rode like the bat out of hell to the colonel, an' I deed not know I was a liar when I say I saw you killed. The leetle señorita cried. The beeg black man bawl like a hurt bull. To theenk I took all that gol' to the colonel! I weel be an hones' man yet, if I do not watch out!"

Then the half-breed grinned slowly, put a hand into his pocket, jingled coin. "Know what? When I come to town et is like a nest of hornets over that newspaper. Old Jerym send for me, an' he ask weel I keel you for a hun'ard dollars? I say, 'Sure!' But he weel not pay me in advance, so I won' keel you."

Enzo's hand came from his pocket in the offer

of a handshake. "Goo'-by. I go south to Mexico."

"But aren't you working for the colonel?"

"Work, me? When the colonel give me a hun'ard dollars more for breengin' in that gol'? Ho! An' I deed get ten from old Jerym too. He is seek at home, an' keep a chain on the door. He is so 'fraid of you he had me take a shotgun to the blacksmeeth shop to be made short." Enzo's slow grin became a chuckle. "He weel keel you heemself an' save some money. I hope he use it on you soon!"

"Thanks!" said Rodiker.

"Sure you weel thank me!" Again the coins jangled. "Now I am reech—for a week! Suppose I die before I spend it all? No, no! That gol' music weel make the leetle señoritas say how beeg an' fine I am."

Rodiker watched him ride off and wondered just what devilment the half-breed had been up to that made him seem so pleased and almost merry.

When he rode up to the mountain ranch the dogs barked, and Maw Rodiker looked out of the door, then waited on the stoop. He wondered that her thin shoulders were still straight, when she worked so hard and wasn't young and from the War years on had carried the kind of load that bends stiff backs. She smiled through the wrinkles when he put his arm about her.

"You've heard?" he asked, and her eyes were bright as she said, "Yes."

Few people came this way, and he asked, "How'd you learn?"

She said, "Come in an' set. You hungry? It's good to look at you. Now you're tired and troubled, too, I see, but there's no coiled-up fear squeezin' around your heart."

She turned into the cabin, and he followed. "How'd you learn?"

She said, "Paw and Ronnie rode up to the meadow this mornin'. A black bear killed a cow yest'day. We've got no cows to spare! There's cold beans in the pot if you want a snack."

He took off his gun and belt, and hung them on a peg. It was the first time in years that he had deliberately let his firearms be beyond reach, and it eased him like drawing a long breath after laying down an uphill burden. He sat on a stool, dropped his hat on the floor, stretched his legs. "How'd you learn?"

Maw Rodiker said, "Paw an' Ronnie'll be back 'fore dark, but ain't you hungry now?"

He stood up and gently put both his hands to her wrinkled throat in pretended menace. "I choke things out of people. So tell me, how'd you know about the colonel taking off that reward?"

Maw Rodiker looked straight at him. "Has Cora Arnold talked like you wanted?"

His hands dropped. "She will," he said, and turned to the stool, pushing it near the table, then sat down. Cora Arnold's lure touched his memory, and his distrust of her somehow did not lessen the enticement she seemed to offer. He walked to the fireplace and rested an elbow on the mantel.

"I first asked, 'How'd you hear?' just curious. But you don't want to tell me. It's not like you to hedge and dodge. Now I'm in a fret to know."

Mrs. Rodiker's stiff back stiffened as she sat down at the table and brushed some crumbs that weren't there to the floor; then she drew her elbows tight to her waist and let her hands rest on the table's edge with fingers intertwined, and her head lifted in saying, "I went myself to Yank Arnold and gave him a talkin' to!"

He left the mantel and straightened, putting his thumbs into the front of his belt, and stared in quiet amazement.

"Does Paw know?"

"No, he don't!"

He sat on the stool again and rested on his elbows to watch her face, as she said, "Some days ago Paw'd gone up in the timber to help a man for an overnight stay. So I fetched down my old sidesaddle from the loft. After Ronnie had told about you bein' there at Arnold's and how Yank hisself acted and what you'd done to Bill Brody, I said to myself, 'Yank Arnold is maybe too much man to turn his face from the truth when it is give to him straight.' So I rode over there. Took near all day.

"That big darkie was mighty polite in sayin' I couldn't see the colonel, but I up an' told him, 'I am Ronnie Rodiker's mother. Your colonel was good to my boy. I've come to tell Colonel Arnold some things he ought to know.'

"So I was asked indoors to wait while he went upstairs, then soon I was asked up. Yank Arnold was in bed and had me set on a chair close to the bedside, and I right out and told him without any beatin' about the bush that the man he thought was named 'Jackson' was Jack Rodiker hisself.

"An' you could have knocked me over with a wren's feather when he said quiet-like, 'Yes, ma'am, I've thought that for some days now. And I have wondered why—why he is here.'

"I said, 'I don't know for a fact, but I think he come to see if he could find out why you an' that Cora Arnold joined up to lie about him. I know he thought you both was chin-deep in it together.'

"Yank Arnold looked at me for a long time, like he was turnin' over things far back in his head, then he asked, 'What does Jack think now?'

"I said I didn't know, at least not from havin' talked with him. I said, 'Maybe now he thinks Cora Arnold fooled you.' I said, 'He wouldn't hang around, playin' like he was a man's friend if he wasn't.' I said, 'He may be hard and sometimes mean, but he ain't never sneaky.' I said, 'He's got good cause to hate you, an' I've done it, too, and do yet some. You'd do it too if a rich man put money on your boy's head that kep' folks spyin' around your place with guns in hand, hopin' to catch an' shoot your boy so they'd get some blood money. Wouldn't you now?'

"And Yank Arnold said, 'Yes, Mrs. Rodiker, I would.' And he said he was right away going to take off that reward. He said he knew now that Jack Rodiker wasn't the kind of man that could be hired to shoot somebody. He said he was more sorry than he would even try to say, and that he was glad I had come. And was there anything he could do to part way make up for the wrong he had done us Rodikers. And I told him no, there wasn't a thing on earth more that I wanted.

"And I said, 'From how you act I think you are an honest man, but you're not smart, or long before now you'd've known that Jack Rodiker don't shoot in the back!'

"And he said, 'Believe me, I have been thinking of that, Mrs. Rodiker!'

"Then he asked wouldn't I care to stay the night, for I looked tired, he said, and it was a long ways home. I told him no. I said I sure wouldn't willin'ly stay under the roof of any rich black Yankee, 'specially not one that had put a dead-or-'live reward on my boy's head. So I came home."

CHAPTER 28

They sat down to breakfast in the candle-lit dawn. Rodiker was leaving as soon as he ate.

When Ronnie asked what would become of the Clayton girls now, Rodiker shook his head. He cut a big bite of tough steak and chewed as the best way to keep from talking.

Maw said that she was sorry about Tex, but it was a fact that he had always been shiftless. Rodiker admitted, "I guess so," but he was thinking of the cripple who had tried to protect a friend by swinging his wooden leg at a man with a drawn gun. Then he spoke up. "I've never seen a braver man. And Slim, too, died from trying to do what he thought was right by us." He had never revealed, and never would, why Slim had so desperately tried to do what he thought was right by the Rodikers.

Maw said, "O' course Tex was brave, but bein' brave ain't everything. Bein' honest is the nearest to the best anybody can be."

Rodiker told her, "You're prob'ly right. But lots of honest men are that way on account of being timid. They are scared of trouble. The Claytons didn't scare. I'd been a gone goose if Sue hadn't got in front of me like she did."

Ronnie blurted, "You love her, Jack?"

"Don't you?"

The kid flushed, looked down, grinned. "I like her a lot, but she allus said that she liked me so much only because I looked like you! She said a man was just a man to Bess, and if one wasn't around, another'n would do! Don't you like Sue best now?"

Rodiker put another big bite of steak in his mouth and chewed, but Maw Rodiker set down her tin cup so hard that some of the coffee splashed. Her voice was sharp.

"First it was Bess, and now it is Sue, is it? She's no more'n a child! And can't you look nowhere but toward the Clayton girls?"

Ronnie said, "Miss Kate acts like she liked you a whole lot, Jack."

Maw demanded, "Who's Miss Kate? That Arnold girl?"

Ronnie said, "Yes."

Maw then got up from the table with a kind of angry quickness and brought more biscuits from the Dutch oven. They were hot, but she handled them without a fork or cloth. When she sat down again she said, "Jack, would you marry Yank Arnold's girl?"

He said, "Oh hell!" then smiled grimly in trying to make a joke of, "I ain't been asked to yet."

Maw spoke sternly. "I never thought I'd live to see the day when a son of mine would make up to a Yankee woman!"

Rodiker said, "Her mother was Southern. She married him at New Orleans during the War." Which, right off, he saw was the wrong thing to have said.

Maw Rodiker's fingers became fists. "A Southe'n woman—durin' the War! Make up to a Yankee! No decent woman could love a damn-blackyankee—not durin' the War!"

Paw Rodiker got up quietly. He was a big man with bowed shoulders and the gentleness of one who knew his own strength and is careful never to misuse it. He said softly, "Maw, the War is over—and has been over quite some years. True, folks like us can't forget. But we can act like we don't remember."

He went slowly out of doors and left silence behind him. Soon they heard his ax with almost rhythmical thud swinging into a cedar log; already he was cutting wood for the winter.

Near the foot of the mountain road Rodiker met Steve, whose young face grinned lazily as he explained, "I've been sent to look for you. They told me at Clayton's which way to come. Somebody brought out a copy of that Moheela paper to the Colonel, and it done him good. It told him you wasn't dead like that half-breed said. He read about Jerym and laughed. For a fact, laughed like a man who has drawed to an inside straight and got himself a straight flush."

They rode stirrup-to-stirrup with the Santsander's valley rolling before them, and they went so slowly that the soft murmuring creak of leather was like a quiet voice using words that didn't make sense.

Steve said, "He sent me to say your job is perm'nent, but he wants that you stay in town to make sure the sheriff toes the mark and don't let them rustlers get away, like Frank Pierce done. He says Jerym'll maybe lose some hide because he's in a tight place to squirm out of, but he'll squirm, and you are to watch out. He wants to make sure the rustlers go to prison. He wants law in the land. He says law-punishment will discourage brand-twisters more than what he calls personal vengeance. He wants you to see that law does like it ought."

Rodiker let his gaze drift beyond the valley and up into the far red mountains, where the earth-makers had built a towering jagged wall, barren, colorful, forbidding. Colonel Arnold wanted to set up law in the country. Law was what everybody said was best. But law wouldn't make any accounting of the honorable and brave qualities in men like Tex and Enzo and Clary. It seemed that law drew a line, and if you crossed that line, no matter how or why, you needed punishment. And the law could be sneaky too—like Deputy Sheriff Joe turning his badge out of sight when he helped rustlers.

Because he had liked Tex so much, the

rightness of law seemed insolubly puzzling, until his thought drifted back to the cabin he had left not long ago. He knew the sweaty toil and stern hardships that had gone into the making of that home, and often there wasn't much to eat and only old clothes to wear, but there had never been any grumbling or thought of how to take something without pay from somebody else. And as he brooded, he realized that whatever pleasant and good traits men like Tex, Enzo, and the rash Clary might have, they couldn't be pardoned and let go unpunished if they stole, especially from honest people. He saw it the more clearly because he was thinking of his own folks, and knew how unyieldingly honest and hard-working they were. So the law ought to be strong throughout the land; only then could it protect people of that kind when they were molested.

Steve drawled, half unheard, saying, "Bein' *es*-cort to Miss Kate was not much fun. Soon as we started, she ordered me back. But you'd said to stick, an' I stuck clear into town. She said I was a coward to be ridin' alongside a girl away from trouble when better men than me was headin' for it. I told her I'd had more trouble from pretty girls than from badmen, and she was one of the prettiest that ever didn't like to have me around. And that made her madder.

"You ought've seen her face when she heard her father was in bed at the hotel, havin' come to town just about dead from worry over her. He must've give her hell with the trimmin's. The next day she was what is called sub-dued when I seen her."

"That's hard to believe."

"And," said Steve with a dreamy look, "that Mrs. Bevarts is a powerful good-looker. I et in the dinin' room across from her. I can see why any man'ud be in love with her quick, if she'd let him! How it come, I wonder, she ever mistook you for somebody else that time in the piñons?"

Rodiker said nothing but thought, *Some man told her what to say. It had to be. Maybe she honestly didn't know it wasn't me. I'll soon find out all she can tell.*

When they stopped at the Claytons' a stranger came out.

He said his name was Mr. Tredel, and when Rodiker gave his own name, Mr. Tredel shook hands with interest and warmth, then turned to the door and called, "Ann, my dear, a friend of yours is here."

Mr. Tredel stepped back for Rodiker to go in first. Ann came straight to Rodiker and put her arms about him and hugged him. She wasn't rigged out like a gambler's woman, but looked cool and lovely, though she had been crying. She said that for a long time she had planned to come home on a visit so Mr. Tredel could meet her folks. They had been ready to start when word came about Slim, and when they arrived by stage yesterday, they found themselves just in time for Tex's funeral.

Rodiker went with her to the back veranda, and they sat alone together. Mr. Tredel, she said, was the best man that ever lived, next to Tex. He owned an interest in the Eldorado in Denver, and a pleasant home. They used to live at a hotel, but after Mr. Tredel's sister died they had taken the two little children to raise, and Mr. Tredel said that a hotel was no place in which to bring up children.

Mr. Tredel came out, and when Ann went indoors his eyes followed her as a setter's eyes follow a child. He sat down and offered Rodiker a big cigar and pulled at his white sleeves which had pink holders. It was the best cigar Rodiker had ever smoked, but he didn't know that, and preferred his own cigarettes.

"Of course," said Mr. Tredel, "we'll take Ann's sisters home with us. The house is not big enough, but we'll build on. There are lots of fine young men in Denver. In my business you get to know which ain't fine. A smart feller can bamboozle a woman, but he can't a saloonkeeper. If any tinhorns show up, I'll kick 'em off the front porch."

Rodiker asked what Bess and Sue thought about living in Denver.

Mr. Tredel carefully pushed the ash from his

cigar with a little finger. “Bess is eager, but Sue just looked at me and Ann and didn’t say yes and she didn’t say no. Her brother dyin’, then her father like he did has hurt the girl.”

Rodiker, ready to leave, went into the house, where Steve sat near Bess, and for all his interest in pretty girls, he acted a little afraid, though awkwardly pleased too. Bess stared sullenly at Rodiker, then looked away, and made Steve writhe miserably by putting a handkerchief to her eyes.

On the way into town Steve didn’t have much to say, but what he did say was, “Ain’t it hell for a fellow to go make a fool of himself, then no matter where he finds a nice girl he don’t hardly dare settle down. Anyhow, no girl worth havin’ would take a fellow that’s got nothin’ but a saddle and a job.”

Rodiker said, “If she’s worth having, she would.”

In town Steve said he would eat and leave for the ranch, and asked what word to take. Rodiker said, “That I’m for law too.”

He left his horse at the stable and walked to the sheriff’s office. The door was closed but wasn’t locked, and the office was empty. He went out the back way and into the alley.

The print-shop door was shut, and paper was pasted on the inside over the windows. He knocked, and Purcell asked, “Who is it?” The editor opened the door to a crack's width, making sure, before he let Rodiker in.

Though only late afternoon, it was dark inside, because all of the windows were pasted over with newspapers, and the shaded lamp threw down its glow like something spilled on the unswept floor. Purcell was skinnier than ever. He took up his corncob pipe and laughed uneasily, being scared but proud too. He bragged about having busted the Bevartses wide open, and folks had praised him for his courage to do it.

He said, "My life is in danger, but I won't run away."

The black shoe-button eyes asked Rodiker for some commendation, and Rodiker said, "Good for you." Then he asked, "Has that bank closed yet?"

"Hasn't opened! Jerym sends out word that it will. He keeps himself behind a chained door. The sheriff is sick abed. He appointed a couple of deputies, that some little ranchers hereabouts and businessmen, too, wanted. There is talk of asking the governor to appoint our town marshal as sheriff. He don't look like much, that fellow, but he's not afraid of the devil in the dark!"

"Anything else?"

"Why, yes. The county attorney has helped in Jerym's dirty work all these years, but now he acts astonished. He's bragging about how he'll prosecute at the next session of court. He'd better too. The country is real riled. Jerym'll purt' near be lynched if that bank don't pay off. I hear Dougal has gone to Woodward to try to get some money for the run when it opens."

"Mrs. Bevarts go with him?"

"Don't know. But wouldn't they be settin' pretty if she had brought them half of all Colonel Arnold owns! And I bet that in her heart she blames Dougal for her being beat out of it. He ought've been smart enough to wait until she'd got her share."

"Yes, he ought've."

"Hell yes."

Again Rodiker went to the barbershop and washed in the dark back room with water from a barrel. He thought of Cora Arnold Bevarts, wondering if it could be that she hadn't purposely wronged him that day in the piñons. She must be troubled at learning that "José" was Jack Rodiker. Would she be terrified at meeting him?

It was sobering to recall how Maw Rodiker had jumped down his throat when Ronnie brought up Kate Arnold's name. He thought, *She's got the devil's own temper about having her own way!* unreproachfully meaning Kate, and as unreproachfully he added, *The beatin'est girl for lying I ever knew!*

It was her intrepid lying that had given him the chance to make Colonel Arnold trust him, but such rash judgment as she used couldn't always be lucky, and she was a girl who did rash things. Her readiness with lies made him distrustful, but he liked her. He more than liked her. *If I don't love her, then I don't know what love is like!*

CHAPTER 29

Rodiker didn't see Cora Bevarts at the hotel, but men crowded about him. Now that the Bevartses seemed broken men, everybody was eager to be Colonel Arnold's friend.

The sheriff left his bed and came from the saloon into the dining room to sit by Rodiker. His full face, laced with small blood vessels that showed through the tan, had a wilted sag, and his eyes were staringly unhappy. A short bouncy man was with him: the county attorney. They accompanied Rodiker upstairs to his room.

Only two chairs were in the room, and Rodiker sat on the bed. It had squeaky springs. The attorney flourished a flat pint from his pocket, but Rodiker said, "No, thanks," refusing the friendliness that drinking together implied. He hooked his hands over a lifted knee and listened. The attorney was glib and uneasy. The sheriff laid his hat on the floor and nursed the water glass half full of whisky on his knee, nodding in agreement to the attorney's promises that no guilty man would escape.

Rodiker listened, aloof, unbending, watchful. He got up to turn down the smoking lamp, then put his thumbs to his belt and stood stiffly tall.

"Colonel Arnold wants law. But if the law

won't do what it ought, he'll do what he can to make the law like it ought to be!"

The attorney drank from the bottle, wiped his mouth, spoke rather demandingly. "One thing I'd like to know is how it happens that after all these years you got so ace-high with Colonel Arnold so quick."

Rodiker said, "Ask him!"

Then he opened the door for them to go out.

The next morning he sat up, yawned, stretched his arms, and remembered that Tex would be buried today. The sun laid a golden shimmer on the threadbare carpet, and he stood in the sunlight to dress. No longer did he have to hunt corners and holes and unlighted places to feel safe.

Downstairs he looked over the register and found "Dougal Bevarts and Wife, Room 4," and no notation of departure. He wouldn't ask about her. Asking might make the sort of talk he didn't want.

He rode out to the Claytons' early. Because he was no longer on the dodge, and it wasn't proper to be armed at a funeral, he put his gun and the rolled-up, cartridge-heavy belt out of sight in the house.

Then he walked with Mr. Tredel along the high river bank, where a grave had been dug beside the mound that was still fresh. Mr. Tredel explained, "I'm having plenty of beer sent out from town, but no liquor. An' I ordered the best coffin in town. The preacher will come before noon. No chance to get flowers, only some paper ones from the lady milliner. Tex had lots of friends."

And the friends came. Some nesters from along the river brought their families in farm wagons. Lots of people swarmed up to the house, cowboys from round about, and bearded freighters. His way of dying made folks honor him.

Old Jerym drove out in a buggy, his wife with him, and people wondered greatly that they would come. It was the first time he had been seen out of the house since the newspaper appeared. Jerym wore the long linen duster, and didn't take it off after he got out of the buggy. His thick shoulders were more bowed than ever, and his head distrustfully swung to one side on the twisted neck, and he wouldn't look anybody in the eye.

His wife got out of the buggy by herself. She was a work-bowed, dried-up little woman, with a dress that seemed burdensome to her frail body. Her face under the slat bonnet looked as withered as a frostbitten apple, as bitter as an unripe crab apple.

Rodiker went to the door of a dim room where Sue sat waiting alone. None of the girls owned a black dress, but Mr. Tredel had ordered crepe and veiling, together with black gloves, from town. Sue's copperish hair was piled in coils and overlaid with veiling that was to be pulled over her face when she went among people.

She said, "All this today is nothing. Last night I went to his grave and played my fiddle. Bess called me daft and tried to make me stop. Mr. Tredel said to let me alone."

"When do you leave?"

"Mr. Tredel says soon as we can have an auction. I won't like a place where there's more people than you can know by name. It's lonely where strangers are. And since Slim died, and now Tex, there's a hurt inside of me that won't let up. I used to laugh and tease. Now I wonder how I ever could. Ann says it's growing up, but I don't know. Once I could shout, 'I love you!' and didn't care who heard. Now I can't whisper it to myself even without feeling some red shame." Her voice was quiet, and her clear eyes were level, until she added, "But I still do and always will!" Then her eyes dropped.

During the service in the front room the doors and windows of the old adobe were filled with faces looking in. When the pallbearers lifted the casket that had silver handles, the preacher followed them into the noonday sun. Mr. Tredel and Ann walked behind him, Bess and a young cowboy followed, then Sue and Rodiker.

Men took off their hats and looked down until the casket was lowered and earth began to be tumbled in; then they moved together with voices hushed, or walked away in the thoughtfulness that comes with laying away a friend.

Only a scattering remained about the grave when Rodiker, from some plucking impulse, glanced over his shoulder and saw Jerym some ten feet behind him. The loose linen duster dragged about Jerym's ankles, and his eyes, as deep-set as an ape's, had a meaningful glow. Rodiker saw the hate, and understood why it looked out of Jerym's eyes, and he gave back an unyielding stare, his wonder being that Jerym would come to Tex's burial. He almost looked away, but didn't, for wariness was marrow-deep in him. When Jerym saw that he wouldn't turn his back again, the front of the unbuttoned duster opened and there was a double-barreled sawed-off shotgun that had been slung by a strap over Jerym's shoulder so it would hang out of sight.

Jerym held the gun like a heavy revolver, his left hand steadyingly before the trigger guard as the other hand gripped the small of the stock. Both hammers were cocked, and he didn't have to sight—he only had to point and he couldn't miss. Rodiker was as helpless as if tied to a post. No human move could be quick enough to strike Jerym's finger from the trigger before the hammer fell, and no man out in plain sight could dodge a blast as near as this would be. All of which Jerym knew, and he asked with bitter gleefulness:

"Why else you think I'd come to old Tex's fun'ral!"

Many people were near enough to see, but it was an unbelievable thing, and mouths hung soundlessly open. Without an outcry at all having been made, uneasiness fluttered among those nearby who hadn't yet seen. Voices became silent, and the silence tense. Mr. Tredel said, "My God!" almost quietly, as somebody who wasn't near yelled. "Look out!" and a nester woman from across the grave shrieked, "Don't!" Those close by Rodiker were lurching aside, for it was a fearful thing to look straight into the big holes of a sawed-off shotgun, and so long as Rodiker didn't try to dodge, too, Jerym was willing that others should go.

Sue, the better to see, tore the veil from before her face when she swung about and, without a word, she rushed at old Jerym. The hammer fell, its click like the deadened strike of a clock in a silent room. The ten-inch barrels of the heavy ten-gauge were almost against Sue's breast, and she was fighting for the gun when the other hammer fell. Rodiker's jump and jerk to send her aside would have been too late, and both would have died if the gun had fired. But it didn't.

Jerym stumbled back, cursing and frantic to recock and to snap the hammers again on shells that he knew were fresh and sound, having come from the shelf of his own hardware store that morning.

Rodiker wrenched the gun from his hands, jerked in two the strap that had let it hang from Jerym's shoulders, and men rushed up. Then he broke the gun and looked—it was loaded, all right.

Rodiker took the loads from the guns, and they were passed from hand to hand. The shells' primers weren't dented. He cocked the hammers and pulled the triggers while the shotgun was broken open: the firing pins did not protrude through their apertures. They had been cut off. Then he knew why Enzo had laughed when saying good-by. But Rodiker told himself, *That's miracle enough for me!* and, giving over the gun to Mr. Tredel, he turned to Sue.

She was calmly examining the ripped seams of her new black gloves. He demanded, "Won't you ever learn some sense!"

"That's what Tex used to say."

"If that gun had gone off—"

She snapped at him, " 'If—if—if!' *If* old Satan had died when he was a baby, there wouldn't be any sinners!"

"You know what I mean."

"I know you're always bein' purt' near hurt when you're around me, so why don't you go back to Yank Arnold's and stay safe? I didn't make for old Jerym on account of you, so don't pride yourself. Mr. Tredel was right there and would've been shot too. Then what would've become of us girls?"

CHAPTER 30

Rodiker's chair was tipped against the hotel front in the midmorning shade of the sycamore when a pole buggy with the top up came through the dust, and a saddled horse jogged behind. It was a gusty day. Dougal stepped from the buggy, unchecked the horses, and let them begin to drink at the trough before he started to help his wife, but she, either impatient or angered, got out herself. She held an unopened parasol and wore a long duster; her hat was fastened with a heavy veil that came over her face, and she didn't lift the veil as she came hurriedly up the steps. Because of the veil Rodiker couldn't tell whether or not she looked at him.

Dougal did, then looked away and, lighting a cigar, stared into the wind-shaken sycamore as if admiring the color-tinted leaves. He was a big man and good-looking in a dark, heavy way; his pants' legs were over his boots and, though driving, he still wore silver spurs. He was in shirt sleeves, the painted vest being unbuttoned, and a string tie dangled from the unbuttoned collar of the blue shirt.

The old clerk came down the veranda steps and staggered up with a couple of bags, then Dougal tossed away the unsmoked cigar, fastened the check reins, and drove on to the stable.

Apparently Dougal was unarmed; *But,* Rodiker reflected, *apparently so am I!* since his own gun was under his shirt.

At noon he went into the hotel dining room. Cora Bevarts didn't appear, but, as he was leaving the room, a little colored youngster slipped up and handed him a letter, then vanished as quickly as a shadow can jump.

Rodiker went to the back table in the barroom. Perfume tingled his senses as he opened the envelope. The writing was bold, looked hastily written, and the message was bold too.

> Please will you come to see me? I owe you more than I can ever repay, but I do want to try. He will be drunk or playing cards tonight. Room four. I am more your friend than you can ever dream, and I am so eager to prove it. Cora.

He thoughtfully tore and retore the envelope and note into bits, then scraped them from the table top into his hand, and dropped the pieces into a spittoon.

She knew now that the "José" who had met her at the train was the Jack Rodiker she had sent on the dodge, and she didn't flinch from a meeting, but urged him to come. He looked at his hand and thought of her throat, but shook his head. She was eager to see him. That meant she was unafraid, or laying a trap. He doubted the trap. At least Jerym could have no part in the planning, and he was the forethoughtful, farseeing one.

Jerym had suffered a stroke, and was unable to move or speak, but, according to the young doctor, knew what went on about him, and that was crueller punishment than anything the law could have arranged. And, most unexpectedly, old Jenny Bevarts said that the story about Jerym wanting his bank robbed was true. She was no longer afraid of him, and it may have been a kind of revenge for all that she had endured through the years for her to say that she had slipped downstairs the night Rodiker came and had overheard what was said.

That afternoon Mr. Tredel brought his "family" into town, and put up at the hotel, taking the best rooms he could get. The auction was to be held the following day, and Mr. Tredel told Rodiker, "I won't have my girls grievin' their hearts out to see things they've growed up with going to strangers. No siree, I won't! Have a drink?"

Presently the gangling Steve came in and grinned widely as he walked up to Rodiker. "I'm back again! She didn't make so much fuss this time about me being an es-cort. Her pappy sent her. He told me to tag along. I guess he thinks the Bevartses ain't all dead yet, and one might jump up an' bite her."

Steve had a drink. He didn't know, he said,

what Miss Kate had come to town for, but she'd sent him to look for Rodiker. Then, right off, he asked Mr. Tredel how Bess was. Mr. Tredel said she was fine, and would be happy in Denver. Steve said he had often thought he'd like to visit a big town sometime, and at once got an invitation.

Rodiker found Kate upstairs in a back room and in a temper. The wind had blown hard all the way in from the ranch. She was hot, tired, dirty, and mad as a hornet, a black-headed hornet, and ready to sting anybody. She was a small girl, but now she was stretched into a kind of tallness by anger. She let him stand at the open door as she swung her hand about and stamped a foot—her father owned this hotel, and here she was stuck off in a hole not fit for a kennel. Cora Bevarts and the Clayton trash had the best rooms, and the old clerk wouldn't ask them to move. Rodiker didn't make any kind of a reply.

Finally she said, "The colonel wants you to bid on the Clayton place. He sent me to tell you."

"Steve could have told me that."

"Oh he could, could he?" Kate turned to the wavy mirror and seemed speaking to her own image. "Perhaps there are other things that Steve couldn't tell! You are to bid up to two thousand or a little over. I look a fright!" She turned and eyed him. "You'll be glad to see your Clayton friends get the money, won't you?"

"They are my friends."

She was again scrutinizing herself in the mirror as she inquired in an offhand way, "Is that why you didn't round up old Tex with the other rustlers?"

He hesitated for a reply and almost spoke of how bravely Tex had died, then told her, "Think however you want."

Kate swirled about and stared. "Are you in love with Sue Clayton?"

He hooked his thumbs into the front of his belt, gazed ponderously at her sunburned face, and surprised her with:

"I won't say yes, though maybe I am, for I like her mighty well—better than I ever did Bess, and I was in love then—so I thought. But how's a man to know?"

"You!" Kate's tone was strong with disgust and reproach. "She said she'd get you, and you are just weak enough to let her!" Kate went nearer the mirror and rose on tiptoes to look more closely at her face. But in a moment she turned swiftly and told him:

"I suppose you think you ought to be grateful because you think she acted so brave! Don't you know no man would shoot a woman? So she didn't take any risk at all!"

He frowned, puzzled and not angered. "When it comes to being grateful, there's nobody I owe more to than you."

Her dark eyes were gazing in the mirror; they flashed at him and returned to the glass, then she said bitingly, "You can get gratitude from a beggar for a dollar!" She moved her head from side to side in the mirror. "A fright!" she said. "I feel like gouging my eyes out so I won't have to look at myself."

She waited, but he returned no comment. Then she told her image, "I'm sweaty through and through, and grit-grimy, too, and haven't a thing to change to. Not another dress, and that Sue person will be rigged out like a squaw at a dance!" Then Kate turned and looked straight at Rodiker and spoke with careful malice. "I don't suppose you'd go to a store and buy some underthings for me?"

That jarred him. He knew she was free-spoken and not quite always modest, but nothing before had been so nearly startling, and he said, "No, I won't."

She jeered. "That's gratitude for you. You owe me such a lot, you say, and you are so grateful! But you are afraid to go into a store and ask for a petticoat! Well, just you remember, Mr. Rodiker, that you are nothing but a hired man on my father's ranch, and if you want to keep your job you'd better do as told."

He said, "There's not much you could ask that I wouldn't do, so why you are actin' so spiteful now I can't figure."

Kate lifted her eyebrows in mock surprise. "You can't?"

"No, I can't."

As she stared at him, determination suddenly hardened her face, and she snapped, "Come in and shut that door. I'm going to tell you something."

He did, and stood with a kind of calm uncertainty as Kate's fingers threw back her loose hair, and she glared with a fierceness that seemed hatred. Then her eyes crinkled, and the words came huskily and hurried.

"You great big dunce, you! I love you and I am jealous! There! I want to hurt you, and at the same time I'd throw my body in anybody's way to keep you from being hurt! Now do you understand?"

He didn't, of course, but confusedly said nothing, and she didn't pause.

"I hate that Sue Clayton because she was bold enough to say right out that she loves you—when I wanted to say it myself, and couldn't because there was still a little ladylike shame clinging to me. But that's gone now! I've pulled it off and thrown it away like a dress that's too itchy and hot.

"Oh but it's hard to make your mind be naked and tell the truth! I hate your Sue because she ran right at Jerym's shotgun to protect you. I hate her because she stood up before you when Frank

Pierce and Zig wanted to kill you. Now I'm being honest, and it feels good! I want to do things like that for you myself, but I don't think I'd have the courage. Not a shotgun—ugh! So I am jealous! I hate her terribly and half love her, too, because she is so bold and splendid and frank. I loved you when I was a little girl, and now I am a big girl and I love you. I am not ashamed to say it now, but you'd better hug me and kiss me like you loved me, too, or I'll be ashamed of having been honest—then I will hate you—oh, terribly! And I mean it!"

Laughter ran over her lips as she jumped at his neck with arms outreaching, and he stooped to catch her.

Rodiker avoided the dining room that evening and so did not know that Kate, coming in alone after Mr. Tredel had seated his "family," impulsively walked straight to Sue as to a friend, and Sue was surprised into a gracious but unfluttery greeting. Kate had shopped, and had used rice powder on her sunburned face, and she had bought a gold-covered scarf from a dressmaker. She was comfortable inside and out, since the wavy mirror seemed to say, *Not so bad!* and the memory of Rodiker's yielding seemed to say, *He's yours!*

Mr. Tredel, bustling courtesy, brought another chair to the table, and Ann did what she could to make the colonel's daughter feel at ease. Though

Bess was rather sulky, Kate soon found herself liking old Tex Clayton's girls.

Mr. and Mrs. Dougal Bevarts were coming in, both with lifted heads as if proud, but they may have been merely quarreling. They took a table nearby without apparently seeing anyone. Cora's creamy complexion was marvelous in such a hot, windy country, but she was never out from under a parasol or a heavy veil in the sunlight. Now her red hair was redder than it used to be. Mr. Tredel had seen lots of red hair like it, but he made no comment.

Folks wondered that Dougal could look so spruce and hold his head so high after all the misfortune that had happened to his family. Right now his father wasn't in jail only because he was a paralytic. The bank hadn't opened, and no one expected it to open. And though Dougal himself hadn't been implicated in the rustling, most people thought family shame ought to have made him hide his head. Instead he seemed hopeful of making a living at cards and horse trading.

After supper Cora went upstairs alone. She pulled the curtains and took off the dress and put on a loose blue gown that had lace and ribbons. Her petticoats rustled. With an atomizer she sent a perfumed mist into her hair, along her neck, and over her breasts. She turned down the lamp wick until it barely burned, then, after studying the dimness, raised the flame slightly. It mustn't be too dark for her to be seen as she wanted to be seen, and, though now she could scarcely see across the room, she didn't mean that Rodiker should be across the room from her. With another cigarette she sat down to wait.

She closed the door behind Rodiker, then stood before him and lifted both hands to his shoulders to let them rest there as she smiled earnestly. His face was grimly set, and, remembering her lure from the brief meeting at the railroad station, he knew this too dim room and too much perfume was deliberate, but that still didn't keep her from being lureful. A no-good woman could pull like a dallied rope.

Cora said softly, "At last I have the chance to right the great wrong I have done you all innocently!"

He didn't say anything, but took one hand from his shoulder, then the other. She let her arms hang with an air of defenselessness, and smiled wistfully. Her throat was within easy reach now, and it was white and bare except for beribboned lace, but he had no impulse to clamp his claw-set fingers there. The heady perfume floated about him like an old enticing memory as her body leaned to him with an offer and a promise.

He said coldly, "Let's hear," and put his hat under an arm.

"Oh!" she gasped, and for a long moment

looked as hurt as if bravely not crying. Then she asked gently, "Won't you sit down?"

"I'm not staying long enough."

"If you are going to be that rude, why did you come? Don't you realize I haven't a friend, and that it is all because of you? Dougal mistreats me so since he can't get my money. And I am glad—glad!—the colonel didn't give it to me! Dougal would have got it from me. That's why he married me. And you needn't think it strange that I want you to be my friend! We ought to be friends, our misfortunes are so intertwined! When I saw you at the station and thought you were merely 'José,' I knew you were a strong man, so handsome, and I liked you. Don't you remember, I told you so then, didn't I? Not in words perhaps, but words—pah!"

But he was stiff, unbending, with shoulders rigidly set, as he told her, "What I want to know is why you ever said you seen me shoot Craig Arnold?"

"I never said it."

"You never? W'y, I heard—"

"Never! Sit down and I'll tell you—everything."

Whatever he may have expected of her, it wasn't such a denial, not with such conviction, and that put his thoughts into a groping scramble to remember just what he had really heard about her accusation.

When he turned toward a chair she said, “No, not there,” and led him to the sofa in the dim alcove.

She sat beside him and looked into his face, and told him with frank and unemotional quietness, “You had talked with poor Craig that day, hadn’t you? Well, he told me so. He said he had been talking with Jack Rodiker, who was riding a Lazy S roan, and that it nearly always meant trouble for a Lazy S man to be near the piñons. It was no time at all after that when I heard a shot. I jumped up and saw a man riding away—and I had to think it was you, didn’t I? But honest, I never said it actually was you!”

“Shot in the back—me?”

“Of course I know now you wouldn’t. And I never said it, even then. All I said was what Craig had told me about who he talked with. And I did see somebody riding off, and how was I to know it couldn’t have been you!” Now, in a quiet way, she seemed almost tearful, pleading. “You must forgive me. I harmed you so. And oh, myself too! If you will tell Colonel Arnold just how it was—will you? You will, please, won’t you?”

Her hand fell caressingly on his arm, and she leaned forward, pleading with turquoise-colored eyes, offering her lips. He stared frozenly and could see her clearly, for his eyes were now accustomed to the dimness, and also he could see the promises she offered, and his confused thoughts whispered, *Maybe that is how it was!*

There were heavy steps in the hall, the bump of a body against the door. The door opened and Dougal, not sober, came in and banged the door to behind him.

He said, "Damn it, I went broke. Let me have that ring so—why so dark? Come on, honey. Give me that ring an' I'll break old Tredel 'fore mornin'."

Rodiker stood up. Cora had rushed with frantic, satiny rustle across the room at Dougal. There was a quick shuffle and twist of bodies, a kind of struggle with Dougal's muddled, perplexed voice asking, "What the hell?" Then a shot was fired—the room-shaking blast of a heavy caliber—and Cora jumped away and dropped the derringer on the floor as Dougal reeled back against the wall, threw out his arms, then fell face down.

She ran at Rodiker with, "I saved your life!" and clutched him, pressing close to speak hurriedly. "I knew he'd kill you! That gun—he always carried it hid under his vest. And you—he tried to kill you, but you jerked his gun away and shot him! You must say that! He would have killed you and—and I love you so!"

Rodiker's left hand pushed against her, keeping her away, as he slowly thrust into his waistband the revolver he had drawn from under his shirt. His voice had the hardness of slow, deep-throated curses. "Now I know who killed Craig Arnold, and how." He struck as hard as he could with an open palm that smacked her across the mouth, and she went down as though his palm had been a fist.

He stared down into her terrorized and bleeding face as he slowly, thoughtfully, said, "Craig told you I'd been there an' on what horse, so when you somehow got his gun and shot him in the back, you knew who to blame. I never before thought the devil could wear skirts."

CHAPTER 31

Rodiker put a lead rope on his horse and rode to the auction in a buggy with Mr. Tredel, who wasn't at ease on horseback, though he knew how to handle a high-stepping team. As Tredel drove he talked with an unlighted cigar in the corner of his mouth.

"You can thank your lucky stars it happened as it did!"

"I do."

"Just s'pose Dougal had caught sight of you, and you'd killed him? That woman would have had everything her own way."

Rodiker said, "A half turn up on the lamp's wick, and that's how it would have been."

"You half believed her story, didn't you?"

"More than half."

"I went up this mornin' to see how Dougal's making out. Was in the poker game with him last night. He don't even know the fund'mental," said Mr. Tredel, shaking his head, "just calls, calls, calls. Break any man. But he's right chipper. Was more drunk than hurt. Shot through the side, and not bad. Says he hopes she hangs, but of course she won't, for it wouldn't be right to do that to a woman."

"Just so she goes to hell, I don't care how."

"Dougal was right pleased this morning when I told him the trick me and the marshal played on her last night. Dougal, you know, come to and said she shot him. So me an' the marshal, we went to her and said he died right after he said it. Which made it murder!"

Mr. Tredel chuckled, worked the cigar to the other side of his mouth. "That county attorney, Miss Arnold, and some more folks was in the room with her, an' none of them didn't know that Dougal hadn't died. Only me and the marshal. He let me do the talkin', and it broke her spir't when I said, 'You killed him. He said so just before he died. He didn't even see Jack Rodiker at all!' Her mouth was all swole, and bled from being cut on the teeth. She said you hit her?" Mr. Tredel made it a question.

"Not hard enough."

"She was half cryin' and wipin' at her mouth. With Dougal dead—so she thought!—she didn't seem to mind saying how she'd killed her other husband. And I'll swear she sounded like she felt nobody ought to think so bad of her because he was crippled-like and had her tied down. Awful jealous he was, she said. She said she was young and wanted to go back East and have fun.

"I hear the colonel sent her money back East regular, so I guess she had fun. And all the time he plastered the country with rewards for you!"

"The colonel is all right."

"You don't hold much of a grudge, do you?"

Rodiker thought of the long nights through the years that he had built up his grudge and had planned to ease it with violence, but now he said, "Depends." His grudge against Jerym didn't seem in any way lessened simply because the old devil was in bed paralyzed.

The team's feet trotted rhythmically in the dust as the iron-rimmed wheels ran with a whispering rasp through the gravelly ruts. He tightened his eyes against the sunlight and looked far over the Santsander and on toward the mountain, where his folks had their small ranch, as he recalled Maw Rodiker's talk of a no-good woman. *She draws you on and on, takes all your strength and manhood, leaves you dead, or near it, then calls for some other fellow.*

He said, "Without a good woman I guess a man can't be much good himself."

"That's right! That sure is right!" exclaimed Mr. Tredel. He drew in his breath and held it a little, before he asked quietly, "Are you going to marry Sue?"

Rodiker didn't say anything.

Tex's place being only some three miles out, Mr. Tredel arranged for a restaurant to send lunch at noon. There was lots of beer, but no liquor except what was in men's pockets.

The auctioneer worked hard from a wagon

bed. When he began trying to play on sympathy for Tex's daughters, Mr. Tredel went close and whispered in protest.

Rodiker told no one he had been instructed to bid for Tex's house and few acres, and it was knocked down to him for $1560.

Rodiker left, returning to Moheela alone. It was past midafternoon when he stepped from the saddle before the livery stable, and Steve got up from the chair out from where he had been flipping small pebbles at big flies and grinned.

"I'd come out to Tex's, only Miss Kate told me to wait here and—"

"Now what?"

"We are all goin' to head right out to the ranch. She said as soon as you come in to tell you, so you wouldn't unsaddle."

"Why?"

Steve's lazy voice dropped into a draggy drawl. "On account of old Jerym. I never heard anybody get such a cussin' out without swear words as she give the young doc! Old Jerym pulled a sandy on him. Was no more paralyzed than a hound dog with fleas! The doc said he could have known if he'd thought to stick a pin in him, but he never thought. Jerym just played it that way so he wouldn't be jailed—maybe hung! Folks are that mad about the bank. That shotgun play at the fun'ral too."

"Gone?"

"Hell yes. He was in bed when folks went last night to tell about Dougal. Some went along about noon today and Old Miz Bevarts was laid out on the floor, half killed. I hear she's said it was because she had backed up what you said about the bank. It all happened last night."

Rodiker thought, *Farseein' and forethoughtful.* He said, "Nobody but Jerym would've thought of such a trick."

"Miss Kate says all he wants is to lay for you. She's goin' to make you head for home, so you needn't unsaddle."

"Is she?"

"I'd purt' near bet on it!" said Steve; then he added, "I mean, she's got a way of gettin' her way, that girl."

"I'll agree," said Rodiker, but he led the horse into the runway, took off the saddle, spread the blanket, slipped the bridle, and gave the horse a slap on the rump, then followed, and opened the gate into the corral. He turned in the shadows and told the stable hand, "Grain him," then walked out to where Steve waited.

Rodiker made a cigarette, and they stood together, not speaking, while he smoked. When the cigarette was half gone he stepped on it with grind of toe, and said, "I can't think why she wants me to turn tail and run. Come on."

They came to the sheriff's office and looked inside, then went in. The sheriff had his feet on the desk and his hat pushed back. He looked sick. Purcell was with him. The slope-shouldered marshal pulled at his droopy mustache as if trying to straighten it, before he told Rodiker, "We don't know where to look. He went into his hardware store sometime last night and picked himself a shotgun. He's never handled guns much, so he has to depend on shotguns."

Rodiker said, "Maybe he'll forget it's full of grease."

The sheriff grunted. "No such luck. He cleaned it there sometime 'fore daybreak."

Purcell fidgeted with his pasteboard eyeshade. "The store clerk says he took a lot of shells!" The editor added uneasily, "I bet he'd like to get a shot at me!"

The sheriff laid aside his chewed cigar. "You ain't the only one!" Obviously the sheriff included himself too. He said, "I've doubled the guard at the warehouse. Two of the rustlers there may be crippled, but they're about the only friends Jerym's got left."

Rodiker asked, "Have you looked for Jerym in the bank?"

"We looked ever'where. The blacksmith broke the lock. It's padlocked now. He's holed up some'eres, waitin' for dark. With all them shells he took, looks like he meant to kill some folks. He's smart enough to know he's through."

A thoughtful silence came. Purcell twitched his

eyeshade, asked Rodiker, "Why did the Clayton girls pull out?"

"Pull out? When?"

"Noon stage," said the marshal. "Bess and Sue. Sue looked like she'd been cryin'."

"Half sick, too," said Purcell, "and such a pretty girl."

Rodiker turned inquiringly to Steve, but Steve shook his head. "I heard they'd left. I didn't see 'em go. I'd sort of liked to say good-by."

Rodiker again said, "Come on," and started for the street. Steve fell into the long-legged, hard-thumping stride Rodiker set on the board sidewalk, and thought that Rodiker was surely acting mad all of a sudden.

Kate was alone in a chair on the veranda under the sycamores, and came a few steps to meet them with, "Where are the horses?" and a questioning rebuke was in her manner and voice. She was in her riding skirt, and, though the day was hot, the new golden scarf was tucked about her neck. "Steve, I thought I told you—"

Rodiker said, "He told me."

"Then why didn't you—"

"I'm still boss of myself."

Kate told him rapidly, with earnestness, "Please don't be stubborn like that! We must leave town, and at once! Old Jerym is loose and armed, and what if something bad should happen to you *now?*"

His shoulders were high and stiff as he looked down somberly and said, “It’s not like you. You don’t scare easy. Not you! You’ve got grit from your toenails up. And you are not one to think well of any fellow that turns tail and runs—let alone a fellow who is your father’s range boss! So what’s come over you?”

Kate’s eyes brightened with, “You ought to know!” She glanced aside at Steve, then back to Rodiker. Her voice softened into tenderness. “It’s different now. I am scared! Just when everything is as it ought to be! Oh, if something happened to you now—Don’t you see?”

Steve saw, and looked the other way, walking off, and wished some pretty girl felt like that about him.

But Rodiker said, “I’m still working for the colonel. Jerym’s his worst enemy. If I run, it wouldn’t be doing like I ought. He told me to stay in town and make sure the rustlers go to prison—that they don’t get away. Jerym’s a rustler too—the big one! And now that he’s not paralyzed, he’s going to prison or to hell.”

The wind shook down some sycamore leaves, and they slithered with a silken rasp over the veranda’s boards. Kate knew his stubbornness. She took his hand and said, “Please? For me, won’t you?” Then she pulled a little. “I’ll go back to the stable with you. Come on, please.”

He said, “No,” with gentleness, and pulled his

hand away. "You go, you and Steve. And why did Sue and Bess Clayton leave town this noon, you know?"

Kate looked up staringly and shook her head. She said, "I don't know," as if not caring either, then was again insistent with, "But you are going to the ranch with us! You just are! You must! And we are starting now. You want me to get mad?"

He smiled one-sidedly and told her, "No," but added, "You and Steve light out. Tell the colonel I bought the place for under sixteen-hundred. Tell him that when Jerym's caught or dead there'll be nobody left to try to get the rustlers loose. You and Steve get going. Jerym is just mean enough with hate of the colonel to want to shoot *you,* and I sure don't want that! So good-by."

He turned from her and started for the hotel door. Kate ran after him with surging lift of the weighted riding skirt, and asked breathlessly, "Now where are you going?"

He faced about. "Why, what's the matter?"

"I'm scared!" said Kate.

"No, no, not you! You're just putting on to make me give in." He smiled a little. "Never was a girl to beat you for getting her own way."

"And it's been the best way, hasn't it, always?"

"I can't argy against that, but I'm not leaving town."

He went into the hotel.

Kate lifted clenched hands shoulder high, then

let them fall helplessly, and turned back to the chair, slumped down, and brooded with a hand to her cheek. She muttered, "What will he do? What *will* he do?"

Rodiker knocked on the Tredel door.

Ann smiled, "Why, Jack! Do come in. Sit down. And my congratulations! Just imagine, after all these years when Yank Arnold was such an enemy you are now to be his son-in-law!"

He sat down, spread his palms on his knees, and asked stolidly, "Am I?"

Ann said, "You needn't feel embarrassed about it. I am pleased and proud of you. If anybody has deserved great good fortune, you have! But Sue, poor Sue! She loved you as a little freckled, scrawny brat, and still thinks she does. But she was sweet about it this morning when Miss Arnold told us. Sue even kissed her, and said she hoped you two would be happy. And I don' think she was being a hypocrite, for Sue is honest, through and through."

"Yes, she is."

"But when Miss Arnold left here, Sue let herself go! I think she would have taken it by force if I hadn't let her have the money so she and Bess could catch the stage to Woodward. That is, Bess wouldn't let Sue go alone. They'll wait there until Mr. Tredel and I come."

Rodiker said, "Sorry I didn't say good-by," with rather the dead tonelessness of a dumb man who has just learned to speak, and when he was out in the hall he thought of Kate and said to himself, *I'll be damned!*

He walked down the hall in such a stupor of thoughtfulness that he passed his door, then stopped at the end of the hall. He stood there broodingly. *She tried to hurry me from town before I found out!* He turned back and, still in a kind of a daze, stopped with his hand on the door knob. But his ears were alert; they told him the bed springs had creaked, and all the quick-thinking wariness of his hunted days was aroused.

He hadn't locked the door for there was nothing in it to guard, but someone was there now. Could be 'most anybody, but he thought of Jerym. *And how could Jerym come unseen?* He didn't try to think, for he knew that desperate men do desperate things that seem impossible. He stood to one side of the jamb as he threw open the door, giving a push that swung it wide.

Jerym was out in the center of the room, and his bowed shoulders were hunched, but the double-barreled shotgun wasn't on his shoulders. He held it waist high, pointing directly at the doorway, and he couldn't have missed if anybody had been there. But all he had to shoot at now was one eye and a side of the right cheek as Rodiker peered in, and six feet was too close for the shot to scatter. He'd have to aim as with a rifle. When he fired, the unbraced gun kicked back in his hands, the muzzle tipping up. Smoke burst through the doorway, as if following the buckshot into the wall across the hall. Jerym backed up with a clumsy shuffle and started to throw the gun to his shoulder for an aimed shot. Rodiker killed him.

Rodiker stood close and held Kate's hands, as he told her, "You're pretty and easy to love, and I do. But I don't trust you. You are brave, too, and would back any man through any trouble. Nearly everything good that's happened to me has been through you. You done it by being tricky and telling lies, and the worst was forging that superintendent thing over the colonel's name. I oughtn't maybe bring it up, since it was all for me, and it worked out like you hoped. But I can't trust you. When you'd say something I'd never know if it was true or not. And if you ever took any kind of a little dislike to me, as women are apt to do at times to the men they marry, I'd be just about helpless from how you can pull a jumpin' jack's strings. Why, your mother wasn't even Southern, was she?"

Kate asked, "What difference does that make now?"

He drew a long breath and didn't tell her. He said, "You don't like the word 'gratitude,' and come to think of it, I don't much either, so I won't say it. All I can say is that nobody on earth can have more help from me anytime it's needed than you and the colonel. He don't like your lying either. You told me so. And when you were a little girl you lied about spraining your ankle so I would pick you up and go get your horse. That was cute, and made me do what I never forgot—it was so pleasant, just holding you. But I'll be damned—and probably would, at that—if I'm going to let a woman I know I can't trust have such a hold on me as I'd be giving you."

"But you do love me, Jack?"

"Of course I love you, but I won't marry you."

"Then you don't love Sue Clayton?"

"Of course I love her. A man can love more'n one woman and not be a fool. But he can't try to belong to more'n one and not be."

"And are you going to marry her, Jack?"

"I am, and when I do, I'm hers, and she is mine, and I won't say to any other woman that I love her. That's how it is, and will be. So now good-by."